PHANTOM

THOMAS TESSIER

Copyright © 1997 by Thomas Tessier
ISBN 978-1-63789-102-5
Macabre Ink is an imprint of Crossroad Press Publishing
For information address Crossroad Press at 141 Brayden Dr., Hertford, NC 27944
www.crossroadpress.com

Cover art by David Dodd

First Crossroad Press Edition - 2024

For Sam

The Supernatural experience always appears as the transfiguration of Natural conditions, acts, states....

—BARON VON HUGEL

If there is any place truly haunted, it is one that men have discovered, lived in, left, and forgotten.

—DONALD CULROSS PEATTIE
The Road of a Naturalist

THOMAS TESSIER: A MAN OF FEW WORDS

An Introduction by Bob Booth

Thomas Tessier is a man of few words, in all senses of that phrase. For his admirers, and I count myself among them, he is not nearly prolific enough. Since 1970 he has published three slim poetry collections, one collection of short fiction and ten novels. That's a book every three years or so, in an age when genre writers produce at least a book a year, sometimes more.

On top of that his books are usually on the short side. You won't find any grand epics from Mr. Tessier, nor any trilogies.

I'm not the only one who feels this way. The eminent genre critic Don D'Ammassa said: "Tessier's fiction comes only at unfortunately long intervals. Even his lesser works have interesting elements, and his better stories are beautifully written and hard to forget." (*The Encyclopedia of Fantasy and Horror Fiction*, Checkmark Books, 2006)

Tessier doesn't just write succinctly, he speaks that way. Long time genre observer Stan Wiater has produced a whole shelf of books that depend on author interviews. I've just proof-read one of them, *Dark Dreamers on Writing*. The book is a collection of advice and commentary by "fifty masters of fear and suspense" arranged by topic. Some of the writers take the opportunity to go on for paragraphs (sometimes pages) to express their thoughts. Not Tessier. Here are a few examples:

"I don't plan. I don't analyze, I write intuitively." and "Resignation, not satisfaction, sets in around deadline time."

Doesn't that tell you all you really need to know about his writing process? I don't picture him studying the markets to see what's hot. I don't see him creating bulletin boards full of index cards, or laboring over extensive outlines. Rather I picture a writer, like Hemingway, alone with his notebook and No. 2 pencils, telling a good story he knows and then working with it, shaping it, sculpting it, until he has to give it up.

His ideas on his chosen genre are equally condensed. Wiater captured them in another book, *Dark Dreamers: Facing the Masters of Fear* (with Beth Gwinn). Typically, Tessier's contribution is the briefest of them all. Channeling Hemingway again though, it is what Papa called "iceberg writing"—you only see about one sixth of what the author knows. The rest is there, under water as it were, and if you read carefully and think about the words that are there you can intuit those the writer has left out.

Tessier said: "I don't worry about running out of strange ideas, because what I try to write about is not so much the mere strangeness but the people, the characters and what happens to them. Life is full of terror and beauty, and they can't be ever separated, and in that conflict is our endless drama."

Doesn't that brief paragraph get to the essence of why those who write horror fiction do it, and why those who read it do so? A few words, carefully chosen, like a fine book collection. Tessier only tells stories he knows and has fully digested. As a reader you get the feeling that he has thought about each tale a long time and only lets you have it when he is ready, when he knows he can do it justice, when he believes it will mean something.

Tessier was born in Connecticut in 1947, a great year, producing Tom, Richard Laymon, Stephen King, and less brilliantly, me. He went to University College, Dublin, after which he spent several years in London. He was friends there with another young poet who was to turn to horror fiction, Peter Straub. During that period he produced three slim volumes of poetry as well as three plays that were professionally staged (but not published) before writing his first horror novel.

Phantom, the book you are getting ready to read, was published in 1982, his fourth novel. Briefly, it is the story of Ned Covington, a ten-year-old boy, who explores an abandoned building near his home and what he finds there. According to D'Amassa it "is a quiet, modernized ghost story that derives most of its impact from descriptions of the boy's reactions to what he discovers and his growing isolation from the world of the living."

The critical response was immediate. Douglas E. Winter in *Faces of Fear* (Berkley, 1985), published a mere three years later, listed it as one of the books that he considered "the best of the modern generation of horror fiction." It was also included on a similar list published as an appendix to Stephen Jones' and Kim Newman's *Horror: 100 Best Books* (Carroll & Graf, 1988).

Winter was also the author of a justly famous article called "Writers of Today," published in *The Penguin Encyclopedia of Horror and the Supernatural*. Tessier, who had earlier written *The Fates* (1978), proved himself one of the major new talents in horror fiction with a little-known supernatural romance, *Shockwaves* (1982), and a compelling humanist ghost story, *Phantom* (1982)."

In Neil Barron's *Horror Literature: A Reader's Guide* (Garland, 1990) the reviewer (Keith Neilson, Cal State Fullerton) said: "A touching, scary book. The child's point of view is handled quite believably and sensitively, and Ned's final hallucinatory confrontation with the 'woman' is as harrowing and imaginative as anything in current horror fiction. The unanswered question of whether the phantom is real or a projection of Ned's emotional confusions adds additional ambiguity and tension to this fine novel."

Phantom was nominated for a World Fantasy Award in a very tough year. I know. I was a judge. I can tell you that one of the books we considered was Ray Kinsella's classic *Shoeless Joe*, the basis for the film *Field of Dreams*. It didn't make the final ballot.

Phantom's competition on that final ballot was Charles L. Grant's *The Nestling*, the book Charlie himself considered his "breakout novel;" George R. R. Martin's original take on vampires, *Fevre Dream*; Gene Wolfe's *Sword of the Lictor*, third in his groundbreaking "New Sun" series; and *Nifft the Lean*, a highly original fantasy by relative newcomer Michael Shea.

The judges (myself aside) were as distinguished as the nominees. Alan Ryan and John Coyne, two horror novelists themselves were joined by two acquisitions editors Sharon Jarvis and Elizabeth Wollheim. We all met one Saturday at a bar in New York (I think it was called The Brass Rail). We drank, we ate, we drank some more, and we talked horror and fantasy fiction for the better part of six hours. We all agreed on most of the categories without much debate. Best Novel was the exception. John, Alan and I argued strenuously for *Phantom* while Sharon and Elizabeth pushed for *Nifft the Lean*. The split was right along party lines, as it were. The men, all with horror backgrounds, supported the horror novel, while the women, both involved in fantasy publishing, supported the fantasy novel. *Nifft the Lean* won, and it is a worthy book, still, as a horror guy....

I've gone on too long introducing a novel that really needs no introduction. Such is my passion for this writer, and particularly this book. Read it for yourself and marvel at the economy of prose and the depth of insight it contains. Like I said. Thomas Tessier is a man of few words, but they are always well chosen.

Bob Booth
Publisher, Necon E-Books
September 28, 2010

THE NIGHT THEY CAME

A child hears best what happens in the night. He may be awake or asleep, or his mind may be roaming the dreamy gray landscape in between, but his ears cannot fail to pick up what takes place on the dark side of the day. Nor is it necessary for a child to understand what is heard: things have their own mysterious meanings beyond the realm of mere words. It does no good to explain the Sandman when the Sandman will still be there, waiting for the chance to sneak in and stop you dead by filling your eyes and ears and nose and mouth with hardening sand.

Ned Covington, not yet five years old, was in his bed and almost asleep, but he was aware of the noises coming from the other side of his bedroom door. Footsteps in the hallway. Bare feet. Coming this way. But there was something wrong, something about the way the sound moved, falteringly, that told him it wasn't just his mother or father making a routine trip to the bathroom. Ned turned toward the window but no light penetrated his eyelids, so he knew it wasn't yet morning.

There was a funny thump from the hallway, as if the person out there was unfamiliar with the place and had bumped into a wall. Then, silence. Ned struggled to wake himself more. It couldn't be his mother or father; they didn't move like that. He knew every sound they made in the apartment, the way they walked, the weight of their steps. This was clearly different. Had someone broken into their home, a bad person, or, even worse, a night thing? Were his parents all right, or were they already lying dead in their room? Why wasn't his father awake and doing something?

Ned wanted to get up and run as fast as he could to his parents, but they were at the end of the hallway and he would have to face whatever was out there before he could get to them. He could shout—but no, that would reveal his presence for sure, and besides, his mother and father might not hear or be able to do anything in time. The best thing to do was to slide way down under the covers and hope that it would pass with the night.

Ned felt safe in his bed, but there was one lingering problem.

Cocooned in his blankets, there was no way he could see anything. The door to his room was always left an inch or two ajar at night, so whatever was in the hallway could crawl right in beside his bed without Ned knowing it until it was too late. Many times he had carefully scattered his toys on the floor, making a perfect alarm system, but his father always made him put them away before going to bed. It was too late to move now. But regardless of the drawbacks, Ned still felt reasonably safe where he was.

He knew there was only one way out of a situation like this. You couldn't move. You had to remain completely covered up and perfectly still. As long as you did that, you wouldn't be harmed. And, although he had never been foolish enough to try, Ned also knew that if you violated this rule by getting up or even just peeking out from under the bedclothes, then, for sure, someone or something horrible would be standing there and reaching toward you, and there wouldn't be a thing in the world you could do to save yourself. At the wrong time, if you merely poked a hand out to test the air it could be chopped off or turned to stone.

The noise was so close now Ned was certain it was at his door. He wanted to jam his fingers in his ears, but even that limited movement seemed too risky. He must not stir at all. It was the sound of breathing, but there was nothing at all normal about it. An open mouth trying desperately to breathe, but caked with a thousand cobwebs or thickening sand—that was what Ned heard. He wanted to scream so loud the window would fly open and fresh air sweep in, blowing it away, but now more than ever he had to keep still and silent.

There. It had turned away from his room. A few seconds later Ned recognized the change in sound as bare feet went from the hallway into the bathroom. Then a heavy thud suggested someone half-sitting, half-falling onto the toilet seat. Ned thought it must be one of his parents after all. He sat up sharply in bed, all demons banished for the moment.

That awful gasping sound continued, and then Ned heard a short mechanical click followed immediately by a tiny gusting noise. Of course, it was his mother's medicine. He had seen her use the inhaler many times, and while he didn't know what it was for, he had no doubt about the sound it made. But could that really be his mother? He had never heard her breathe like that before.

Ned climbed out of bed and made his way across the room to the door. He peered through the narrow space. The bathroom door stood wide open, and as his eyes adjusted to the dark Ned could dimly see his mother slumped on the toilet seat. Her nightgown defined her, a pale, white shape in the darkness. At first Ned was reassured that no phantom or night thing had come to menace their home, but then another vague fear began to grow in his mind. What was his mother doing sitting there like that? Her head was bent forward to her chest and her hair hung like a rough curtain in front of her face. That was wrong. Had she fallen asleep? She wasn't making any of the sounds people make when they use the toilet. In fact, she wasn't making any sound at all. Even that terrible breathing noise was gone, Ned realized. He was shivering and his feet felt as if they were glued to the floor. Fear of a different kind started to fill him from within.

His mother's hand relaxed slightly and the inhaler clattered on the bathroom tiles. It was shockingly loud to his ears, and Ned flinched. Something inside was trying to get him to move, to run to his mother and do whatever he could for her, but he was unable to budge from the spot. His bones had become iron rods welded tight and he could only stand there, fixed in one place like a scarecrow.

Then his mother slid forward off the toilet seat and crashed to the floor with such force that the walls seemed to shake. The sound was a bottomless thunder that roared in Ned's brain. The next thing he knew, the hall light came on like an explosion and pain stabbed his eyes.

His father, wearing only underpants, had come into view, but Ned was looking again at his mother, who lay sprawled face up on the floor, half out of the bathroom. Her eyes were partially open but they appeared to be filmed over, like a car window in winter. Her cheeks were incredibly white and her lips-her lips were turning blue, and then purple, even as he watched. *She's becoming a ghost,* Ned thought, and he really expected her to fly away from them forever in the next few seconds.

"Oh, God, no." Michael Covington bent over his wife and put his ear to her lips. "Breathe, Linda, breathe."

Michael snatched the inhaler off the floor, but when he tried to put it into Linda's mouth he found that her teeth were clamped tight and it was impossible for him to force her jaw open. He slapped her cheeks lightly, then harder, but it had no effect. He splashed her face with cold water from the bathroom faucet, but that too failed to bring any response. Again Michael pressed his ear to her face. Nothing. If she's not breathing, he thought, she's dying. Now. Here. On the floor of their apartment. He grabbed her wrist, but his own hands were shaking and he was sobbing now, so he couldn't tell whether she had much of a pulse or not. He turned and rushed to the living room to call for an ambulance. Somehow, he dialed and got through.

"… Severe asthma attack …"

He heard them, but the words meant nothing to Ned. All he knew was that a phantom had come and done something monstrous to his mother. Any second now she would disappear before his very eyes. Then she would be caught, she would be one of them. and he would never see her again. Then what? Another night, soon, they would come back and take his father. How could he stop them? Ned would be left all alone. Until, at last, they came for him, and he knew that when that happened nothing, not even the borders of his own bed, would save him.

Michael Covington returned to his stricken wife. He placed a pillow beneath her head and wrapped her in a wool blanket. He raised her feet and rested them on the edge of the toilet seat so more blood would flow to her head. Still, she looked like a dead woman. Michael hurried away to put on some clothes.

A few feet away, in the darkness of his room, Ned gazed through the one-inch gateway to hell. Perhaps he had seen too much; certainly, he had heard too much. Overloaded, he was going numb, vacating himself to deeper, inner havens. Like everyone else, Ned lived in two worlds: day and night. But this was reality of another kind. Bizarre and disturbing as the night, it was nonetheless the daylight life of his mother and father, now torn and twisted. Within the space of a few minutes the two worlds had been thrown together in a way Ned had never experienced before, and it was a diabolical mixture. That was his own mother out there, propped against the toilet like a stray plank.

Even now he couldn't move. Rooted. A scarecrow. Just beyond the light's reach, out of sight, but close enough to see. His thoughts were like giant amorphous blobs that collided and drifted awkwardly in his mind. He hadn't moved. He hadn't done a thing to help his mother. She had been left to battle, and lose, alone, while he cowered in his room. Now it was too late.

They had tricked him. That was the worst part. Ned could see now what a fool he had been. You think you understand, you think you're doing exactly what should be done, and then *wham*, you find out you did it all wrong. What was the rule, the one saving provision? Simple: once you have drawn in beneath the covers and sealed yourself in the protection of your bed, you must not move out of it again until morning. If you break that rule, if you so much as stick out an eyelash, the terror will be there. And that's what had happened. Ned had popped up out of the blankets like a jack-in-the-box and gone to see what was happening. Now he was seeing it, and the terror was real. He would continue to see and see and see, until it was all over for this time. Because there is no way back under the covers.

Fully dressed now, Michael returned and pressed the back of his hand to Linda's forehead. As if by magic, she stirred and moaned faintly at the touch. Michael was startled, but a little relieved. Then there was a knock at the door and things began to happen fast. Ned saw his father admit two men in white uniforms. One was carrying a folded-up canvas chair with wheels. They both looked older than Ned's father. The three of them stared at Ned's mother, as if wondering what to do with a big mess that had been left on the floor. Is she dead, the boy wondered. No, she just moved and made a noise.

"She's had an asthma attack."

"Has it happened before?"

"Never like this—she never passed out."

"Does she take anything for it?"

"This." Michael held out the inhaler. "I tried to give it to her but I couldn't get her mouth open."

The two ambulance men studied the object briefly and then handed it back to Michael.

"Okay, let's take her in."

One of the men started to set up the wheelchair.

"I don't think she's breathing," Michael said nervously. "Would you please check?"

"In the ambulance."

"Do you have any oxygen?" Michael asked. "I think she should have some oxygen. Fast."

"In the ambulance. We got to get her in the ambulance," the man with the wheelchair said. "That's the first thing."

His partner was down on the floor, examining Linda. He checked her pulse, parted her lips, and he held the dial of his watch to her nose.

"She's sorta breathing," he announced, standing up with a loud sigh. "Best thing is, get her to the hospital where a doctor can take a look."

The wheelchair was ready and the three men tried to lift Linda into it, but suddenly she began to wave her arms and kick her legs, violently resisting any attempt to move her.

"Hey, hey, what's this," one of the ambulance men said.

"Linda, honey, just relax and let us lift you into the chair," Michael said.

"She don't wanna go."

Ned saw that his mother's eyes were wide open now. They darted about wildly, frantically. It was as if she was seeing a different world, or some other, unknown dimension. She showed no signs of recognizing her husband or the apartment.

"Okay, let's go."

"One, two ..."

They lifted again, and again Linda lashed out with her arms and feet. They couldn't get her off the floor, where she huddled to herself.

"What's her name?"

"Linda."

"Last name?"

"Covington."

"Mrs. Covington, we're gonna move you into the nice big comfortable chair now," the ambulance man said sweetly. "It's much nicer than where you are now, so just enjoy the ride and let us do all the work, okay? Ready?"

"One, two ..."

He sounds like a goddamn Lawrence Welk, Michael thought angrily.

This time Linda pushed one of the ambulance men away, breaking his grip completely, and her foot caught Michael on the side of the jaw, knocking him over. The other man, who hadn't gotten hold of her at all, looked on in disbelief. Linda curled up on her original spot, half in and half out of the bathroom. Her eyes danced.

The ambulance men looked unhappy. They picked up the inhaler and examined it a second time.

"She take a lot of this?"

"She takes it when she needs to," Michael said defensively. Something was pushing up, trying to break the surface in his mind. Something ugly.

"You ever seen her like this before?"

"No, I told you. The worst that ever happens is she gets breathless and a little dizzy. She takes the inhaler and sits down until she feels better."

"You say it's asthma, but I've never seen anybody with asthma act like this."

"No way," the other ambulance man added gratuitously.

"Can't you do something?" Michael begged.

"Not until we get her in the ambulance."

"What is that, some kind of law?" Michael shouted.

"You ask me," the ambulance man went on calmly, "I think she OD'd on this stuff." He held up the inhaler like exhibit number one in a court case. "Took too much, you know, pop, pop, pop. That's why she's acting crazy like. Now she's off on a little trip."

That didn't sound right to Michael. He had never heard of an asthma inhalant doing that to a person.

"Will it wear off soon?" he asked. "Should we wait a few more minutes before trying to move her again?"

"Beats me," one ambulance man said as the other shrugged. "I suppose you could call her doctor and ask him about it."

These guys are truck drivers, Michael thought in despair. They've probably been doing this for years and they probably mean well, but they don't know a damn thing. They might as well be here to collect a load of old newspapers. What did they handle most of the time— gunshot wounds, stabbings, drunks? They might well know what to do with those cases. But asthma? Forget it.

"She needs oxygen," Michael heard himself say. "At least give her that."

The ambulance men exchanged glances, then nods, and one of them went out to get an oxygen tank.

"I don't know if it'll do any good," the one who remained said. "But we'll give it a try." He looked at the inhaler again, as fascinated as a man who has just discovered a whole new life form.

"Don't you have a set procedure for dealing with asthma attacks?" Michael asked.

"Too many pops," the man muttered.

Ned's eyes were on his mother's. She looked like a trapped animal, eyes ricocheting around in their skull sockets, breath coming in short, husky grunts. It seemed like she was a hundred million miles away. *They* have her, Ned thought. She's here, but they have her.

The other uniformed man came back into the hallway with a long metal tank and a plastic face mask.

"Mrs. Covington, we're gonna give you some nice fresh air now, okay dear? Just relax and breathe it all in nice and deep."

Before the mask reached her face Linda was squirming and thrashing, twisting her head away and striking out at the three men around her.

"Aw Jesus Christ, this is not like anybody with asthma that I ever seen. What the hell has been going on around here?" the ambulance man asked accusingly.

Michael ground his teeth like someone trying to bite through a two-by-four. Something was pushing harder, closer. Something ugly. The thought formed: irreversible brain damage.

"She needs oxygen," Michael said furiously. "She has had a severe asthma attack and her brain is starved of oxygen. Now give it to her."

Michael jumped on his wife and pinned her arms to her sides. One of the ambulance men held her head while the other one slapped the mask to her face and turned on the oxygen, Linda writhed in agony and shrieked like a grievously wounded beast. They wrestled to keep her in place for a long minute, two. She roared and brayed and howled, and finally wailed with diminishing strength, She looked like one of the earth's dying creatures at the end of the world. When it was all over she subsided on the floor. Her face was streaked, her hair and nightgown drenched with sweat. She was a heap of bones in a flimsy bag of skin. Only Linda's eyes were still alive, racing feverishly.

"I'm okay, I'm okay, I'm okay." The words rattled off her tongue in a rush. "I'm tired, I'm so tired."

"I bet you are," one of the ambulance men said with a smile. "I'm tired, too."

"Linda, honey!" Michael exclaimed. He could hardly believe that she might actually come out of It.

"I'm tired, so tired," she repeated.

"Sure you are, honey," Michael said. "You're going to be all right, but you have to go to see the doctor now."

"Okay, but not yet," Linda said wearily. "I want to rest here for a little while."

"You rest, honey, that's right. We'll move you."

"No, don't move me yet." A hand fluttered weakly. "In just a few minutes ... " Her eyes closed.

"Lookit that, she's asleep," one of the ambulance men said after a minute.

"Wish I were," the other remarked.

At last they were able to shift Linda into the wheelchair and fasten a restraining belt around her. They were ready to go.

"Do you want to come with us?"

"Yes—oh, no, I can't," Michael said. "We have a child sleeping in there." He gestured towards Ned's room, without noticing that the door was open a crack.

"Just as well," one of the ambulance men said. "Nothing you could do at the hospital anyhow."

"Get some rest now," the other advised. "You can see her later."

Michael was smiling as he stood by the door and watched them go, which seemed strange to Ned. True, his mother hadn't flown away or disappeared, but she was gone all the same. How could his father look so happy?

Michael walked into the living room and wrote down the name of the hospital and ward the ambulance men had given him. He was to phone in a couple of hours and find out what the situation was. Now he collapsed on the sofa. He brushed his hair back and noticed that it was damp and matted. Quite a wrestling match for a while there, he thought. Thank God she's all right ... if she is all right.

What would have happened if he hadn't heard the sound of the inhaler and then Linda falling to the floor? What if he hadn't dragged himself from sleep to go and see what was the matter? Would she have died there on the floor, head sticking out of the bathroom, a corpse waiting for him or Ned to—

Ned!

Dear God, I hope he slept through it, Michael prayed. It was hard to move from the sofa, but he went to check on his son. He knew that Ned's door was always left open a crack, but in all the commotion he hadn't thought to shut it or make sure the boy was sound asleep.

"Oh, no," he whispered to himself. Ned was still standing on his spot, staring sadly ahead. One hand held his penis through his pajamas. "Hey, what're you doing up?" Michael forced his voice to come as close to normal as possible. "Do you have to go pee, Ned?" He scooped his son up in his arms.

"No." So tiny and forlorn.

"Well, you should be in bed sleeping. It's the middle of the night." Michael carried the boy across the room and set him down on the bed. He brushed the fine light hair away from Ned's face. "Are you sure you don't have to go pee?"

"Yes." A little waver. Perhaps close to crying.

"Okay, how about sleep then?" Michael hugged Ned. "You know, the Hulk has to get his sleep, otherwise he won't be strong in the morning."

"No, I don't want to."

"Are you all right, Ned?"

"Where's my mommy?"

There it was.

"Mommy got sick, Ned. She had to go see the doctor, but she's going to be just fine, and tomorrow you and I will go see her. Okay?"

"But where is she?"

"Gone to see the doctor."

"But I want her."

"Hey, come on, Ned. I told you we'd see her in a little while. You want your mommy to get better, don't you?"

"Yes."

"Well, she has to go to the doctor to get better, and we have to get some sleep so we'll be wide awake when we go to see Mommy later."

"But I want to see her."

"So do I, Ned, but the most important thing right now is that she go to the doctor. You love Mommy and I love Mommy, and she loves us. We all love each other, but Mommy has to go to the doctor now. You don't see me crying about it, do you?"

"No." How could a four-year-old make a word sound so stony?

"We should both be happy that Mommy can go to the doctor and get better, right?"

"I want my—"

"I'd really like to sleep here and cuddle with you, Ned. Is that all right? Can I do that? Then we'll get up and go see our mommy in the morning. Is that okay? Can I sleep here with you?"

Finally: "Okay."

"Okay, good. Come on now, give me a big cuddle." Ned hugged Michael's neck but there was no strength in his arms. Michael pulled the blankets up over them and held his son close. The gray light in the window made him wonder how much time had passed. It seemed like hours since that first dreadful sight of Linda on the floor, but it probably hadn't been very long at all. The images that filled his mind were too vivid—he had to lose them in sleep, if that was possible.

Ned clung tightly to him, which was a good sign. Michael couldn't bear to think about how much the boy might have seen. And Linda, dear Linda.... What the hell had happened to her? She had asthma, yes, but she had never had an attack even remotely as serious as this one was. What had caused it? She used her inhaler three or four times a day, a little more on especially dry days, but that was it.

Now this. She had been hysterical, delirious. Off the goddamn wall, with that kicking and punching and ungodly screaming. The ambulance men thought she was doing drugs, that's for sure, and not just the inhaler. It hurt him to recall how they had taken in the view when, in Linda's thrashing about, her nightgown had jumped up her thighs. And the way they had looked at Michael, as if he had done something and it was all his fault that she was in such a state.

Michael sighed deeply. The boy seemed all right. Whatever he had witnessed earlier, he was clinging to his father now and breathing with the even rhythms of sleep. It'll all seem like a bad dream to him when the sun comes up, Michael thought. Kids are tough.

Linda had to be okay. Everything was just starting to go well for them in Washington. Our lives are just beginning, he thought, she has got to be okay. And Ned too. Let this not be a trauma, let there be no mental scars. Let there ... Michael fell asleep.

Ned was close to sleep, but his mind hadn't let go completely yet. Snug in his father's embrace, he felt safe and comfortable. One of the rules was that if you were with either or both of your parents nothing, but nothing, could happen to you. If only he could sleep with them every night—but, no, they didn't allow it. Ned couldn't understand. It was as if they were actually looking for trouble.

What had happened before—he couldn't think about that now. He was too weak and tired. Besides, it didn't matter. His mother would come back, or she wouldn't. It made no difference as far as the real problem was concerned. Ned knew what had happened. A phantom had come and turned his mother into a raving mad dog of a person. Even if she survived somehow and came home again, the point had been made. The line had been crossed. Day and night were mixed, once and forever.

That was just a demonstration.

If they could do that to your mother, just think what they could do to you....

CHAPTER 1
LYNNHAVEN

It wasn't much of a town anymore. You could ride the old Coast Turnpike every day and hardly notice Lynnhaven. Those who did take a look invariably described it as sleepy. Local pundits often used the word "coma," while the Town Clerk was fond of saying that Lynnhaven was in a period of transition. If so, it had been going on for thirty or forty years. Lynnhaven was not so much a town as a fishing village, and even the fishing activity was residual now. More and more of the young people regarded fishing and crabbing as hard, poor-paying work at a time when better opportunities could be found elsewhere. If Lynnhaven had a future it was probably in the direction of light industry, tract homes, condos, shopping plazas and fast-food chains, but the new era had not yet arrived. Lynnhaven was a forgotten pocket of a community, waiting half-heartedly to be rediscovered.

There were other towns up and down the shore, larger and suburbanized, so the rest of the world began nearby and Lynnhaven didn't really seem like an isolated or remote place. But inland, on the other side of the low hills, the earth was an expanse of undeveloped, uninviting woods and swamps that stretched for miles. Lynnhaven was merely one of the smaller and less conspicuous stops along the Chesapeake from Annapolis to Norfolk.

In the old days, before the Depression and scandal shut down the spa, Lynnhaven had a population of ten thousand, but it had dwindled down to a third of that now. The Sherwood family was dead and gone, their spa nothing more than a ruin on the hill. Housing was no problem in Lynnhaven; a number of fine white clapboard homes stood vacant and shuttered, ready for new buyers. There wasn't a wharf along Polidori Street that didn't need some repair work or general sprucing up, but no one bothered; there didn't seem to be much point. It was a place of flaked paint and driftwood grays, and if it had long since stopped taking itself seriously, well, maybe life was a little easier for that.

The spa on the hill had been Lynnhaven's claim to fame back in the Twenties. The Sherwood family, who built it, brought relative prosperity to the town for a few years. Local old-timers who could still remember something of those days tended to regard the spa as a folly or a sucker-farm that had sprung up in their midst and then, in the manner of such things, collapsed. The money had been nice, but too many years had passed for Lynnhaven to feel anything more than indifference to the dim memory buried in the tumbledown estate high on the edge of town.

Lynnhaven was neither gloomy nor unpleasant. Some people even thought that its slightly shabby, slightly run-down appearance made it quaint and pretty. But the town didn't have a good beach or much of anything else to draw tourists. Those who did pass through Lynnhaven usually continued on their way after cruising the few central streets.

Blair's Market still sold bottles of Lynnhaven Water, but they moved very slowly. The mineral content, which included sulfur in strength, may have been good for one's health, but it left something to be desired in the flavor department. Chief among the other stores in town were a couple of boat and tackle shops, a vintage Western Auto, Mae's Candy, which specialized in undistinguished saltwater taffy, and Marine Antiques, which was open whatever odd hours suited its proprietor, Monroe Tillotson.

Two of the town's larger and more elegant homes had been converted to boarding houses, providing inexpensive accommodation for some of Lynnhaven's solitary folk—widows and widowers, spinsters and bachelors, people without relatives or money enough to live anywhere else. They survived on Social Security and miscellaneous jobs. Everyone knew Miss Merrion, for instance, who had a room at Laurel House. She sold magazine subscriptions and stuffed envelopes for a company a thousand miles away in Minneapolis.

If there was nothing particularly attractive about Lynnhaven, neither was it the worst place in the world to live. If you liked seafood it was possible to eat very cheaply there. The boats went out every morning and came back every evening, and bargains could be had when they unloaded. Moreover, Lynnhaven was a completely safe town. For more than forty years the police force of two had had little to do other than keep their one squad car polished and the drunks in line. Miss Merrion and others like her could walk home alone after bingo on the darkest night without fear of being bothered. Even the town dogs were well behaved.

Lynnhaven had to do without some things, inevitably. It had neither a local newspaper nor a library, and the Rialto movie house had been turned into a warehouse years ago. In fact, the last film shown there had been *Abbott and Costello Meet Frankenstein*, in 1948. The nearest A & P was ten miles away and the only church in Lynnhaven was Saint Paul's, which retained a small but reliable congregation of Lutherans. The fire department was strictly volunteer and was put to the test only a few times a year, dealing with things like a grease fire in the kitchen or a small electrical blaze caused by old wiring. If a real fire had ever started, especially on Polidori Street where the buildings stood one to another, half the town could have been wiped out in very little time. But nothing so dramatic ever happened in Lynnhaven.

There were those who would say that the last time the town ever got worked up about anything was during World War II. A group of local men, who for one reason or another had not been called into the war effort, formed themselves into a kind of unofficial home guard, armed with guns, clubs and fishing spears. They patrolled the shore and kept watch day and night. It would be just too bad for any German sub they got their hands on. But not even the Nazis bothered to visit Lynnhaven.

Presidents took office and departed without having much impact on the townspeople. Few registered, and of those fewer still got around to voting. Politics, like crime, was something that took place elsewhere. You could keep track of it on television if you were interested. In spite of, or perhaps because of its proximity to Washington, Lynnhaven could not boast a single nuclear fallout shelter. What was the point? Only one of the town's sons, Marv Wilcox, was dispatched to Vietnam, and he came back with a lot of souvenirs and a tidy bankroll. Marv went into business for himself down in Newport News, doing contract work for the Navy.

All towns have their secrets, and Lynnhaven was no exception. But secrets are not secrets unless almost everybody knows something about them, and then they become an accepted, if submerged part of everyday life, too familiar and mundane to be of lasting interest to any but a few gossips—and poor fare for them. Adultery, cock or dog fights staged in the woods—the Lutheran minister, Reverend Harnack, would address himself to these goings-on one Sunday out of every four, but even he could muster only routine disapproval. Secrets? Yes, all the usual ones.

More or less.

CHAPTER 2
THE BAITHOUSE

The old man tied one end of the string tightly around a three-inch strip of pork rind. "That's all there is to it," he said.

"Aren't you going to use a hook?" Ned asked.

"Don't need no hook to catch crawdads. You just wait and see."

The old man tossed the pork rind into the water and played out a short length of string. Ned watched it drift briefly on the current before sinking out of sight.

"Now what do you do?"

"Just wait a few minutes, give 'em time to gather round for a bite of lunch. Won't be long."

"What's this stream called, Peeler?"

"Ain't a stream, it's a creek, and it's called Old Woods Creek. All this stretch of land is Old Woods."

"Old Woods Creek," Ned repeated. "What's the difference between a stream and a creek?"

"If you can jump across it, it's a creek. If you can't, it's a stream."

"What's the difference between a stream and a river then?" Peeler snorted. "River's just a stream somebody decided to call a river, that's all." Then he added: "Unless you're talkin' about the Mississippi and such. They're your bona fide rivers, but there ain't so many of them. Most rivers are just over-growed streams."

"Think you got anything yet?" "Let's see."

Peeler hauled in the string. Four crayfish dangled from the piece of pork rind.

"Wow, look at them!" Ned exclaimed.

"Greedy little cusses," Peeler said, smiling. "Old Mr. Crawdad is such a fool he won't let go of his food, even if it means he gets caught and ends up being used for bass bait hisself."

"Can they hurt you?"

"Big one can give you a pinch, I guess, if you're not too careful with 'em. But these lowly fellers can't do nothin' to you."

Peeler gently separated the crayfish from the line and dropped them into a pail of water. Then he and the boy moved a few yards farther along before plunking the bait back into the creek. Peeler rummaged around in the old burlap sack he carried and pulled out a can of beer.

"Can I have some?"

"How old are you, Nedly?"

"I'll be ten in August."

"Good enough," Peeler said, grinning. He handed the can of Iron City to Ned, who took a sip and grimaced. "Better not tell your folks I give it to you."

"I won't. I don't like it anyway."

"Wait a few years and try again."

"Peeler?"

"Hmmn?"

"Is that your real name?"

"Is now."

"Did you used to have another one?"

"'Fraid so."

"What was it?"

"Now that's a secret."

"I won't tell anyone."

The old man arched an eyebrow in mock-seriousness and studied his young companion for a few moments.

"How do I know you won't tell anybody?"

"I promise."

"You do?"

"Honest."

"Okay, I'll trust you, but you better keep your word or you'll get in big trouble."

"I will, I promise."

"Okay. My name was Hamish."

"Hamish?"

"Yep."

"What kind of name is that?" Ned asked. He had never heard it before.

"Goddamned if I know," Peeler replied. "Always hated it."

"So why are you called Peeler now?"

"Better'n Progger, ain't it?"

"Progger?"

"Yep."

"Is that a name?"

"Could be," Peeler said as he took three more crayfish from the pork rind.

Ned watched silently. Sometimes the old man didn't make much sense, or if he did it wasn't always easy to follow. But that didn't really matter. Ned just enjoyed being with Peeler. They had met only a few weeks earlier, shortly after the Covingtons had moved to Lynnhaven. On one of his first rambles around the place, Ned came across a long, low shed on the spot where a street ended and an open field began. He could just make out the word BAITS in faded paint on the gray boarding. Curious, Ned walked through the thick and tangled grass to the open doorway. Inside, all was darkness and the faint sound of running water. Ned almost turned and left, but he noticed a little light coming in through two small windows in the middle of the shed. He stepped through the doorway and let his eyes adjust from the bright sun outside to the gloomy interior. The air was cool and had a rich, sweet smell, like freshly turned soil. Ned could see why. There was no floor, just bare earth. The shed was full of wooden tables with boxes built on top. In each box was a layer of dirt several inches deep, home for hundreds of writhing worms. A perfect place for a vampire, Ned thought. A little further into the shed he found two chipped and battered bathtubs holding dozens of crayfish. It was the first time Ned had ever seen one, although he knew what they were from pictures in books. A hose had been rigged up to run a thin stream of fresh water through both tubs. Other tables held large metal washtubs full of what looked like clumps of weeds in water, and boxes of sand and moss. Ned couldn't see any sign of animal life in these containers, but he wasn't about to stick his hand in and poke around. The two windows were so fly-specked and dirty they provided only the barest illumination.

When Ned turned to leave he saw the figure of a tall, heavy man standing in the doorway. In one hand the man held a wire basket full of live crabs, clicking and crawling over each other. Ned jumped in fright. But then the man was laughing good-naturedly and he came and introduced himself as Peeler and made the boy welcome. Ned ended up staying more than an hour, talking and watching Peeler dismember the crabs.

"So you just moved here from Washington, D.C.?"

"Yes."

"Lot different here, ain't it?" Peeler reached into the tub full of weeds and came up with a can of cold beer.

"It sure is," Ned agreed.

"Your father work in Washington?"

"Yes, he does."

"He drives back and forth all that way every day?"

"Sure."

"He must love his car."

"It's brown, with a white vinyl top."

"I'll be damned."

Peeler was a tall, solid man who had to walk slightly stooped in the baithouse. His face was as rough and weathered as the sign outside, but it was not without a measure of warmth and friendliness. When he smiled, which he did almost every time Ned said something, it came entirely from his eyes. To the boy, Peeler might have been a hundred years old, but he was an immediate, natural friend. His hands were like those of a giant, huge and leathery, but surprisingly nimble as they took apart a crab or tied a complicated knot.

Ned also met Cloudy, an elderly black man with a shiny moon face, gold teeth and a silver halo of hair. Cloudy was Peeler's "partner at baitin' and crabbin' and so on."

"He tell you how he caught them crabs?" Cloudy asked.

"No."

"I didn't think so. Well, I'll tell you. He goes down to where the water's shallow and he knows there's some crabs, and he sticks his big white toes in."

"His toes?" Ned wasn't sure whether to believe it or not. "That's right, and when he feels the clappers latch on, he knows he got a crab."

"I'd like to meet the crab who'd touch your toe," Peeler said.

In the days that followed Ned stopped by to visit Peeler and Cloudy as often as he could. They were always the same, joking, telling stories, glad to see him. And they always wore the same clothes. Peeler's outfit was a flannel shirt, green work pants and heavy shoes. Cloudy had on a suit and sneakers. In each case the clothes were wrinkled and torn in places, and appeared to be about as old as the men who wore them. Sometimes Peeler wore a washed-out gray-and-green baseball cap. The breast pocket of Cloudy's jacket held a plastic case crammed full of ballpoint pens, none of which Ned ever saw the man use.

The baithouse was a place of wonder. At the far end, beyond the tables and tubs, was a cleared area. Two beaten old armchairs without legs sat on the ground, along with the front seat taken from a car. The walls here were covered with tools and equipment, every item of which was a mystery in itself to Ned. Rusted beer cans lay all around the place, and new empties were constantly being added to the collection. It was a crude and trashy shed, but to a boy of nine-going-on-ten recently delivered from city life it was a place of enchantment, a cool dark comfortable haven from the heat and light of summer.

"That's enough for now, I guess," Peeler said. The pail of water teemed with crayfish. "They'll start eatin' each other pretty soon if I don't get 'em into the tanks."

"Eat each other?" Ned asked. "Like cannibals?"

"All I know is the longer we take the more of their arms and legs you'll see floatin' around loose in there."

Back at the baithouse, they found Cloudy sitting outside on a wooden crate, leaning against a pile of old tires.

"Look at that lazy son of a biscuit," Peeler said loudly. "Hey, ain't you got enough tan on you already?"

"Lunchtime," Cloudy said without bothering to open his eyes.

"He always sleeps through lunchtime," Peeler explained to Ned. "You won't never see him eat no lunch."

Peeler went inside the baithouse to take care of the crayfish, but today Ned hung back, standing a few feet away from Cloudy. He was curious about something, and it didn't seem right to ask Peeler.

"Cloudy."

"Mm?"

"What's that?"

Cloudy opened his eyes a crack and saw that Ned was pointing to the shack out behind the baithouse. It was a tiny structure, four walls and a flat roof with a chimney pipe sticking out, a door and a single window. Altogether, about twelve feet square. Nearby was the wreck of an old car; the windows were still intact but the body was covered with rust and the bare wheels were overgrown with wild grass. It was a Studebaker, but now it looked like the remains of a beached monster from another age.

"That? That's Peeler's house."

"Oh. I thought that's where he lives," Ned said, nodding.

"He don't live there," Cloudy corrected. "That's his house but he don't live in it. Oh, no, he *can't* live in it."

"He can't? Why not?"

"Go see for yourself," Cloudy suggested with a wave of his hand. "Go ahead, open the door."

"Won't he mind?"

"Naw, Peeler don't mind. He show you hisself if you ask him. Go ahead."

Ned went over to the door of the shack and hesitated briefly. What did he expect to find—a gutted interior, a caved-in floor, a swarm of rats? It had to be something serious enough to drive a man from his own dwelling. Ned pulled the door open and jumped back a step. Empty beer cans, dozens of them, tumbled out of the shack and onto the ground. Ned could hear Cloudy laughing behind him.

"Wow," Ned gasped. "Where did he get all these cans?"

This made Cloudy laugh even more. Ned moved to take a closer look. The inside of the shack was a lake of empty beer cans, four or five feet deep, wall to wall. Enough Iron City cans to rebuild Pittsburgh from scratch, if that were ever necessary. The top of a broom handle was just visible, sticking up in the middle of the single room like the mast of a sunken ship. Any other furniture or contents the place might hold could not be seen. Ned couldn't begin to guess how many cans there might be.

"He got some good old ones in there," Cloudy said. "Down at the bottom."

"Gosh, where does he live now?"

"In the car, where else."

"The car?"

At that moment Peeler emerged from the baithouse and threw a handful of crab scraps into the little vegetable patch a few yards away. He glanced up at Ned.

"Damn good car it is, too," he said before disappearing back inside.

"Only one he ever owned," Cloudy elaborated lazily. "Kept it all this time."

"Like the beer cans," Ned said. "He must have every one he ever drank in his whole life."

"And then some. The rest is underground hereabouts, I forget exactly where."

"Underground?"

"Sure. He used to bury them all, till they finally got to be too much work."

Cloudy made it sound like the most natural thing in the world, burying your empty beer cans, but it was too much for Ned to figure out. He went to take a look at the car. The weeds and flowers were so tall and thick around it that the vehicle looked as if it might have grown there, the exotic offspring of soil, sea and countless subterranean beer cans. The front seat was gone, undoubtedly the one removed to the baithouse. The floor of the car was covered with blankets and there was a pillow propped in the back left corner. All very tidy.

"Sleeping in a car, that's neat, but doesn't it get cold in the winter?"

"Oh, he got the heater and radio workin' in there, and he just have to recharge the battery now and then."

"Why does he do it?"

"I never did know that one, Mr. Tadpole." Cloudy thought about it again, and then shrugged. "For some unforesaken reason, I guess."

Peeler returned, a beer appropriately in hand, and dragged a crate across the ground to sit down with Cloudy and Ned.

"So this old squirrelbait told you about my house, eh? That what I heard?"

"Yeah, it's great. I wish I could sleep out in a car."

The two old men laughed.

"But why do you have all those cans in the house?" Ned asked. "Why don't you just throw them all away?"

"I did. I used to dig a hole in the ground and dump 'em in and cover 'em up again. When I got tired of that I started tossin' 'em in the car, but that was no good because the car filled up in no time. So, instead of livin' in the house and throwin' the cans in the car, I decided to live in the car and throw the cans in the house. Took me long enough to figure out, but ever since things've been fine. It works just right."

"It's a system," Cloudy chipped in, as if explaining everything.

"But why don't you just have the trash man take them away every week?"

"If the trash man came here he'd take everything, lock, stock and barrel," Peeler said, and then he and Cloudy roared with laughter.

"Where do you live, Cloudy?" Ned asked.

"Oh, I stay in town."

"At the Capitol Hotel," Peeler said sarcastically.

"Down near Polidori Street," Cloudy went on, ignoring his partner. "Yeah, I got me a room there."

"I didn't know there was a hotel in town," Ned said truthfully. To him a hotel was a big building with a big sign, and he hadn't seen one in Lynnhaven.

"You wouldn't notice it," Peeler said, laughing.

"There used to be lotsa hotels here, back in the days of the old Lynnhaven spa."

"Spa?" Ned didn't know the word.

"Yeah, certainly. All the rich white folks from Washington, D.C. used to come down here to take a bath."

"In more ways than one," Peeler added.

"That's for sure," Cloudy agreed.

"A bath?" Another one of their incredible stories was taking shape, but Ned could tell he wasn't being joshed.

"Yeah, I'm tellin' you," Cloudy continued. "The rich boys in the govamint come down here with their wives and girlfriends and what not, and they took the hot baths at the spa. Supposed to be good for you or something. Right here in Lynnhaven. This used to be quite the town once upon a time."

"Even had a train station," Peeler said. "Direct line to and from Washington."

"That's right. Lynnhaven Depot, it was called. Then when it all ended people just started callin' it Lynnhaven. They forgot about the depot part of it."

"What happened to the place?" Ned asked.

Cloudy held his hand out, palms up.

"The waters went bad," Peeler said.

"Oh, that's what it was, huh," Cloudy said. "I never did get the right of it."

"The waters went bad and somebody croaked and the next thing was they shut the spa down. And then they took away the train tracks and that was that."

"How could the water go bad?"

Peeler smiled at the boy. "Nedly, anything goes bad if people make it go bad. Somebody put something in the water or in the ground there that made the water bad. That's what happened."

Cloudy frowned. "They prove that?"

"Nobody proved nothin' ," Peeler said emphatically. "Which only goes to show I'm right. You and me must be the only ones left here who remember anything about it, Cloudy."

"That's right."

"And you don't remember much...."

"And Mr. Muckle down to the hotel. He can tell you about it too, he was around then."

"I thought Muckle was dead," Peeler remarked.

"Not so's you'd notice."

"Cloudy?"

"Yes, Mr. Tadpole?"

"Is Cloudy your real name?"

"You are one for names," Peeler said, shaking his head.

"Is it?" Ned asked again, to keep the question from being sidetracked.

"I won't tell you my real name," Cloudy said with a broad grin. "But I will tell you how I come by the name of Cloudy."

"Okay." That was good enough for Ned. "How?"

The black man sat forward on his crate and stared hard at Ned. "Look at my eyes," he said. Ned did so. "Now tell me what you see there."

"Well ... " Ned concentrated. "Big brown eyes."

Peeler laughed out loud and took another swallow of beer. The can was empty and he tossed it at the shack.

"What else?" Cloudy demanded. "What about those eyes'?"

"I don't know. They're just eyes, that's all."

"Aw, you ain't lookin' right, Mr. Tadpole. Okay, I'll tell you. When I was a boy like you my momma look in these eyes one day and she say, 'Your eyes is cloudy. Cloudy.' And one of my brothers, fast's can be, he says, 'Is your eyes cloudy, Cloudy?' And I say, 'No, just cloudy, I guess.' And ever since that day they's called me Cloudy. That make sense to you?"

"Your eyes aren't cloudy, are they?" Ned couldn't tell. What did cloudy eyes look like? He'd never heard of such a thing.

"They must be, everybody says so."

"Do you have, like, trouble seeing?" Ned asked.

"No, I see just fine. But everything do look a little cloudy."

The two men cackled with laughter again and Peeler punched open another can of beer.

"Want to know my middle name?" Ned offered.

"I surely do."

"Yeah, what is it?"

"Michael. It's my father's name."

"Michael," Cloudy pronounced. "That's a name, all right."

"I can tell you because you're my friends."

"Why thank you, Nedly," Peeler said warmly, giving the boy a thumbs-up sign.

"Everybody should have friends in low places," Cloudy said, shaking with mirth. "Now you got 'em."

The afternoon wound on, interrupted only by a couple of people who drove up to buy some sand worms. Ned told Peeler and Cloudy more about what it had been like living in an apartment in Washington, and how his parents had waited until his school year had ended in June before making the move to Lynnhaven, even though they had bought the house two months earlier.

"That's the old Farley place you live in now," Peeler said.

"The Farley place?" Cloudy's eyebrows moved up a notch. "That where he live?"

"What's the Farley place?" Ned asked.

"Where you live," Peeler said. "What's your daddy do in Washington ?"

"He works for the Internal Revenue." Ned realized that by answering he had let Peeler change the subject again, but it wasn't any big deal: a conversation with Peeler and Cloudy could go here and there, around and around, like a fishline bird's nest.

"Eternal Revenue," Cloudy intoned.

"That's a good safe job," Peeler said quickly. "Your folks from Washington, or somewhere else?"

"Buffalo, New York. We go there once or twice a year to see my grandparents. Usually in the summer and at Christmas, but we're not going this summer on account of we just moved into the house."

"Buffalo," Cloudy said. "You been to Buffalo. I ain't never been there and I'm old enough for a whole army of you, Mr. Tadpole. What d'ya think about that?"

Long after Ned had left for home and the sky had gathered into a darkening purple dusk, Cloudy kicked the dirt with the toe of his shoe, like a nerved-up horse.

"I got to go to town now."

"See you," Peeler said.

"That boy, he very nice."

"He surely is."

"He live on the Farley land?"

"That's right."

"You know—"

"Bullshit," Peeler cut him off.

"I know, I know."

"Besides, there ain't a Christ-thing you can do about it anyway."

CHAPTER 3
PARENTS

Michael Covington handed his wife a glass of sherry and turned to pour a double bourbon with a splash of spring water for himself. He tested it, approved, and sat down in his sturdy leather armchair.

"We wanted a place that had been overlooked," he said. "A nice, quiet, small, older town. And that's what we found."

Linda nodded. "I know." She hadn't touched her sherry yet, but held the glass stiffly in one hand.

"You don't have to go far down the road in either direction to find the kind of new suburban developments that are exactly what we didn't want."

"I know, and I do like Lynnhaven," Linda said. "It's kind of run-down and over-the-hill, and that's what helps make it charming in a way."

"So?" Michael picked up one of his pipes and idly toyed with it. He hadn't smoked indoors at home in years, but he still carried at least one pipe with him at all times.

"That's just the problem," Linda said. "Lynnhaven suits me fine, and you too, as far as I can tell, but—"

"Absolutely."

"—but I'm not sure it's right for Ned."

"Now that's where you're wrong," Michael asserted. "He's loving it here, and you don't need a degree in child psychology to see that. Getting him out of D. C. was the best thing we ever did for that kid."

"Don't call him 'that kid,' Michael. Please."

"Listen, honey, it's like he's discovering the outdoors for the first time in his life. He's got the woods and the fields and the brooks to explore, the beach, he can watch the fishing boats go out and come in and unload. I think it's all terrific for him, just terrific, and he seems to be having a great time." Michael sat back with the look of a man who has just reached the bottom line on a dream of a balance sheet.

"All that is true," Linda admitted, "and it is important and I am happy about it." She spoke slowly and methodically, as if she were trying to explain her doubts to herself as much as to her husband. "But, I don't know … I guess, well … He still has no friends here."

"He will. Give him time. We've only been here a month."

"That's just it. Kids make friends in a day or two, or an hour or two even. But the other children around here are either too old, in high school, or just babies and toddlers."

Michael sighed. "When he gets into his new school in September he'll be surrounded by kids his own age and he'll make plenty of friends then."

"Maybe, but they'll probably live miles away."

"Honey, you're worrying too much about nothing. Really. Let's just take it easy for a while and see how things develop. I think it's going to be fine. Ned's really come to life out here."

Linda looked at the glass of sherry in her hand as if noticing it for the first time and sipped.

"Maybe if he were involved in some team sports …"

"You know Ned doesn't go in for that kind of thing," Michael said patiently. "I tried it with him—baseball, basketball. Remember? He just didn't take to them. He has his own interests and you have to let him follow them. I'm not going to be one of those nutty fathers who drives his son to be the best damn pitcher or quarterback in the neighborhood."

"No, no, I wouldn't want that either." Linda made a face, annoyed that she was unable to put her finger precisely on the source of her doubts, nor even to articulate fully what those doubts comprised.

Maybe it's nothing, she thought. And maybe it's everything. Getting older. The usual magazine and talk-show crisis of those in their thirties. But the problem was real, she didn't doubt that. Ned was her only child and she knew she could never have another. And it's so hard to know what is right and good for a child, and what isn't. You keep thinking and hoping that it will get easier as the child grows older, but it doesn't. It gets worse, and harder.

She looked at Michael. A good, well-meaning man. Solid and reliable. It had been a pleasure to watch him grow over the years from a nervous and somewhat awkward youth into an assured and sociable man. A devoted husband and father, too. If at times he seemed a little complacent, if the edge was softening—was that so unexpected, so terrible? It happened to everyone. Didn't it?

As for herself, Linda knew she wasn't making much of an effort to fight the tide, real or imaginary. Your body slackens, your face changes. After all, she had been a mother for nearly ten years now. The mind shifts as well. She was aware of the fact that she read more magazines and fewer books than she once had. It seemed that any old radio program would do, whereas in the past she had searched out good classical broadcasts. And, worst of all, she surrendered now to television shows she would never have even glanced at a few years ago. At her gloomiest Linda felt as if she were caught in a vast process of attrition, the slow but inexorable obliteration of herself as a person.

Day after day
In every way
I'm turning gray.

On the other hand, Michael's mind never seemed to stray within a thousand miles of such thoughts. He had reached the point where he took life as it came and rode with it, lucky man. He was so remarkably free of uncertainty that Linda didn't know whether to be envious or frightened.

Their lives were one thing, but what was important above all else was to make sure that everything was right for Ned. Insofar as it was humanly possible, Linda was determined to see that it was done.

A child is all you have.

One boy-child.

"Hey honey, why the face?"

Oh, yes, and a husband. Linda smiled mechanically and took another sip of sherry.

"Game of cribbage?" Michael asked.

"I couldn't pay attention to the cards tonight. Do you mind?"

Michael shrugged. "Okay. I just asked."

"Do you think Ned spends too much time with those men at the bait place or whatever it is? I worry about that."

"Oh, I think it's all right," Michael answered after a few seconds' thought. "I asked Bill Fischer next door about them and he says they're just a pair of harmless old coots."

"You don't think they might be a little … funny? With Ned being a pretty, young boy, you know, they—"

"Nah listen. There's no gossip at all about them, and there'd be plenty if there was even the flimsiest reason for it. You know that. Besides, Bill said they've been here practically since the last Ice Age and never any trouble."

"Well, it still doesn't seem right to me," Linda persisted. "He goes over there to see them almost every day."

"So he *has* found a couple of friends."

"Michael, they're a couple of old wharf rats who live in a setting that belongs on Tobacco Road."

Michael frowned at his whiskey. "That's rather judgmental, don't you think?"

Linda looked away. "I'm sorry," she said. "Maybe it was, but he is our son."

Michael rose and went to get another bourbon. He could see that this had the makings of a three- or four-drink discussion.

"Look, honey, Ned's grandparents are way the hell up in Buffalo and he sees them only once or twice a year. So it shouldn't come as any surprise to find that when he has the chance he enjoys the company of a couple of older people. That's natural and good for a kid. It increases his perspective. And secondly, whether you like them or not, and you don't even know them, what are you going to do? Tell Ned he can't see them, that he has to stay away from that place? What would that accomplish?"

Linda shook her head unhappily. "No, I don't suppose that would do any good."

"Of course it wouldn't. More sherry?"

"No, thanks."

"Linda, if you want, I'll ask around some more about those two old-timers, maybe even go down there myself and check them out. But I really think all we have to do is what we have been doing: watch out for anything that might go wrong or harm our son, but otherwise leave him room enough to grow his own way."

"You're telling me I worry too much."

"We already know that, honey."

Michael picked up the remote control for the television. Like a fisherman casting onto a lake, he raised his arm above his head and then swung it down, pointing the device at the set and at the same time thumbing a button to turn it on. He repeated the movements half a dozen times, patrolling the channels until he found one that was acceptable.

Poor Lin. She did get in these moods from time to time. There wasn't much he could do about it either, except to be as calm and reasonable as possible. He knew there was really no way to talk her out of it; you just had to try to help her work her own way back. It was understandable. First, there was the move to Lynnhaven, coming after years of living in a city. That would take her a while to adjust to, but he was confident she would with no real trouble. The move itself wasn't wrong, it was in fact the very thing they had worked for for so long. Second, of course, was her health—not always a conscious fear, perhaps, but a very real one all the same. She must wonder every day if she might be about to suffer another devastating attack like the one five years ago. The doctors had no explanation for it either. Linda had been asthmatic from childhood, she had bouts of wheezing and troubled breathing now and then. The inhalers kept it under control very nicely. But that attack, the overwhelming severity of it ... It had happened only that one time in her life so far, but the threat of a rerun was a terrible thing to live with. Well, he had made their house as safe as he could. They had enough air conditioners, purifiers, dust removers, humidifiers and ionizers to open a small appliance store. Third, Ned was their only child. If they'd had others, even only one more, maybe the focus of her anxieties would not be so circumscribed and intense. But the doctors had advised against another child. Not the happiest of situations, but it was obviously more sensible to make the most of it and enjoy the one child they were fortunate enough to have than to ache for the ones that would never be.

Michael was sure that everything would sort itself out in time. Lynnhaven was a nice town and they had a lovely house. He could be happy here for the rest of his life. The house had character. A large and roomy saltbox with two fireplaces, it was situated on a good four acres of land. A sensational investment, too. Sooner or later, sadly but inevitably, more people would rediscover Lynnhaven, and when they did property values would soar. Not that Michael could ever imagine selling the place, but it was nonetheless comforting to know that his home was destined to appreciate significantly—dramatically, even—in the years to come. All in all, they had done well and were in a good position.

But try to tell that to Lin.

CHAPTER 4
A VERY SPECIAL ROOM

It was the best room in the house. It was outer space and inner earth, the triumph of a young boy's mind.

It was: stamps and coins and a handed-down set of old Hardy Boys mysteries and crab shells with bits of gooey stuff still sticking to them in places and strangely colored rocks and dried out worms and acorns and horse chestnuts and a microscope and a telescope and a salamander in a bowl of mud and comics and all kinds of cards and a cherry bomb hidden for an occasion that would be known only when it came and carved sticks and a jack knife and waterproof matches and a canteen and a pocket magnifying glass for frying Japanese beetles and a rabbit's foot and a shell plugged up with a dead snail and ...

It was the best room in any house. It was a boy's room. Here and only here could magic forces be found. The Invisible Weights, which on certain mornings anchored your arms and legs so that you couldn't get out of bed until they decided to let you go. The Moving Pebble, which might change position only an inch or two but was never in the exact spot where you left it. The Night Fire, which could only be seen in a mirror in the dark when you brushed your hair (you know it's static electricity, but if that's all you know, you don't know anything).

It was a small, narrow room, and Ned had chosen it over the other available bedroom for just that reason. He knew it would be tricky enough for him to keep track of every square inch here; the bigger room would have defeated him. Besides, a large room feels loose and vacant, no matter what you do with it. This shoebox with the angled ceiling was perfect.

A measure of confinement isn't necessarily a bad thing either, so one window is better than two. The view from the porthole: the backyard, an expanse of grass that Ned's father would have to rehabilitate, future flower beds and a vegetable garden, some lawn chairs and, farther out, a couple of stately sugar maples and a scattering of gray birches. The land rolled away, beyond the limits of the Covington property, to a broad meadow that had, over the years, spoiled with thick brush and undergrowth.

The only thing that stood out in that unremarkable landscape was the stark remnant of an ancient scarecrow, a mute and forlorn reminder of other, presumably better times, when the meadow had been tilled. Ned had inspected the scarecrow the first day they moved into the house. Only a few strips of rotting cloth remained, but the "body" was still firmly fixed in the ground and the rope binding the "arms" had tightened so much Ned's fingers found no give in the knots.

When he wasn't outdoors Ned spent most of his free time in his room. Aside from a few favorite programs, he did not watch much television because it made him feel tired. And the room, which was after all a very special place, always offered more to occupy Ned's mind than the flat TV screen.

For one thing, magic. Not just the Moving Pebble, but the magic that lies beyond such phenomena. The magic of the unseen. Ned believed in it, without knowing what it was. You had to have a special feeling for it, be in a special place, otherwise there was only the ordinary. The twin alarms of fear and excitement were signals Ned had come to know well. When it was finally definite that the Covingtons were going to leave Washington, Ned had worried that the magic in his room would be lost forever. But the first day in Lynnhaven, when he chose this room, he knew that everything would be all right. Perhaps it was nothing more than the aspect of light, or the way the air felt, that almost tangible charge that, even at its weakest, bespoke secret powers. Magic is an imprecise term, but if Ned couldn't say what it was, he did know it was there.

"Is there such a thing?" he asked Peeler one day.

The old man considered this for a moment, composing his face in a serious expression. "I believe so," he said at last. "Could be."

"What is it?"

"Ain't nobody knows that, no matter what they might tell you to the otherwise." Then he held up one finger to emphasize his next point.

"But I do know this. It ain't rabbits outta hats or card tricks or parlor stunts like that."

"Well, if nobody knows what it is and you can't see it, how do you know for sure that there is such a thing?"

"Sufferin' hellcats, you sure can fish an unrewardin' mudhole when you've a mind to, boy. You can't see the air neither, but you know it's there. Maybe magic's like that, although I can't say I've had the experience of any since I don't know how long."

"Are there real magicians, people who can use it and do things with it?"

"Never seen one," Peeler scoffed. "Nor never heard of one who wasn't just doin' tricks and stunts. Them fellers are a dime a dozen."

Ned was pleased. It would be great to have a real knowledge of magic but something told him that was not possible, and now Peeler was saying much the same thing. Magic was a property, a state, something you might come across from time to time and take little notice of, like a cold spot or a patch of fog. But the fact that it was so elusive didn't mean a boy couldn't look for it all the time, and perhaps even find it.

"Are there night things, phantoms, Peeler?" Ned already knew the answer to this, but he wanted to hear what the old man thought about it.

"Tell me what *you* mean by that, and I'll tell you my answer."

"I don't know what they are," Ned said. "I don't think you can see them but sometimes you know they're there, in your room at night in the dark. Strange creatures, like, and you can't move from your bed or they'll get you."

"Oh, yeah, I think I can remember what they're like," Peeler said. "They're a part of magic, I'd say."

"Can they hurt you?"

"I don't guess so."

"Do they go away when you get older?"

"Everything goes away when you get older." Then, seeing the look on Ned's face, Peeler smiled and added, "But other things come along, Nedly, better too, if you keep your eyes open for 'em."

"Does Cloudy know about magic and stuff?"

"Cloudy's same as me. He don't know nothin' about nothin' from nothin', and that's a fact. You ask him, he'll tell you so hisself."

"But you know a lot."

Peeler just laughed.

Ned knew the phantoms very well; it seemed he'd been aware of them for most of his life. He'd never seen one, of course, and he had to admit he'd never even actually been touched by one, but he knew them all the same. Sometimes, when they weren't around for several nights in a row, perhaps a week or more, he thought he missed them. But then they would be back, surrounding his bed, shivering his nerves and stirring up fears so that he'd give anything to have them go away for good.

He tried to picture what they looked like. Two-legged, deformed subhumans with huge blind eyes, from the bowels of the earth. Hideous plant-men that moved on stalks. Large mossy valves that could swallow a grown person whole with an oozy slurp. Or the Sandman, who was not a man at all, whose every gesture and movement was accompanied by a horrible, gritty, grinding noise that was like cutting glass, only a thousand times worse. Or a fat, lurching bag of soupy slime you could poke your hand into, but if you did ... They came singly or as an army, in more shapes and forms than anyone could count. Unseen and untouched. But they came, they were there. A while ago Ned tried to pin them down in his mind, to make individuals of them and give them names. Bronk, Lorp, Tsull, Naurgub—but it was like trying to fix a snowflake on a fishhook.

Another time, years ago, just after his mother had come back from the hospital, Ned had asked his parents about night things and phantoms. It was at the dinner table, and his father herded peas around the plate before answering.

"It's just your imagination, that's all. People imagine all kinds of things, but that doesn't make them real."

"Like bad dreams, nightmares," Ned's mother had said. "You've had them. You know they're very frightening at the time, but you also know they're not really happening and you can't be hurt by them. They're only in your head."

"That's all," Ned's father confirmed.

Ned decided there were some things it wasn't very helpful to talk about with his parents. It was not like something wrong, a secret that had to be kept from them in nervous desperation, but rather he had just come to the conclusion that it was pointless to raise such matters with them. Magic and phantoms didn't exist for them. It seemed to Ned that his parents had won, in a way. They were free of the fear and menace that darkness brought. But if it was a victory for them, Ned sensed that they had simply landed on the shore of neutrality and the diminished nature of that achievement held no appeal for him.

It still frightened him to recall what had happened to his mother that night five years ago. In spite of his worst fears, she had returned and life went on much as it had before. But even if the doctors had words for it, even if his parents thought they knew what it was, Ned was convinced that he alone understood what had truly happened that night. A phantom. The dark magic of the night world. It didn't help to know this, in the same way that it didn't seem to hurt his mother and father not to know. Either way, it was all beyond the realm of human influence or control. If it was going to happen again, Ned knew that all the medicine and machines in the world could not prevent it. You lived with it, or—or who knows what? But there was no avoiding it. Nobody could do that.

One night, not long after the day he and Peeler had pulled crayfish from Old Woods Creek, Ned fell asleep early. In Washington he would have been awake in his room much later, reading by flashlight or creating mental pictures to go with the sounds of the city outside. But in Lynnhaven, more and more it seemed, the combination of sea air and the extra outdoor activity he got up to hit Ned as soon as darkness fell.

"Work hard, play hard and sleep hard," Ned's father had declared shortly after their arrival in the fishing village. "That's what you want to do out here, and that's the way it should be."

But some things didn't change. Night things.

Ned's eyes opened, and the room seemed to be bathed in a pale, lunar light.

Here there was nothing to use, no rumbling truck or beeping car horn for the suddenly awake mind to fix on, if only for a second or two. Here there was nothing but the silence of the Lynnhaven night. The house was just a little too far away to catch the sound of the breakers on the shore, or the random clatter of the bell buoy in the bay.

That light.

Ned had never seen it before. He had never seen anything before, however many times he had tripped into consciousness in the middle of the night. Now there was light, a thin, washed-out illumination that gave the room the eerie look of an aquarium.

To wake with your eyes open and your head out from under the covers—that was the chanciest circumstance of all. You might yank the bedclothes up over you in an instantaneous move, but the slightest twinge of hesitation would bring immediate paralysis, and then you could only hope to endure.

Ned lay there like a rag doll, body limp and eyes wide open. What was this light? He could almost make out certain features, specific objects in the room. They were fuzzy suggestions at the edge of his sleepy vision. But his mind was awake enough to recognize the ghostly light as unique. He managed to shake his head briefly, but the glow remained, imprecise and persistent as the afterimage of a camera's flash.

"What is it?"

Ned realized it was his own voice, although it sounded small and distorted, as if it were echoing up from the bottom of a very deep well. A moment later he began to doubt that he had spoken at all.

"What is it?"

Now his voice startled him, it was so close and loud. He blinked his eyes rapidly, hoping the movement would plunge him back into familiar darkness. But no, the light was still there. It was real, neither a dream nor an optical side effect of waking fast. He had pictured a hundred, a thousand different creatures, but he had never conceived of such a chilly, diffuse phosphorescence.

This does not happen.

Rooms don't behave like this. Rooms don't behave at all. Rooms are just—rooms.

This does not happen, but—

It suddenly occurred to Ned that he wasn't frightened. He felt no fear, in spite of the fact that he was lying there exposed and defenseless. It was because now he could see something, whatever it might be. He was surrounded, enveloped in a room full of the stuff, but he felt no apprehension, only puzzlement.

"What is it?"

Nothing.

"Who is it?"

Nothing.

"What do you want?"

Nothing, nothing, nothing. Ned wondered if, when you came right down to it, his parents might not be right after all. This was nothing.

Nothing.

Was he just a silly little boy with a vivid imagination, peopling his mind with ridiculous creations that had no basis in reality? Were the phantoms just that—phantoms of his mind? Ned screwed his eyes shut and mentally counted off the seconds of a long minute. Then he let his eyes open again.

Still the light.

Now the fear. He could be wrong, wildly wrong. He could be underestimating what was going on, assuming it was nothing when in fact it was more, so much more that he couldn't even begin to grasp it. Ned's body was shaking now.

"Hello?"

It was the voice of surrender, and he hated it as soon as he heard it come from within him.

Then the light was suddenly gone. Not a slow fade or a smooth disappearance. The light was there, and then it was gone. This was even more upsetting to Ned, because it seemed a kind of awful proof of what he had feared. It was not nothing that he had seen. He had been let off this time, but that hardly made any difference. He felt invaded. There had been a light, unlike any other light on earth. It had held him in its grip, but still it hadn't taken him.

Yet.

CHAPTER 5
OLD WOODS TALES

"Cloudy."

"Yowsir?"

"Is Progger a name?"

"It surely is."

"It is? What's it mean?"

Cloudy was perched on his crate by the pile of old tires. He was trying to fix an electric clock he had found. It was plugged into an extension cord that ran to the baithouse nearby. The second hand swung around the dial as it should, but the minute and hour hands wouldn't budge from ten past two. Cloudy set the stubborn device down on his lap and looked at Ned.

"How come you wanna know that?"

"I never heard it before."

"You never heard it before, then how you know it to ask me what it means?"

"Well, I did hear Peeler say it once."

"Peeler said it, huh." Cloudy resumed his efforts with the junked clock. The faulty hands moved smoothly enough when you pushed them with your fingers, but if you let the clock run on its own they stayed where they were. "Peeler should say it, he bein' a progger hisself."

"He is?"

"'Course he is."

"But what is a progger?"

"What's a progger? Mr. Tadpole, you don't know nothin' at all, do you?"

"Nope."

Cloudy put down the clock again and assumed the look of someone who has been called on to explain two plus two. Actually, he was glad to have a diversion, since he was getting nowhere with the infernal timepiece.

"A progger, he's a person spends his time proggin' around, you see. Now, proggin' is just pokin' around the swamps and marsh creeks and potholes to catch somethin' you can use. Could be crawdads—"

"I did that with Peeler."

"See? You been proggin' and you didn't even know it."

"What else?"

"Any thin' you can get, that's what else. Crawdads, catfish, muskrat, mink, any old critter you can trap or hook or bonk on the head. Dippin' for peeler crabs or jiggin' for eels, and such like that. Clappin' and hollerin' for a snappin' turkle, a progger do that too sometimes."

"Turkle?"

Cloudy nodded enthusiastically. "Lotta them around, but you must do a regular song and dance to make 'em pop up so's you can grab 'em, and then you better make sure he can't get you. Big snappin' turkle, he can chomp your little finger clean off."

"You mean a snapping turtle."

"That's right, snappin' turkle."

Cloudy prodded the clock tentatively with one finger as if he half expected the machine to lunge suddenly and bite him.

"Are you a progger too, Cloudy?"

"I'm what you call your weekend progger, like Grandma Moses. I'm a part-time progger, you see, I do it when I ain't got nothin' else to do. Now you take Peeler, he got proggin' in his blood, he's the real progger."

"Peeler sure drinks a lot of beer." Ned didn't know why he had just changed the subject; maybe Peeler's style was rubbing off on him.

"He likes the beer," Cloudy agreed.

"But you don't drink it, do you, Cloudy?"

The black man looked somewhat indignant. "Oh, Lord, no, no, I don't drink at all, not no more I don't." Now he held up the clock and studied it as if it were some remarkable object from a strange civilization in the far reaches of outer space.

"How come?"

"How come what?"

"You don't like beer, is that it?"

Cloudy turned his attention to the boy again. "Don't you never start, Mr. Tadpole. What happened to me, I used to drink all the time. Like beer? I loved it. Every chance I got, I took a drink, 'cause when you're younger you think you can do whatever you want and it won't bother you none. But the thing of it is, I had a friend, name of Mr. Eustace Boggs." Ned laughed at that. "You think that's funny?" Cloudy continued. "Well, everybody called him Useless. That's the truth. Useless Boggs. Anyway, he was in an accident one day, I don't remember exactly what it was, but old Useless, he lost his legs or he couldn't walk no more, somethin' like that, and then he really was useless. Stuck in the house, in bed most of the time, and oh, he had a plague of a wife. Marylou Boggs. Talk? That woman'd make the wallpaper curl up and block its ears, the way she'd go on. It was Useless this and Useless that, and poor old Useless couldn't do nothin' 'cept sit there and listen. Well, I don't know why, but I kinda liked that poor sucker. I guess I'd knowed him a long time. So I used to take the newspaper up to him at his house every day and tell him what's goin' on, jokes and gossip and stuff like that. Nobody else bothered with him, so I was his only contact with the outside world, you see. Now, we had a little system goin' between us and it was a nice one. I'd wrap up a bottle of rye whiskey for him, smuggle it in past Marylou, and Useless'd pay me for it. Sometimes he give me a ten, sometimes a twenty, and I got to keep the change, so we both done well out of the deal. He had a lotta money, see, on account of the accident. He got a big payoff for losin' his legs, so money was no problem.

"At first I didn't like the idea, you know. I said to him, 'Useless, did your doctor tell you not to take no drink?' He says, 'No, the doctor never say nothin' like that to me. My wife did, but she's no doctor.' So you see, Marylou was the one who didn't want him to have a drink, but what else has the poor man got? He can't go nowhere, nor do nothin' without his legs, so I had to help him out. I don't know what he did with it all, maybe he watered the plants with it too, but he had to have a new bottle every single day. Imagine that. Boy, we sure had some kinda system goin' there for a while. Then it stopped."

"How come?"

"He died, for cryin' out loud. Fell right outta his bed onto the floor. Useless Boggs, dead with a pint of rye whiskey in his hand. Didn't spill a drop, neither, I heard. I don't know, the doctor must've talked to somebody.... I never did notice it myself but they say his liver was the size of a basketball. And that's when I stopped drinkin' myself, right then and there."

"A basketball, gosh."

Cloudy began to laugh. "Yeah, it sure killed him good, and I learned my lesson. That was the best payin' job I ever had, and what I'd done was kill the goose that laid the golden eggs, see. If I had it to do all over again I'd make Useless take it a little slower like, so we'd both get a little more mileage outta the situation. But you know one thing I never did find out about him?"

"What?"

"How'd he get rid of all them empty bottles? I give him a new one every day, but he never give me no empties to smuggle out. I don't know how he did it. Maybe Marylou had somethin' to do with it, maybe she wasn't really so bad after all...."

"How old was he?" Ned asked.

"Oh, just young, about forty or fifty, I guess."

"Was this here in Lynnhaven?"

"Over in Old Woods, that's right."

"By the creek where Peeler and I caught crawdads?"

"Over that way. All that way is the Old Woods, Mr. Tadpole. That's where Useless lived, till he escaped this world. They say he was swamp folks, you know, but that ain't true."

"Swamp folks?"

"Yeah, they're the people who live deep in the swamps, back of Old Woods. Nobody don't go in there too far, but they're some folks hid up there, leastwise they used to be. They're supposed to be pretty bad too, cut your throat and cook you up for dinner, that kind of thing, or worse. I don't know, but I tell you: nobody goes up there for a picnic. Now, Useless always seemed okay to me, but they say he had swamp blood in him. I don't know, I think he was just another oyster shucker. He—"

"They kill people up there?" Ned was more interested in hearing about the swamp people than Useless Boggs now. "Today? They still do that?"

Cloudy laughed.

"Oh, I bet if you was to go up through the Old Woods now you'd find the swamps all drained out and a bunch of white folks beatin' up golf balls and drinkin' cocktails instead. That's what I think. Probably ain't no more swamps there nowadays, and no swamp folks neither. I expect they're long gone in this world."

"Really?" Ned's disappointment was obvious.

While the boy's mind filled with images of the dread swamp people and the terrible things they got up to, Cloudy stood up, placed the impossible clock on the ground and stomped it to pieces. Enough is enough.

"On second thought," he addressed Ned, "I probably wouldn't go pokin' around up there Old Woods way. Just in case I was wrong, you know, and them swampers was still hangin' around...."

CHAPTER 6
THE FARLEY PLACE (1)

What's the purpose of this little expedition, Michael wondered as he set off down the street. To put Linda's mind at ease, he hoped. An exercise in reassurance, that's all. Besides, it wouldn't do any harm for him to meet either or both of the two old-timers who had befriended his son. In fact, it was probably a good idea if he did. Not that he expected anything special to come of such a meeting. Michael was sure he would find out what he already knew, namely that these men were a pair of harmless old coots who entertained Ned with their fishing talk and country ways. Ned was most likely the only person around who would bother to listen to them.

That suited Michael just fine. In time, certainly when he settled into his new school in the autumn, Ned would make friends his own age and lose interest in the old men. Linda was always trying to steer Ned, to guide him this way or that, and Michael knew there was a danger of overdoing it. His job was to make sure a proper balance was maintained. Right now the important thing was to remember that only very recently Ned had been thrown into a completely new environment, different in every way from what the boy had known for the first nine and a half years of his life. Michael and Linda were there to help him land on his feet, which he seemed to be doing very well, but they would have to do it as unobtrusively as possible. Let Ned adjust to his new surroundings in his own way and at his own pace. These early weeks and months might be a difficult period for him, and they had to provide love and support as they were called for, but too much parental interference wouldn't help at all. Linda knows all this, Michael reflected, but she has a harder time restraining herself.

It was a shame, really, because all three of them should be getting the most out of their new life. Michael had waited patiently and worked hard for the day when he could buy the right house on a decent-size piece of land, and now that he had finally achieved that goal, he was determined to enjoy it to the utmost. He wasn't about to cheat himself of the experience, and anyway, he was sure it was the best thing he could do for Linda and Ned. Michael had been married to Linda long enough to know that it would take her, not Ned, longest to settle in and relax. She couldn't be jollied along or nudged, but the more she saw of a full, happy transition in her husband and son, the more she would come to feel at ease.

As for Ned, all the evidence so far seemed to indicate that he was having no problems at all. He sometimes had that funny, distant look about him, but then Michael had to admit that there was nothing really new about it. Ned had always been something of a dreamy kid. Of course, there had to be a certain amount of inner conflict and uncertainty in the boy but nothing serious. Ned was apparently responding well to the new house and to the town. Michael mentally repeated one of his favorite maxims: Kids are tough, adults are the ones who need help.

Another thing that Linda had not yet fully accepted was the fact that Ned was, by his own nature, one of those youngsters who tend to keep to themselves. He was bright but quiet rather than boisterous and outgoing. He might have trouble picking up the social graces when he got a little older, but so what? Michael had a feeling that Ned would always run by himself, not with a pack, and the thought was pleasing. If nothing messed him up, he should grow into a strong, self-possessed individual. Working in a bureaucracy helps you appreciate those qualities because they are just the ones you've lost yourself, Michael thought sardonically. The point was valid, however, and sometimes it annoyed him that he had to make it over and over again to his wife; but he understood what her problem was. Linda's touchy asthmatic condition and the fact that they could have no more children combined to create in her a desperate fear that Ned was somehow uniquely vulnerable. So she wanted to see him as healthy and active as possible, which was fine; and she was constantly encouraging the boy to become involved with sports, which was not so fine because Ned simply had no interest in them.

"You want him to be Teddy Roosevelt," Michael had once said half-jokingly to his wife. "Just let him be himself." The hurt look in Linda's eyes had told him he'd made a mistake, and ever since then Michael hadn't prevented her from airing her anxieties by urging Ned to take up athletics. But he was careful not to join her cause, telling himself that as long as he abstained from the discussion, if not actively taking Ned's side, the boy would keep his equilibrium.

Michael realized he must have walked too far and taken a wrong turn, as he was now circling down toward the town's main street. It wouldn't do to get lost in a place this small. He backtracked, and a few minutes later found the dead-end road he was looking for.

It was the first time Michael had actually seen up close the place that was so popular with his son. What could you expect of a baithouse? This crude structure seemed appropriate. He could see, out back, a small and dilapidated house-that must be where the old guys live, Michael thought. His eyes took in the other features: the vegetable patch, the jalopy that looked like it hadn't been driven since the day it rolled off the assembly line, the pile of old tires, crabbing gear and junk that had accumulated around the yard. Yes, just the sort of place that would worry a mother. But to a boy it would be fascinating, and even to an accountant father it was not so off-putting.

"Hello," Michael called out, wondering if he had chosen the wrong time to visit. There didn't seem to be anyone around.

Peeler came out of the baithouse a moment later. He knew at once that this man, casually dressed but in city clothes, was not here to buy perch eyes.

"Yes, sir, what can I do for you?"

"Oh, hi. My name is Michael Covington. I'm Ned's father."

"Is that right? Well, I'm pleased to meet you, Mr. Covington, I truly am. How are you?"

"Fine, thanks," Michael said, noting the other man's warm smile and firm handshake. Nothing wrong there. "Nice to meet you. I gather Ned comes around here quite a bit. He talks about you all the time, so I thought I ought to come around and introduce myself."

"Glad you did, glad you did. That's a fine boy you got there, Ned is. Awfully fine."

Michael nodded. "He's a good kid. I just hope he doesn't get in your way or make a pest of himself when you're working."

"Not a damn bit. Ned drops by most every day, and we're always happy to see him. He's mindful and polite as can be. A credit to his upbringin' I'd say."

"Thanks, it's good to hear that."

"Got a million questions, of course, but what feller his age doesn't?"

"Yes." Michael realized that the old man had set one hook in him: how many questions did Ned ask his own father? Some, but not that many.... Well, trust a fisherman to exaggerate.

"No," Peeler continued, "he don't get in nobody's way, no how."

"I'm glad of that," Michael said, wondering whether he had just heard a triple or quadruple negative. "You're in the bait business, I see."

"We sell bait, that's for sure. Do some fishin' and crabbin' as well, and some repair work."

"Really?" Michael tried to sound impressed.

"Yeah, there's always somethin' to do," Peeler said. "If not one thing, then another comes up. No end to it."

"You're a jack-of-all-trades, it sounds like."

"You could say that, I guess." Peeler knew when he was being condescended to, but it didn't bother him. "And you work in Washington, I believe. That right?" He could put a little tone in his voice, too.

"Yes, it is."

"But you're not a politician?"

"No." Michael smiled. "Just an accountant."

"That's good, I don't think too highly of politicians."

"Who does?"

"Remind me of a bunch of angle worms crawlin' around in a knot at the bottom of a jar, a scummy mess. It seem that way to you?"

Michael laughed. "It does, sometimes."

"So, you bought the old Farley place."

"The Farley place?" Michael was puzzled. "We bought the saltbox on Chestnut Street."

"That's it."

"But we bought it from the Winslows, an elderly couple who were moving down to Florida."

"Yeah, the Winslows was there for a good few years," Peeler said. "And the Petits before them. But someways down the line that was the Farley place. I think they was the ones who built the house in the first place."

"Really? I don't know the whole history of it," Michael said, genuinely interested now, "but I was told that the house isn't actually all that old."

"No, it ain't."

"I mean, it's old enough, about eighty or ninety years, but not as old as a lot of saltboxes."

"But you like it, huh?"

"Oh, yes, we love it. Of course, it needs some fixing up. You know what they say: the only thing that works in an old house is you. But they're small things, and we're just really very happy to have found the place."

"That's nice," Peeler said, but he had a doubtful expression on his face.

"Is that what everybody still calls it? The Farley place?' Peeler nodded. "Why is that?" Michael asked.

"I don't know," Peeler said. "Just outta habit, I guess."

The conversation meandered on for a few more minutes, but it lacked a natural impulse of its own because, it was clear, neither man really had anything much to say to the other. Michael was checking out his son's elderly friend, a man with whom he would otherwise not come into contact. Peeler knew well enough what was going on, and he wert along with it. He just had to avoid saying anything outrageous. It would be a big mistake to give Michael Covington any reason to keep his son away.

"Where's your partner?" Michael asked as he was about to leave for home.

"Cloudy? He's in town, I expect. He's got a room there and things to do."

"Oh." Michael immediately felt relieved.

"He ain't out here all the time, no," Peeler went on. "Cloudy's what you might call a half-assed partner, y'see, he helps me out some of the time, but he's got other work he tends to as well."

"Sorry I missed him, but I'm sure we'll run into each other one of these days."

"Sure you will."

Michael left, pleased that he would be able to give Linda a reassuring account of his meeting with the old man. Peeler and Cloudy. She would be particularly glad to learn that they didn't live together in that tiny house. As for the rest, what was there? A couple of odd names, some colorful talk and a thicket of grammatical contortions. None of which was worrying. Ned undoubtedly heard worse in the school yard. Michael had to laugh though-these old-timers sure loved to play the part.

Peeler went back into the baithouse, snatched a can of Iron City from the tank and sat down in his favorite falling-apart armchair. He hadn't invited Ned's father in to sit down and have a drink because you just didn't do that with a taxman, even if he was on a social call (funny how he had neglected to say who employed him as an accountant!). But Peeler had to admit that Michael Covington was a reasonable enough man, of his kind. A bit better than he might have been. Good at his job, probably, but otherwise pretty useless, a city type who would always be a city type, no matter how much he tried to settle in out here. But not an offensive man. The important thing was that he apparently had no objection to Ned's spending time with Peeler and Cloudy. I may be a washed-up old fart, Peeler thought, but I sometimes have a sense about things, and right now it tells me that something is coming, a change of a sort, and that it's important I have that boy near to hand.

Otherwise ...

CHAPTER 7
IN THE RUINS

... there would be death here.

No one thing sparked the thought in Ned's mind, but he couldn't doubt it. He had followed the track bed of the old rail line and climbed the hill to reach this gloomy spot. It was the long way, Ned knew from a previous scouting mission, but it was his decision to approach the place from the back. The hill wasn't steep, but it was thickly covered with bushes and brambles, so the going had been slow, and there were always enough trees to obstruct the view ahead-making it hard to know how far he had wandered from a straight line on the way up. He had started this expedition shortly after lunch, but already the afternoon seemed to be winding down and he had only reached the outside wall. It was a mass of gray-brown bricks, at least ten feet high but rotting. The wall stretched away to the right and left as far as Ned could see. Even on a hot day like this the bricks were cold and clammy to the touch.

He followed the wall for what seemed a considerable distance before it curved sharply. Beyond that bend, Ned found a tree that had fallen down, its upper branches caught on the top of the wall. Blown over in a storm, probably, Ned thought. He figured it was the best point of entry he was likely to find, so he took it. Parasite suckers had claimed the tree, smothering it with hundreds of viney arms that made it difficult for Ned to find a place to put his feet. Slipping, wedging his sneakers into the tangled, decaying mess, he pulled himself up the trunk of the tree. Ned stopped when he got near the top of the wall. He reached out, but his whole body began to slide and he quickly clamped his fingers around a sucker as fat as a bullwhip. His position was precarious: he needed both hands and feet just to stay where he was. How could he get onto the top of the wall only a yard or so away? Not far, but too far, it seemed. Ned looked down and was alarmed to find that the distance of ten feet to the ground looked far greater from up here. Perhaps he could ease his way back down the tree trunk a few inches at a time. But when he tested his maneuver Ned rediscovered the principle of many old traps. The suckers all grew up the tree, of course, pointing in his direction, and it was virtually impossible to go back down against them. He couldn't see what he was trying to do and his feet could find no hold. Ned felt like a foolish kitten stuck in the tree of curiosity, but he knew that no firemen would ever come to this place and get him down.

He looked at the wall again. Maybe it wasn't as much as a yard away. Besides, it was the only way to go. Ned hauled himself a little higher, narrowing the gap slightly. This would have to do; any farther and the clump of dead branches and slimy suckers would make it too tricky to use the top of the wall. Ned knew he shouldn't do it, but he looked down again. It was more like fifteen or twenty feet to the ground-no, he told himself, that can't be right. He was letting his imagination get the better of him. Still, it was obviously enough of a drop to break bones. Don't think about it.

What he had to do was this: reach out in one swift but sure movement, grab the top of the wall and pull himself onto it. The most dangerous part would come when he let go of the tree with his other hand and swung it across to the wall. Then all that would hold his body over the gap would be one hand and the toes of his sneakers pressing hard against the slippery suckers. One way or another, Ned was about to find out how strong he was.

But he almost didn't. The first time he gripped the top of the wall a brick tore loose in his hand. Ned let it fall at once and clung fiercely to the tree, waiting for the surprise, the shock to die down in him. For some reason he had given no thought to the possibility that the wall itself, that massive presence, might be unreliable. Now his whole calculation was thrown in doubt. Question: What would Ken Holt, boy detective, do if he were in this situation? Answer: Try again.

Ned did, and this time the bricks held. The rough edge of the masonry dug up the skin on his forearm, causing Ned to regret that he hadn't worn long sleeves. He barely paused, however, before letting go of the tree. His upper body arched across the open space, his toes pulled free of the suckers and pushed off, and after a brief scrambling flurry Ned was lying face down on top of the wall. A little sloppy, he thought, but who cares? He felt as if he had just conquered Everest, and for a while he didn't move, enjoying the sensation of having arrived where he was.

When Ned finally looked around to survey the new territory, what he saw took his breath away. Lynnhaven's old spa was situated in a gentle hollow at the top of the hill, and Ned was evidently perched on the outer wall's highest point, for the entire inner acreage sloped gradually away, giving him a disturbingly good view of the place. The main building, a grotesque double-winged structure with turrets, stood on the far ground several hundred yards away from Ned, looking like the shattered castle of some demented and defeated prince. The vast expanse in between was a jungle of choked and twisted vegetation, broken up by an astonishing network of lower inner walls. It was a honeycomb, a maze—but no, as Ned studied the scene more carefully he could see definite patterns emerging. This was no random piece of work. Here the walls were built to form an equilateral triangle, there a perfect circle and, farther over, a rectangle. Other shapes suggested themselves to his eyes, but in many places the growth of stunted trees and layered vines made it impossible for Ned to be sure. It was clear, however, that all the inner walls were connected, forming a multitude of geometric figures running to the outer wall in places and also right to the main building. To Ned's mind the whole remarkable panorama conjured up images of forgotten history and legend—a small medieval town with its royal palace, say, or an ancient Inca stronghold and sacred temple. Strange people once dwelled here, and perhaps strange creatures too, for which there were no names. Now all were gone and dead—yes, that was it. *There would be death here.* Even from outside the walls Ned had sensed it, the afterglow, the radiation of death that lingers so long.

But it didn't bother him now. Ned felt as if he had just set foot on a new continent, and he all but trembled with the excitement of it. This was more, much more than the ruin he had expected to find. It was a puzzle on a monumental scale, and it raised Ned's exploration to a dramatic level of challenge.

Not far from where he sat, another wall offered access to the interior. When he reached it Ned was pleased to find that the inner walls were only about eight feet tall, a height much easier to cope with. Taking care, he could stand erect and walk on the tops of the walls from one end of this incredible place to the other, back and forth, until he had seen anything there was to see. Then he could easily find the best place on the outer wall from which to jump down.

The first few areas of the estate that Ned inspected were disappointingly alike: snarls of thorny weeds, man high, filling the divided spaces so that he had to look hard along the base of the wall to see the ground. They were like enormous, vile salads, Ned thought, and there was no way of even guessing why the walls had been laid out the way they were or to what use the enclosed sections had been put. He did notice, however, that every inner wall had a door or an archway built into it. Many of these openings were bare, but quite a few of the original doors remained intact—heavy slabs of bleached, warped lumber. There were no passageways or lanes between walls; one area opened directly to each of those that surrounded it, and thus all were connected. The plan may have been very clear and simple, Ned thought, but you would still want a map to find your way around down there, especially if you were going from the main building to a crescent-shaped pocket like this one, where only a couple of people could fit in at a time. What was the point of building such a tiny enclosure—or indeed what was the point of building the whole place like this? Ned walked on, but the more he saw the less sense it made to him. Didn't Peeler and Cloudy say people came to the spa to do something about their health? But this place didn't look like any hospital or clinic Ned had ever seen.

Nor was it uninhabited. Almost as soon as he moved away from the outer wall Ned heard the noises—a stirring here, a brushing whisper behind him, the soft tramp of steps taken off to one side. Now and then he would turn quickly, in time to see a branch still shaking or to catch a glimpse of some undefined figure moving in the undergrowth. At first it meant nothing to Ned. Just animals, he told himself. But the sounds worked away at his mind and eventually he stopped, cold and nervous. What about the swamp people—could they be up here, a gang of them hiding out in the abandoned ruins? He looked all around, but the only thing he noticed was that the outer wall now seemed to be dangerously far away. Ned had gotten himself pretty much into the center of the ruins. He continued on toward the main building, half expecting a crowd of deformed savages to leap out of the flora at any moment and pull him down from the wall. Don't think about it, just hurry up and get out of here. *Otherwise ...*

Ned stopped when he came to the circle. It was much larger than it had looked from the outer wall. In fact, it now appeared to be the single largest part of the place he had seen yet. But that wasn't what stopped him. The circle had the same dark green foliage as the other areas, but here it halted in the center, forming a second circle of open space with a diameter of about ten feet, as far as Ned could judge. He couldn't see the ground at that spot, but the hole in the middle of the weeds was unmistakable. Thus the circular wall seemed to be filled with an immense wreath. But if this was puzzling, it had other, more unnerving features. Ned heard the sound that came from the center hole—a steady, deep slurping noise, as if the earth itself had formed a terrible mouth there, gurgling, sucking.... And, rising through the air above the vegetation, was a mist so thin Ned hadn't seen it until he had come to the circle, a stream of pale vapor issuing from that giant, unseen orifice.... An image came to Ned's mind of a mythical ogre, a monster buried in the earth, pinned in place by the chain of walls and dense ground cover, breathing smoke from the "Only part of him exposed to the air, waiting for the chance to break free and stalk the land.... Grateful that he couldn't actually see what was down there in the center of the circle, Ned hurried on, trying not to make the least sound that might disturb a sleeping giant.

As he drew closer to the main building he became aware of a change in the sectored grounds. The jungle of wild growth thinned out somewhat, and in places it consisted of nothing more than brindle grass stitched through with the usual brambles. Now Ned knew what it was that bothered him about this berserk garden. Wherever he looked, whatever grew, the color was not quite right. All of the greenery had a bluish-black tinge to it. Ned thought his eyes might be playing tricks on him, or that it was simply the way the sun hit the leaves in a thin, brittle shine, but the more he studied the scene the more he became convinced that these were bizarre and poisoned plants, varieties that continued to grow but that had gone bad over the course of many years.

In the shadow of the mansion Ned saw the remains of several small outbuildings—windows, doors and roofs all destroyed. Perhaps they had once been cottages, bath houses and changing rooms. A bent, rickety skeleton was all that was left of a greenhouse. The inner walls ended here, about forty yards from the main spa building, looping around to the right and left to join the outer walls at the extreme end of either wing. The scrubby open ground was broken only by wide stone stairs that led up to a terrace and the tall, boarded-up doors of the spa. Large urns still stood at various points along the balustrade. The lower windows were all blocked up with sheets of corrugated metal, while the upper ones were as open as the eye sockets of a skull, but inaccessible.

Maybe I won't be able to get into the building after all, Ned thought, but perhaps that isn't such a bad thing. The place looked anything but inviting, and Ned had visions of ghastly things lurking in dark corners within—an army of rats, spiders as big as a grown man's hand, trapdoors that opened to nests of snakes and swooping vampire bats....

He stayed on the wall and decided to follow it around to the place where it met the outer wall and the right wing of the building. Ned took another look back at the route he had just covered, and he felt both thrilled and relieved, like someone who had just tiptoed through a perilous no-man's-land between the edge of the world and the abyss of hell. Now all he had to do was lower himself down from the outer wall and head for home.

But then he saw that it might yet be possible to gain entry to the spa building. The last window in the right wing was only a couple of feet from the spot where the walls touched and at about the same level as the coping stone on the outer wall. The corrugated metal in this window appeared to be loosely propped in place, not nailed tight. If it had been a matter of hopping from the wall to the window ledge, with nothing to hang onto, Ned might have decided it was too risky, considering that the drop to the ground was about ten feet here. But this window, like every one in both wings, had a low wrought-iron grille set in the concrete casing—and that made it easy.

Ned knew it was late in the day and that the sensible thing would be to go home so that he would be there in plenty of time for supper. He had found the way, he could return whenever he wanted, tomorrow even, and resume his exploration of the spa. Yes, that was the sensible thing to do.

But ... Ned was here now, and it seemed silly to have come so far only to turn away just when he had reached what might be the best part of the expedition. If he left now he would be awake all night, wondering what he had missed. The corrugated metal leaned there, glinting dully in the sunlight, so close, an invitation rather than a barrier. How easy it would be to push it to the inside, to the fortress heart and headquarters of the dead spa. To the center of it all. The ruined walls outside were amazing, but who knew what might be found inside? The rusty hulks of Frankenstein machines, perhaps, or a closet full of skulls and bones.... It was frightening, but there was no other way of seeing what the spa was like, and maybe even finding out what people had done there. It was frightening, but irresistible. No, of course he couldn't leave now. There might not be enough time to go through the whole place, nor even all of this wing, but he could look at a few rooms and then, having planted his flag, make it home before supper had gathered too much dust. Ned moved.

What followed was a far more threatening version of his first attempt on the spa wall. As soon as Ned got his weight onto the grille, part of it ripped free of the weak, powdery cement and tilted out away from the building. Terrified, he could do nothing but hang on, and then it gave way completely, rushing him to the ground below. He landed on his back in a patch of spongy plants that cushioned the blow and spared him serious injury. But the wind had been knocked out of him and for a while all he could do was lie there, stunned, until things slowly began drifting back into focus and he realized what had happened to him.

I'm trapped.

Before, he had been above, looking down from the safe height of the walls, surveying the grounds almost casually. But now he was down, well and truly caught within the confines of the spa. There was a feeling of dread in him, the fear that he had crossed an invisible line, taken that one step too many—and that now he would pay for it. I have to get to the terrace and find a way out of here, Ned told himself urgently. *Otherwise ...*

Ned shoved the treacherous wrought-iron grille off his chest, and in doing so became aware of the fact that *he was sinking*. Something cold and wet oozed through his clothes and it felt as if the earth were trying to draw him into itself. He tried to push himself up, but his hands plunged into creamy black mud that nearly caused him to vomit. Dimly, it made sense to him. This corner of the property, well shaded by the building and wall, had turned to swamp, and he had fallen into it ... quicksand? Ned had never seen quicksand, except in the movies, but in his mind the word was as touchy and potent as nitroglycerine. One person alone could never escape from it. When it got in your ears you stopped thinking, your brain was instantly dead. Like the Sandman, it filled you, seeping into your nose and mouth, blinding your eyes. And in the end, you disappeared forever.

Ned forced himself to concentrate; panic would only make matters worse. If that was possible. He remembered what he was supposed to do. Lie flat and make no violent moves. Your body is light, he thought, even if it doesn't feel that way. It is light enough to stay on the surface, if you let it. Eyes closed, Ned lay still. It's all part of the same rule, he reminded himself. The only difference is, you're not in bed now and you can *feel* the demon danger through your clothes and on your hands, you can smell it. Ned expected the awful slime to flow into his ears at any second, but it didn't. The rule was working once again. Finally, he opened his eyes. The forbidding face of the spa building towered over him, and Ned wouldn't have been surprised to hear it boom out, *What a puny fool you are to enter here.* Ned turned his head slightly and saw that he hadn't sunk any farther. It might just have been the pressure he'd exerted trying to push the heavy grille away, or so he tried to convince himself. Anyway, the springy clumps of weeds seemed to be holding him up somehow, and he would have to use them if he was going to escape the foul mire.

Slowly, patiently, Ned raised his body an inch or two and shifted it sideways. He made progress this way, as long as he kept his movements short and gentle. But if he reached too far or pushed a little too hard, his hands would slip through the bog plants into the muck again.

"Aaaugghh!"

He had come face to face with a fat, shiny creature about three inches long that looked like a snail without a shell. Ned grabbed the disgusting thing with the tips of his fingers and flung it as far away as he could. Was it a leech, a bloodsucker? It must be, and if there was one there would be others.... Ned shuddered and worked backward, awkwardly inching his way across the swamp. He saw himself, in his mind, as a kind of human crab crawling laterally on its back.

Abruptly, he discovered that he was on firm ground—had been for several yards. He jumped up, patting down his hair and body until he was sure there were no leeches on him. Ned trembled—from the damp, he told himself. Now he looked around to get a better idea of his position. He didn't know how much time had been lost, but he no longer cared how late it would be when he got home, as long as he did get home. The terrace still appeared to be the best, perhaps only chance he had, and Ned started for it. Along with the two huge doors, a number of windows faced onto the terrace, so he would try to get into the building through one of them and then out again on the front side. If that didn't work, he could stand on the balustrade and look for a place where he might be able to get back up onto the wall.

Before Ned reached the terrace, however, he stumbled through a brake of brushwood and found himself looking at a door set in the base of the building. The cellar, naturally—any building this big was sure to have one. He hadn't seen the door sooner because the plants had screened it from view. The door was wedged into its stone frame, but after repeated yanking it popped open, rattling on its corroded hinges.

Now the way was clear, the fortress breached, but Ned hesitated. The late afternoon light illuminated only the first few feet of the interior, leaving the rest in utter darkness. He would be wandering around in that darkness, in the bowels of an enormous mansion he was completely unfamiliar with, unaided by the flashlight and matches that were in his bedroom at home. Was this really such a good idea? Ned blamed himself again for being so careless. You think you know what you're doing, but you always find out the hard way that you don't. This moment seemed to sum up everything about the day's venture. With luck, or else by doing something the wrong way, Ned had made progress. But he had reached the threshold in more ways than one. He knew it wouldn't be wise to suppose he had any luck left, and he also knew that if he did something wrong inside the building it would be his last mistake. His allotted number, Ned sensed, had been used up. Once he got in there, could he find his way out of the building by himself? Could he deal with whatever he might encounter in that darkness (at least he had been able to see that leech)? The answers to these questions were Probably Not and No. Well, he could still try the wall again.

No. The door was open and Ned decided that he might as well finish what he had started. Besides, his eyes would adjust to the darkness so he wouldn't be totally blind. Some light must get through in there. It required a certain amount of caution and common sense, that was all. This door led to the basement beneath the right wing of the building, so he would just have to work his way to the left until he found stairs. When he got out of the cellar the going would be much easier; plenty of light must filter in on the upper floors. It seems like a hard thing to do, Ned reasoned with himself, until you take a second look at the problem and break it down, and then you find it's simple. Sort of.

It was like stepping into a black pit where the air conditioning was on high. The temperature in the cellar felt thirty degrees cooler than outside. Enough light came through the doorway to show Ned that he was in a small room, and he could just make out another door in the wall ahead of him. It opened easily, but the outside light died at that point. Ned moved into the next room and waited for his eyes to adjust. Every room must have a door, he thought. Rather than walk straight ahead it would be better to follow the wall until he found the next door. At last Ned came to the conclusion that his eyes were as ready as they would ever be, and that he. was not going to see much of anything. Taking a deep breath, he turned left and walked. The rectangle of pale light at the outside door was gone now, so it was all the more important that he concentrate on what he was doing. Ned kept the back of his left hand pressed against the wall, and he walked by sliding his feet along the gritty floor. He held his right hand out in front to warn him of any object in his path.

He continued this way for a while, and then his left hand tapped wood instead of the rough stone wall. Okay, here was another door. Ned was about to open it when he paused to think again. He had been moving more or less parallel to the outside wall of the building, which meant that this door probably opened into a room similar to the first one he had entered. If so, it was of no use to him. Of course, it was always possible there was a stairway in there ... but probably not. Ned left the door shut and went on, encouraged by the possibility, a new one, that he was in a corridor that ran the length of the wing—and that he was advancing right to the center. Although it was uncomfortable to be in such overwhelming darkness, Ned tried to ignore it by closing his eyes and pretending the place was actually lit up, making a game of his task. It seemed to work, as he felt better and was moving faster. But then he opened his eyes, annoyed that he had been so foolish. With his eyes closed he would miss the telltale shaft of light that might signal stairs. Some game: he could wander here forever with his eyes shut.

Ned passed another door, then a third, and after that he didn't keep count, but there were several more. He would like to explore them all, but not today, not without a light. For now, he had to stay on the straight line he was following.

How far had he walked? Surely he had come under the center of the building by now. That was another small mistake: if he had counted his paces he would at least have a rough idea of where he was. Ned tried to draw a picture of the whole building in his mind, a transparent diagram of the structure, and then he plotted his course from point of entry. He should be about—but it was no good, just guesswork. He could be anywhere along that straight line. If it was straight. Ned went on, knowing it would be yet another mistake if he were to change his plan now. He walked at almost his normal speed, anxious to come across something, anything other than those useless side doors.

Ned hadn't known what to expect inside the building, although the usual images had come to mind: creaking floors, heavy cobwebs that wrapped around you, the sound of trailing footsteps, clanking chains, the squeal of hungry rats, maybe even a mummified corpse whose eyes would fly open the moment you saw it. But he experienced nothing like this, only the cold air which thoroughly chilled him. And the silence, so vast and conclusive that the small sounds of his own movement seemed more than sacrilegious. It was a silence so profound that simply to be there seemed an affront. It was a perfect place for ghosts, Ned knew, but he had the feeling that even ghosts would feel unwelcome here.

Ned stopped. *Too far, I've come too far.* It was impossible to think otherwise now. His senses couldn't deceive him that much—could they? Perhaps he had marched on into the left wing without realizing it. There comes a time in the execution of every plan when the drawbacks can no longer be ignored. Sooner or later, if the wall led nowhere, it would be necessary to open a door, try something different. But Ned didn't want to move. The wall was a comfort, his lifeline back to the outside if he gave up in here. Although even that thought was rapidly losing its appeal. By the time he got outside it might well be too dark to find a way back over the wall. He had reached the point where all plans seem unworkable. Ned knew that if he sat down and cried he would eventually feel better, but he wasn't ready to give in to that, at least not yet.

So he couldn't go back. That meant he would have to make do with the emptiness and the sense of going nowhere inside. Walls and walls and walls ... Ned wanted more than anything to lie down, fall asleep and wake up tomorrow morning in his own bed. Or to see flashlight beams knifing through the pitch black, to hear shouting voices and to run crying into the arms of his father. But things like that didn't happen, not in real life. If he was going to be rescued, he would have to rescue himself.

He could follow this wall, or ... He could find out if he really was in some sort of central corridor. Walk straight out away from the wall, count the steps taken, and he should come up against another wall. If it seemed like he was going too far to be in a corridor, he could always turn around and count his way back to this wall. Ned considered the idea at length before deciding it was a reasonable experiment.

Two ... Eight ... Twelve ... He would stop at twenty ... Twenty ... Well, say twenty-five and that's it. ... Twenty-five. Nothing. It was hard to imagine a corridor this wide or wider. But if it wasn't a corridor, what kind of room was it? Ned stood still in the dark, trying to figure out what to do. Returning to the wall as planned seemed pretty tame, and once he got back his only choices would be to resume the blind walk or retreat to the outside. However, Ned knew that it made even less sense to wander around aimlessly in a space that might be so big he could end up going in circles for hours. Stick to the plan, he argued. Count back twenty-five steps.

But even before Ned turned, he froze. He saw no light or heard even the faintest sound, but something stopped him. He couldn't explain it to himself because it made no sense, but a new, powerful wave of terror surged through him, and his body refused to turn around. Without understanding how, Ned knew beyond any doubt that if he went back now, even only a few paces, he would be in great danger. Sweat trickled down his face—crazy, in a cold place like this. Ned scarcely breathed, but his mind worked quickly to come to terms with this new situation. The rule here would have to be much the same as it was in other circumstances. If he turned around now, *something* would be there, right behind him, waiting. Ned's body was moving as he completed the thought. The only safety lay in continuing to move ahead. He should have known: Once you leave the covers, or in this case the wall, there is no way back. Keep moving and *it* will stay behind you. Please let that be so, Ned prayed.

He had no idea where he was going. He tried to steer himself along an imaginary diagonal that continued to the left and toward the center of the building, but he couldn't be sure he was actually achieving that. And even if he was holding such a course, there was no guarantee it would lead anywhere.

This time when Ned came to a door he opened it without hesitation, mildly startled, but pleased that he hadn't run into yet another wall. He was rewarded by the barest hint of gray light in the distance. It might only be an illusion, but it was enough. There was no question of turning around; the force of fear was still as real as a hand on his back. Ned pulled the door shut behind him, although he knew it was a meaningless gesture. What frightened him couldn't be stopped by doors or walls.

He continued forward in the same awkward but steady sliding motion that had to be wearing down the soles of his sneakers. But in spite of his careful progress, Ned tripped and sprawled on the stone floor. His hands groped wildly in the darkness, and every nerve in his body screamed that he was vulnerable. Ned jumped to his feet, frantic to maintain his sense of direction. Some piece of equipment or heavy machinery had caused his fall, but he sighted the gray patch ahead and started for it. Almost at once he stumbled again, flopping into what felt like a tub or a vat of some sort. Ned cried out in anger. He got back onto the floor and tried to move a little to the side, but a wall pressed him back. Now he really was in a corridor, he realized, one that was narrow and evidently full of old junk. The feeling of a dreadful presence right behind him grew more' acute, but it also spurred Ned on. He bumped into unidentifiable bulky objects at almost every step, and he climbed over them or crawled around them as fast as he could. The scrapes and bruises he suffered were annoying, but there was no time to dwell on them. If I get out of here I'll come back with a light and a big hammer, Ned promised himself, and I'll smash all of this stuff to pieces. But then he knew he would do no such thing. The truth is, if I get out of here I'll never, ever come back to this place.

An iron rod protruding from some unseen apparatus caught Ned in the stomach, doubling him over in pain. He rolled off it and hit the floor again. This time he stayed there, gasping, and then sobbing to himself. He didn't want to move anymore, come what may. If there really were phantoms, let them come and take him, once and for all. Get it over with. But nothing happened. Ned lay in darkness and silence, the only sound that of his own breathing. He felt vaguely embarrassed as if he were too small and insignificant for *them* to bother with. Ned forced himself up and went on toward the gray light. In his mind he could almost picture the presence at his back, a shadowy figure that sneered down on him, saying, *Go, little boy, you are safe now but you can be taken anytime, anywhere....*

The light, what little there was of it, came from a stairway. The door at the top stood open. Now that Ned had finally reached this point he felt no joy or relief, just an odd sense of deflation. He walked up the stairs and came out in a large round room. Ned guessed it had once been the spa's lobby and reception area. Now it was empty, the floor strewn with chunks of plaster, broken glass, beer cans, Twinkies wrappers and other rubbish. Paint hung in long, tattered strips from the walls. A massive staircase circled up four flights around the open well to the uppermost floor, which was topped by the framework of a huge skylight. Most of the glass was broken, by storms and vandals and sheer neglect, Ned thought, but he could see how impressive the place must have been at one time. It still was, in a way. He also noticed that his sense of time was apparently way off the mark. Wandering through the cellar had seemed to take hours and he thought it would have to be after nine o'clock by now, but the sky was still too bright. Could it be only six-thirty or seven? Maybe this was a place where time slowed down…. An abandoned paper wasp's nest lay on the floor at Ned's feet, and he kicked it away idly. He had won. He had explored the spa from its far outer wall to this front room. He had made it, in spite of all the obstacles and difficulties. So why did he feel confused and even defeated now?

The front door was boarded up, but several of the lower planks had been kicked loose and Ned saw that he would have no trouble crawling out. Like a puppy. Before he got to the door, however, he came to an abrupt stop. Words were scrawled in the thick dust and grime on the floor. The letters seemed to writhe like hideous snakes, but they held their shape.

YOU WILL BE
MINE AGAIN

All the blood in Ned's body rushed to his heart, which thundered and felt like it was about to explode. Trembling but deliberate, Ned rubbed out the words, one by one, with the toe of his sneaker. Then he was running as if his life depended on it, running down the long sloping drive away from the spa, through bushes and across the disused railroad bed, running from he knew not what, slowing a little only when he found himself at last on familiar streets with regular houses.

For an hour and a half the fear and anxiety had been building up in her. Linda's body felt like a bunch of steel rods. Her imagination had staged an anthology of short plays, each one a mother's nightmare. Then, in the single good moment of the entire day, it all dissolved as she caught sight of Ned coming across the backyard. He had never been late like this, never. Linda fought back the tears. She was so glad to see him alive and home! Of course, as soon as he opened the door and came into the kitchen, the joy she was experiencing transformed itself into crystalline anger.

Ned's sneakers were caked with mud. His clothes were muddy and his back was coated with the stuff. It was in his hair and on his face, and his hands were black. Linda noticed a long scratch on his right forearm; no doubt other injuries awaited discovery beneath the grime.

"Hi, Mom."

For a nine-year-old Ned was remarkably nonchalant. He walked casually across the room to the cabinet by the sink and took out the container of Borax.

"Where were you?" Linda screamed before Ned could start to wash his hands. "Look at you! You're covered with mud, you've got a cut on your arm and you're over an hour late! Where were you? What were you doing?"

Ned was paralyzed, all confidence blown away by his mother's outburst. He started to say something, but his throat had dried up so fast the words came out strangled beyond recognition. He gulped and tried again.

"I was just hiking in the woods," he said feebly.

"Hiking in the woods?" Linda raged. She wanted to shriek out every terrible thought and fear she had suffered while waiting, praying for Ned to come home. She wanted him to know how helpless and frightened a person could be. But then the tears were in her eyes and on her cheeks, and there was nothing she could do about them.

Ned hesitated briefly, then went to her. Linda felt his thin arms around her and she hugged him tightly, still crying. Then she was aware of Michael, who had appeared at the edge of her blurred vision. She blinked several times rapidly, wiped the tears away and sniffed.

"How could you, Ned?"

"Well ... I don't have a watch," he said reasonably.

"Yes, but you know when it's time to come home," Linda went on. "You know how ..."

Ned nodded silently, prepared now to let his mother have her say. He wouldn't argue. Why bother? He knew he had no defense. A glance at his father told him there would be another lecture from him after his mother finished. A double bill. Followed, no doubt, by some form of punishment.

But Ned didn't mind. In fact, he was glad to be there, glad to take whatever was coming to him. He was a lucky fellow. Only a little while ago, and not very far away, he had escaped something far worse. Five words still burned in his mind, so he wouldn't forget.

CHAPTER 8
POLIDORI STREET

Michael deliberately chose what seemed to be the seediest bar along the waterfront. Polidori Street was probably the oldest street in Lynnhaven, and it looked it. This is where you'll find the old tars and soak up local color, Michael thought, poking fun at his own intentions. The potential foolishness of the evening's quest did not escape him, but neither did it deter him. I'm not a gawking tourist, he reasoned, I live here too now. Besides, he knew he wouldn't find anything interesting in the Washington Irving Inn or the Patrick Henry Rooms or the Edison Restaurant Bar or any of the other Musk and fake leather lounges along the highway outside of town. They were clones, from Anywhere, U.S.A.

The bar Michael went into was so unassuming it didn't even have a name. Only a Budweiser neon light in the window marked the place. The first thing Michael noticed when he stepped inside was that the floor tilted away from the door, giving him the distinct sensation of literally going downhill as he went to take a seat at the bar. Appropriate, he thought, I like it. But the bar was almost deserted. Two customers sat together at a shaky table in one comer. They stared silently at their drinks, as lively as a pair of potted plants. Maybe they're joint owners of an uninsured boat that has just sunk, Michael mused. The only other customer was a young man with curly hair. He wore a sweatshirt with cut-off sleeves and he was sitting on a stool at the end of the bar. The bartender listened impassively as the young man explained something in great detail, underlining every word with elaborate hand gestures. Michael couldn't catch what was being said, so he occupied himself with filling a pipe (he had taken care to bring the most battered briar in his collection). The mirror behind the bar was festooned with postcards, paper money from foreign countries and pasteboard plaques with catchy mottos like A HARD MAN IS GOOD TO FIND! and ONLY SAILORS GET BLOWN OFFSHORE!

The bartender saw Michael and came over to serve him.

He was a heavyset man who might have been thirty-five or fifty or any age in between. He had the lumpy, nicked features of someone who has taken at least as many punches as he has thrown. His crew-cut hair was a neutral lichen on a skull that presented new horizons in phrenology.

"Bottle of Bud," Michael requested.

He got four dollars and fifteen cents change from his five. The bartender went back to the curly-haired youth who now addressed him as Ted. Ted, the bartender, took in another minute or so of Curl's ongoing saga before shrugging and walking away. He stuck a toothpick in his mouth and took a closer look at Michael.

"You from here in town?" Ted asked, making it sound like an accusation.

"Yeah, moved in not too long ago."

"That right?" Ted had heard stranger things. He chewed his. toothpick.

"Quiet night," Michael observed.

Ted grunted ambiguously. At that moment three more young men came into the bar and joined Curly. They called for 7 & 7, a mix of Seagram's rye and 7-Up that Michael loathed. Ted started pouring and Michael's eye fell on a card that said OUT TO A DRINK OF LUNCH! He noticed that all of the messages ended with an exclamation point.

One of the men at the bar proceeded to tell a story in a loud voice. It was about a sailor who, after months at sea, prowled the bars and finally found a prostitute he liked. They went back to her place, he paid her five dollars and they got down to it. But the sailor had had too many drinks and he wasn't making progress. Still, he labored on, and at one point asked the bored girl how he was doing. "About three knots, sailor," she said. The sailor wondered if she was making fun of him, so he asked her what she meant by that. Her answer: "It's not hard, it's not in, and you're not getting your five dollars back." The four young men rocked on their feet with laughter. Michael smiled. Ted, who had heard that joke many times before, studied the serial numbers on a handful of dollar bills.

A woman entered the bar and, after a quick glance around, sat on a stool next to Michael. Right on time, he thought. Just as he had cued the arrival of the noisy trio by remarking how quiet it was, so their little story had cued the entrance of this shady lady. The only cue in the bar that wasn't working was the exclamation point: so far it had failed to produce a single laugh. Ted must have known the woman because he brought her a rye and ginger without having to be told. Then he stared at a large jar full of pickled eggs, perhaps trying to guess their number.

"Hi," the woman said with a smile.

"Hi," Michael said.

"The place is busy tonight."

"Quite a crowd," Michael agreed with a touch of sarcasm. It was easier and safer to take a look at her in the mirror behind the bar. She had the bright, artificial face of a child's doll. It probably took her longer these days to assemble all the components, but she hadn't reached the stage where no matter what she did she would always look frayed. That might be the next comer, but she hadn't quite got to it yet.

"My name is Vy," she said. "Short for Viyella, as in Viyella shirts — how's that for a name? Everybody calls me Vy. What about you?"

"Dave," Michael said. It was his middle name.

"That's a nice solid name," Vy said. "I find names fascinating, don't you? My first husband was named Orlando and everybody called him Or, which sounds funny but actually suited him very well. He could never figure out what kind of person he was going to be or what he was going to do. He was a kind of human *or*, stuck between all kinds of alternatives and directions, never knowing which of them to take up. He was an *or* all the time I knew him. Probably still is, the poor bastard."

The more Vy talked, the less Michael wanted to hear. He asked just one polite question — "Do you live in Lynnhaven?" — and that was all Vy needed to grab the conversational reins.

"Lynnhaven's a funny old town," Vy said. "Cute and dumb, you know? It's kind of nice, I suppose, but it sure isn't the liveliest place in the world. In fact, it's pretty darn slow when you come right down to it."

Michael nodded agreeably. There was no point in telling her that was one of the reasons he liked the town.

"I've been thinking of leaving," Vy went on. "But I don't know where I'd go, that's what's keeping me here. I've been like this for the last six months—how's that for indecision? Ever since Ralph died. Maybe I'll go to Arizona or Oregon, I hear they're still real natural. But then, I remember reading something about the Mafia taking over Arizona. I guess it's only a matter of time."

She's not shady, Michael decided. She's just a birdbrain. Now it seemed to him that, yes, this was a silly little excursion he was on. He had a wife and son and plenty of booze at home, so what was he doing in a nameless joint like this? What was he looking for? Nothing, really. Just a pleasant walk, a beer in a local bar and another pleasant walk home. That was enough. Enough to remind him of what he was lucky to have. The world was full of bruised souls and stunted personalities, like Vy and Ted and those potted plants over there. People with not a whole lot going for them. Even Linda, his own wife—where would she be without him? She was a good person, and full of love, but could she hold herself together alone if she had to? Did she have the necessary inner strength? Michael wondered. Of course, Ned would be there, but a child can be as much a drain as a help. If anything ever happened to Michael, Linda would need all the help she could get. Including, eventually, another man. She just wasn't the kind of person who could make it alone. Perhaps Michael should increase his life-insurance coverage, so that Linda would have plenty of cushion if the unthinkable ever came to pass. You can never be too secure.

" ... on the rebound," Vy was saying. "So Bruno and I got married, just like that. That's the kind of people we were. But the whole thing lasted only one week. We went to Haiti for our honeymoon, which was handy because you can get a divorce there too, pronto, which we did. Don't ask me why, who knows about marriage? It's a funny business, that's all I can say. Anyhow, I found out later that Bruno was running guns into Nicaragua and he got very rich. Just my luck. He sold guns to both sides, all sides—that's the beauty of free enterprise. But what a way to make a living. I finally understood why he was such a nervous guy."

Vulnerable, Michael thought. Yes, that was one part, a large part, perhaps, of what had attracted him to Linda. She was one of life's vulnerable people. She needed to be looked after and protected. She was his special project for life, and just thinking about it gave Michael a good feeling inside.

"Funny the things you think of when you're in a bar with strangers," Michael said absently. "Things that never occur to you at any other time or place."

"You're telling me," Vy agreed.

Michael looked at the woman again. Not bad, really, he had to admit. Something of a good shape there, too. He might almost find her attractive. If he thought about it for a while.

Good thing he was a happy man.

CHAPTER 9
UNDER THE HALF MOON

Before bed.

Sitting by the window.

He and the spa were a film playing over and over again in his mind.

Then the scarecrow moved in the light of the half-moon.

Broomstick arms, first one, then the other, swung around to wave and point.

At Ned.

CHAPTER 10
LINDA

She was waiting for a sign.

Her husband thumbing through the latest issue of *Business Week*? Her son quietly watching "Buck Rogers" on TV? The slosh and hum of the dishwasher in the kitchen? No, none of these.

Linda thought the problem might be that she was still overly romantic. Too much Wordsworth in college, or something like that. You could spend a lifetime waiting for a sign that the ideal, the idyllic, the dream had begun. But it would never happen. Even when every circumstance seemed to be right and the dream within your grasp.... How hard it was to close your fingers around it. Memories? You could try to cast them in a magic light, but at the same time you knew they were only ordinary.

But Linda was waiting for another kind of sign. One that would herald the arrival of trouble. It was not something Linda looked forward to, but neither was she so foolish as to assume it would never come. Having only one child heightens your awareness of dangers. The sign, if and when it came, could mean anything, but what she feared most was illness. Although Ned seemed to be a perfectly healthy boy he could be carrying her own physical weaknesses in him like a time bomb.

There are many myths and misconceptions about asthma. Friends in Washington had told Linda she was crazy to move to the shore, that the damp sea air would kill her. Go to Arizona, they urged her. But asthma affects different people in different ways, and Linda had learned the hard way that a dry atmosphere was much more likely to trigger an attack in her. Even here, in Lynnhaven, they had to have humidifiers on both floors of the house. Another annoying notion was that asthma was purely a mental problem. She had lost count of the number of smug people who had nodded sagely and recommended a good psychiatrist to her. Of course, stress influenced it, but asthma was still a very real physical affliction. The sanest, most well-adjusted people in the world could suffer devastating attacks. But the most distressing misconception was that asthma developed in childhood. If that were true Linda could have begun counting the days until Ned would be safe. A few more years and he would be into adolescence. But asthma could and did surface at any time in a person's life. In many cases it didn't emerge until one was fully adult. So, every day that passed with Ned in good health did offer some relief for Linda, but also seemed to renew the threat. You can never be sure, you can never be safe.

And asthma was only one of many possibilities. A child might suffer and die from a million different things. Drugs and street violence might have been left behind in Washington (at least, she hoped so), but Lynnhaven was still something of an unknown quantity, and it would be a mistake to regard it as a true sanctuary. A cut from a rusty fish hook, a cut so small Ned wouldn't even mention it, could bring on tetanus.

Linda recognized the old trap and once more pulled herself out of it: the more you worried about things, the more things you found to worry about. And down that road lay the twin pitfalls of fatalism and paralysis. Linda knew that the proper attitude was one of vigilance.

Michael was so calm about these things. They didn't seem to bother him at all. She would like to be that way, to be able to take each day as it came, naturally and competently. That's what Linda had always admired about her husband, even years ago when he had still had a lot of boyishness about him. It was a measure of competence she felt all too lacking in herself. Nor was Michael one of life's sleepwalkers. He knew who he was and what he was doing, and he built his life on that foundation. It was a sense of certainty that Linda clung to, even if it did infuriate her at times.

Maybe the trouble was that she and Michael seemed to have so little time together alone. The last time they had been away by themselves was—God, five or six years ago, when they had left Ned with his grandparents in Buffalo and gone to Montserrat for a week. Since then, not even a hasty overnighter in a Maryland motel. Yes, it would definitely be good for them to get away for a while. But it was not going to happen this year, she knew. They had already spent a lot of money on the house and there was still a good deal of work to be done.

They had come a long way, she and Michael, since the days when they'd been students together at Boston University. From there they'd gone to Pennsylvania, where Michael did graduate work. Then Washington, the exciting adventure that, somewhere along the line, had downshifted into everyday life. Linda hated to think of her old art history texts, dusty now and packed away in cartons in the cellar. She couldn't remember the last time she had gone to an exhibition or picked up a new art book. With Michael, the change could be seen in the way he had taken to the dull security of his government job; he no longer talked about moving to one of the prestigious private firms, much less branching out on his own.

It's called life, Linda reflected. Sooner or later, one way or another, you have to strike a truce and settle in.

Now, Lynnhaven. The move from the city. A whole house, not just an apartment. Four acres of land. The next rung on the endless American ladder that goes—where? Maybe that's what it's really all about: the movement, the semblance of change that eventually took the place of change itself. But how could Linda fault it? What more did she want?

Friends. Now that she thought about it, Linda wondered if she hadn't really been speaking about herself when she told Michael that Ned needed friends. Here she was with a child to watch over and a marriage as comfortable as an old chair—but no neighbor close enough to do things with, to talk to, no friend of her own.

In Washington there had been acquaintances, other wives and some good neighbors in the apartment building. But the move to Lynnhaven had reduced contact with those people to occasional telephone calls and vague promises at both ends of the line to get together soon. Is something happening to me? Linda wondered. Do you suddenly become old and boring when you move from a city to a small town? One thing she knew for sure: when you move you lose touch in many ways.

Even with Janice, and that was perhaps the most distressing part. Janice Roberts was Linda's best friend in Washington, and yet in just a few months it seemed they were becoming strangers to each other. They still talked on the telephone, but the conversations now tended to be short and newsy, almost to the point of being impersonal. It was worrying, but Linda tried to convince herself that they were just going through one of those temporary lulls that occur in all relationships once in a while.

Linda and Janice knew each other from college in Boston, but their friendship didn't really blossom until they met again by chance in Washington. Janice had landed a job with a small but up-and-coming public relations firm and had settled into a tiny apartment on the fringe of Georgetown, not far from where Michael and Linda were living. As well as being old schoolmates, the two women complemented each other in certain ways. Janice was living alone and making a career for herself, while Linda was married and looking forward to raising children. It was a friendship remarkably free of tension or competitiveness. Linda and Janice were both happy with their own situations, and so they were able to admire each other's strengths and abilities without envy.

In Washington Linda and Janice did things together regularly, whether it was visiting a gallery or seeing a new film or play, or simply meeting for lunch and a bit of shopping. Even after Ned was born they were still able to get around almost as often as before, since Michael didn't mind taking care of the infant for a few hours on a week night or a Saturday afternoon. And Janice would baby-sit from time to time so that Michael and Linda could go out together. Michael and Janice got along well enough. Although he thought she was somewhat pretentious and she found him rather stuffy, there was no antagonism between them.

But now—what was happening to Linda that was changing her friendship with Janice? Since the Covingtons had moved, the two women had seen each other exactly twice. That in itself was not too surprising, as Janice's work kept her quite busy and Linda had more than she could handle between Ned and the new house. No, there was something else, the tone perhaps, of those two encounters, that bothered Linda.

The first time had been shortly after the move, when Janice came to Lynnhaven to inspect the place. She thought the house and site were wonderful, and she stayed for most of the afternoon. The two women chatted comfortably over wine and pate and coffee and pastry. There had been no awkward silences or strained moments; it had been an easy, pleasant occasion, like many others they had spent together. Yes, and ... ? Linda remembered. A few minutes before she went back to Washington, Janice had looked around and said, "Well, you really are here now." But it wasn't so much what she had said, nor even how she had said it that stayed with Linda. It was the look in Janice's eyes, an expression that was there for a brief instant and then gone. Even now, a couple of months later, Linda couldn't say what it meant. Perhaps nothing. Perhaps she had imagined it. And yet, it stayed with her.

Not long after that they saw each other again. It was a Friday, Linda remembered. She had called the office to say that Michael was sick and wouldn't be to work that day. Actually, he was fine and just wanted a three-day weekend. That freed Linda and she immediately decided to go into Washington. Janice had to be at a reception at noon, but she was able to sneak away early and meet Linda for a quick bite of lunch and a drink. They had a little less than an hour together but it seemed longer, Linda recalled unhappily.

"How was your reception?"

"Terrible, which means good," Janice said. "Full of lecherous cops and ambitious young congressional aides."

"What was it for?"

"Teflon-coated bullets."

"You're kidding." Linda smiled, but then she saw that Janice was serious. "Why—"

"Believe me, you don't want to know."

The conversation moved in fits and starts for the next half hour, going nowhere. Janice seemed not tired but weary. It was strange, and it made Linda feel self-conscious. All of a sudden she realized she didn't have much to say. It was as if a vacuum had formed over the table between them, and they could do nothing about it. Both women felt relieved when it was time to go.

"Are you all right?" Linda asked as they stood outside the restaurant.

"Sure. Why?"

"I don't know. You look like you could use a vacation."

What a terrible thing to say, Linda thought. But it was too late, the words were already spoken.

"I probably could," Janice admitted. "How about you? How are you doing out there in the sticks?"

Linda recalled answering: "Oh, fine."

On the way back to Lynnhaven she tried to reason her way out of her melancholy. Just one of those days. Two people in off-moods. Janice working too hard. Me not yet fully adjusted to my new environment. Et cetera. Blah blah blah. Fine? Pretty good? Okay? So-so? Or ... what?

Since then she'd had no desire to go back in to Washington, but she did hope Janice would come out to visit again. Their friendship was too solid to shake apart in a little turbulence. But she knew now that Janice could not solve her problems for her. Linda had known how easy it was to feel invisible in a big city; since moving to Lynnhaven she had learned that a person could be equally alone in a small town. And the only one who can do anything about it, she told herself once more, is you.

Linda looked up from her cold tea and unopened magazine.

Had she heard something, or was it just her imagination? A voice. Ned was talking to someone. Linda left the kitchen and went quietly through the dining room. She saw Ned standing at the far end of the living room. He was looking straight ahead at nothing.

"Who were you talking to?"

Ned wheeled around, startled by his mother's presence.

"Nobody."

"I thought I heard you talking just a minute ago."

Bright afternoon sunshine poured through the wide window and Ned moved to step out of the glare that only increased his discomfort.

"No.... I guess I just read something out loud from the newspaper." He pointed to the comics page lying open on the coffee table. "That's all."

"Are you all right, Ned?"

"Sure."

"Well, don't forget. Your father wants you to do some weeding in the garden."

"I know. I'll do it later, when it's cooler out."

Ned went upstairs to his room. Linda refolded the newspaper and then wandered back into the kitchen. Out loud? Yes, Ned followed the daily strips and he had stacks of comic books in his room. But reading them out loud—that just didn't seem like Ned's style. Ned loved to read; he took after his father in that respect. Michael, in the absence of anything better to read while sitting on the toilet, would study the labels on bottles of disinfectant or shampoo. Once he had emerged from the throne room denouncing skin cremes as an extravagant waste of petroleum products. But Ned was the kind of boy who could sit reading for hours on end without making a sound. He never even laughed at those comics, let alone read them out loud.

Don't go making something out of nothing again, Linda reproached herself. What did it matter if Ned was reading out loud, or even holding an imaginary conversation? Kids do that all the time. Not only is there nothing wrong with it, but sometimes it's even good for a child, all the books said so. But Ned was almost ten and he'd never done it before. At least, not as far as she knew....

She could talk to Michael about it, but—was there really anything to talk about? He would listen, as he always did, attentive, sympathetic; concerned, but in the end he would say: What did you hear? No single word. Not even a syllable to ponder. Nothing. It's nothing.

And he'd probably be right, Linda thought. She'd just have to be more alert. The important thing was to be prepared if her son was ever threatened, prepared to do whatever was necessary to ensure his safety. She would protect Ned. She would die for him, if it came to that. No question.

CHAPTER 11
EXPLANATIONS

Michael Covington sipped the gin cooler he had made for himself. It was somehow wetter and more refreshing than bourbon on a hot languid evening like this. Washington had been a pressure cooker all day. The air conditioning in the office had broken down for three hours and the humidity was such that sweat poured off people even when they sat still. He felt better now, stretched out on a chaise lounge in the backyard at dusk with a tall drink; better, but still pretty damm hot. And here was his son, sprawled on the grass, looking up, waiting for Michael to say something.

"Ned, I'm going to tell you something that happened to me once, when I was a boy about your age. It's a true story and I can still remember it vividly. Maybe it'll help you understand a little better some of the things you've been wondering about."

Michael paused, staring at the clear, icy drink in his hand as if it were a crystal ball geared to reveal the past in an exemplary light.

"I think I told you before," he went on, "that for a few years when I was a youngster I had a paper route. I used to deliver the Sunday newspapers to a lot of houses in our old neighborhood—in fact, I had a hundred and eight customers at one time, so you can see it was a pretty big route. And in those days we had to handle quite a few different newspapers that no longer exist, like the *Journal-American*, the *Herald Tribune* and the *Mirror*. I even carried a Polish newspaper, but I can't remember the name of it now. I bet I could walk through that neighborhood in my mind and still tell you the names of all my customers and which papers they took…. Not that it means anything now.

"In Buffalo the weather is a lot rougher than down here in the winter. The snow falls by the ton. Remember the pictures Grandpa Fred sent the year before last, with the snow piled up higher than a grown man? Well, it was that bad or worse every winter when I was a boy, or it seemed that way. And you know how fat and heavy *The New York Times* is on Sunday—imagine lugging it through snow drifts that come up to your chin, trying to keep it dry and get it safely behind someone's storm door that is frozen half-shut. I'd be kidding you if I told you I enjoyed it, because I didn't; I hated every minute of it. The weather, the dogs, the waking up at six in the morning, the crabby customers who'd try every trick in the book to avoid paying you a lousy fifteen or twenty cents.... But it was all good experience, I guess, and the money, while it wasn't a great deal, did help in those days.

"Anyhow, the thing I was going to tell you about happened on a Friday night. It was in the summer and it was a hot night like this one. I was riding around on my bike collecting money from some of my customers, and it must have been nine o'clock or a little after, because I remember it was fully dark. I stopped in to Benny's, our neighborhood grocery store, to get some candy. Junior Mints and Necco Wafers, those were my favorites. When I came out of the store and started to pedal my bike away, I noticed the moon. It was huge, it was like an enormous golden pumpkin in the sky, bigger than I'd ever seen the moon before.

"I rode along on my bike, cruising, eating candy and collecting money at a few more houses, but I went more slowly and I couldn't keep from looking at that moon. It was so large it seemed to me there had to be something wrong. And then I began to get scared. The only reason the moon could be growing so big was that it had to be coming closer. The more I looked and the more I thought about it, the more I was sure that the moon was going to crash into the earth that very night. It would be the end of the world, and the worst part of it was that I had no doubt the moon would hit smack in the middle of Buffalo.

"I know it sounds silly now, but I believed it at the time, and boy did it scare me. Could I be the only person in the world who knew what was about to happen? Why were there no sirens, no emergency measures being taken? The neighborhood was perfectly quiet and peaceful. Surely there were scientists somewhere who were supposed to keep an eye out for possible catastrophes like this. But then I thought, maybe there's nothing they could do. How could anybody stop the moon from plowing into the earth, if that's what was in the cards? Maybe they deliberately weren't telling anyone, so there wouldn't be a panic.

"Ned, that moon hung so big in the sky I was sure I was going to die that night, and my family and everyone else in the world along with me. I wanted to race through the streets on my bike, yelling and warning all the people about the disaster that was about to take place, like a kind of newsboy Paul Revere. But it seemed crazy to me that nobody else had noticed it, so I decided to tell one person first, an adult, and see what kind of reaction I got.

"The next customer on my list was Mr. Trunk, an insurance man who took the *Times* and was always nice to me. I rang his doorbell, collected the money and the usual dime tip, and I almost didn't say anything, I was so nervous.

"But just as he was closing the door I said, 'Mr. Trunk, take a look at that moon.'

"He came out onto the front porch and gazed up at the sky. 'Yeah, that's quite a moon,' he said, calm as could be.

"'It's really *big*,' I said.

"Mr. Trunk nodded his head and said, 'Sure is. It's a beautiful moon tonight.' And then he said goodnight and went back into his house. It hadn't bothered him at all.

"The idea that the world was going to end began to fade in my mind from that moment, and by the time I got home I didn't even mention it to anyone in my family. But it was still hard to believe that I could be so wrong. The moon that had filled me with visions of death and destruction, oceans boiling and cities being ground to dust, had brought the completely opposite reaction to Mr. Trunk. He thought it was beautiful, and he was right. I didn't know what to make of it for a while, but I'll tell you this: I was glad when I woke up the next morning and found that I was still alive and the world still existed. And here's another interesting thing: if the moon really was going to crash into the earth, it wouldn't make any difference whether it was day or night, right? But we think such thoughts only at night; they never occur to us during the day, for some reason.

"So you see, Ned, you can look at something and think you know what it is, what it means and what's going to come of it. You can be so sure that your heart booms and you can barely put two words together. But you can still be wrong, one hundred per cent wrong. The important thing to remember is that there's always an explanation for everything. We may not know what that explanation is, or we may not understand it completely, but that doesn't mean that anything our minds dream up is true. It just means we haven't found the truth yet, that it's still hidden, waiting for us to uncover it:

"You asked me if I believe in ghosts and phantoms and things like that, and I have to tell you that I don't. Plenty of people do, even adults. Maybe I'm wrong, but in all the centuries that people have talked about such things no one has been able to come up with a bit of solid proof. And why not? I believe it's because they just don't exist, however much people would like them to. Wouldn't it be nice if we could talk to a friend or a relative who had died? I'd love to be able to talk to my older brother, Jim. I hardly knew him when he was shot down over Korea, but wishing isn't enough, and imagining that something is real doesn't make it real.

"Same thing with magic. Everybody likes to watch a good magician at work, but you have to find the explanation if you want to know what's really happening. Remember the stories about the great Houdini and how he amazed thousands of people in his day? He would be all chained up and in the strongest handcuffs made, and just before they put him in a trunk his wife would kiss him good-bye, like it might be the last time she saw him alive, right? Well, she had a key in her mouth and when she kissed him she passed that key into his mouth, and that's how he could start to get free and make another miraculous escape. But it wasn't a miracle and it wasn't magic; just a simple key.

"That's what you have to look for when you think you've come across something strange or spooky: the explanation behind it. We could sit here for a couple of hours and watch the sky, and sooner or later we might see something unusual. The light of an odd shape or color moving through the night. Does that mean we've seen a flying saucer from another planet? Well, that is one possibility, but it isn't very likely, is it? The chances are it would be a jet plane at a high altitude or a helicopter skimming along the horizon or a meteorite or one of those satellites we've put into orbit—or any number of other things, like reflected light on a dark cloud, who knows what. It may not be as exciting as the idea of visitors from outer space, but that's the way it is. The simplest, most down-to-earth explanation is usually the one that turns out to be true.

"Now I'll tell you one more thing, Ned. No explanation ever makes anything less special than it seems to you. I've looked at that moon thousands of times since that night in Buffalo and it has never, ever been as big as it was then. I don't expect it ever will be, either. That moon, that night, will always be special to me because I saw it the way no one else did. And the fact that I was all wrong can't change that one little bit. Do you know what I mean?"

"Yeah," Ned said without conviction.

"Okay?"

"Okay, yeah. Thanks, Dad." There was much, so much that Ned could say in reply. What about all those unexplained UFOs, what about the cases of people driven from their homes by ghosts or forces unknown, what about the people who just suddenly disappeared in strange circumstances? But his father had had his say and Ned felt it was better to let the matter rest there. "I think I'll go watch TV now."

Michael smiled as his son crossed the lawn to the house.

So much for my big speech, he thought. But maybe the boy took in some of it. If the message gets through, at least subconsciously, that will be enough. The kid's all right, Michael told himself. I wish I had some of his imagination. He should enjoy it while he can. Life gets ordinary soon enough. Wait until Ned has his first wet dream—that'll crowd some of this stuff out of his mind.

Linda came out the back door of the house and walked toward him. Michael saw again how attractive his wife could be. She looked good in shorts and a light summer blouse. The ghost of the nineteen-year-old college girl whose appearance used to give him instant, embarrassing erections, could still be seen in this woman. If the heat wasn't so draining Michael could almost think about chasing her upstairs.

"That was quite a conference you two had out here."

"Just men-talk."

"Telling your son about all the wicked women in your past?"

Michael chuckled. "Not that kind of men-talk."

"You were getting pretty animated there for a while. What were you doing, reciting 'The Cremation of Sam McGee'?"

"No, just probing a few soft points in the Special Theory of Relativity."

"I love you, Michael."

"That's good, because I love you."

CHAPTER 12
THERE IS MAGIC ... AND MAGIC

"Well, well, well," Cloudy exclaimed. "If it ain't Mr. Tadpole hisself."

"Hi."

Ned smiled sheepishly as he greeted the two old men. Cloudy held a portable electric mixer in one hand and its two eggbeaters in the other. Peeler was sitting back with a can of beer, his face shaded beneath the visor of his baseball cap. He cracked one eye open to see Ned, then shut it again.

"I thought maybe your daddy was keepin' you away from here," Peeler said.

"No, why?"

"He come around to see me a few days ago."

"He did?" Ned was puzzled to learn this. "What for?"

"Just to say hello and tell me who he was. Last week some time, I guess it was. I was afraid maybe he didn't like what he seen and decided you should stay away."

"No, he didn't say anything to me about it," Ned said. "I didn't even know he'd been here."

"So where you been?" Cloudy asked.

"Oh, around home."

"Around home, huh?"

"I was being punished," Ned admitted.

"You was? What for?"

"Last week I went up the hill to explore the ruins of the old spa."

"You went up there? Alone?"

Cloudy looked genuinely surprised, and Peeler pushed his cap back, taking notice.

"Yeah, and I got home late and my clothes were muddy and I had a few scratches, so my mom and dad were kind of sore at me and I had to stick around the house for a few days."

"I bet they was sore at you," Cloudy said. "You shouldn't never oughta go up to that place, Mr. Tadpole. Never."

"It's dangerous," Peeler said. "You could break a leg and be stuck there and nobody'd hear you call for help."

"I know, I know," Ned said, almost enthusiastically. "I nearly did get stuck there. It's the most incredible place I've ever seen."

"You fall into one of them gardens," Peeler warned, "and you won't never climb out again, no how."

"I know. It's like a jungle in there."

"Worse," Cloudy said.

"What did they have all those walls for, anyway?"

"They was gardens."

"They had all kinds of gardens and things in there," Peeler went on. "In one garden they'd have a certain type of grass growin' so that when you walked on it, it give off a pretty smell. Another garden'd be full of some kind of flower, just the one, so you'd get that smell. And the next garden, somethin' else, and so on. Every one of 'em was different, who knows what all for."

"The gardens was quite the thing in their day," Cloudy put in, "White folks come from miles around and plenty kept comin' back for more. They paid a lot to stay at the spa." He shook his head, as if still amazed at the idea. "That was back in its heyday, of course."

"Some of the walls had shapes—like, one was a rectangle," Ned said.

"That'd probably be the old tennis court," Peeler said.

"Oh ..."

"They had lots of stuff like that there, too."

"And one wall formed a circle, and there was a gurgling sound, and smoke came from the middle of it. But I couldn't see because of the bushes."

"You know what that might be," Peeler said.

"What?"

"That just might be the mud."

"Mud?"

"That's right. I heard they got a pit of some sort up there, with hot mud and steam that perked up from underground, kinda like a geyser, only different. And they say folks used to take all their clothes off and get right down in that hot mud and waller around for as long as they could take it."

"Like Georgia hawgs," Cloudy added, grinning.

"Why would they do that?" Ned asked.

Peeler shrugged. "Somebody musta told 'em it was good for their health, or some such nonsense like that. Or maybe they was just havin' fun. No tellin' why folks do the things they do."

Ned tried to picture grown men and women, naked, slithering around in hot, steamy mud that made that horrible slurping sound. The image was at once exotic and disturbing.

"You know," the boy said, "I heard lots of things moving around in the brush. I could never see anything, but I always had the feeling that somebody or something was following me, watching me all the time. What do you think that was?"

"Animals," Peeler stated flatly.

"That's what I thought," Ned said, a little disappointed.

"Raccoon, fox, possum—all kinds of animals would've moved into that place over the years."

"I bet there's a big, juicy snappin' turkle in the lily pond," Cloudy said. "If there is a lily pond." He thought about it some more. "They must be, a place like that."

Ned decided to try his most daring speculation: "I was wondering if any—you know, swamp people, might be living in there now...."

"I don't guess so," Peeler said.

"Too close to town," Cloudy elaborated. "Swamp folks, they don't like a town nor other people bein' too close to them. They hide out far away as they can get, that's why they ain't too friendly if you wander into their patch, see,"

"If I had an old map of this area I could show you where the swamp people lived," Peeler said. "They had their own places, like Mud Hen Gut, Dolly's Quarter, Middle Runt Creek and Jenkins Dip—they was swamp folks hangouts."

"I remember some of them places," Cloudy said. "Pissholes, every dad one of 'em too."

"Were they real little towns, like?" Ned asked.

"Naw, not hardly," Peeler scoffed. "Nothin' more'n a bit of marsh staked out by this family or that, and twenty or thirty idiot kids shacked up in a pigsty. That's all. But you run into the wrong bunch of 'em and they'd really have your nuts in a noose faster'n you could blink."

"That's the truth," Cloudy agreed.

"Are they still around?"

"I don't care if they are, and I don't care if they ain't," Peeler replied promptly. "Last time I come across one of them fellers was ten or twenty years ago. I was pickin' berries and I guess I strayed some, when all of a sudden I notice this guy watchin' me. I could just see his face in the shadow of a tree about a hundred yards away-well, maybe not that far. Anyhow, I didn't act like I seen him, but I just kinda backed away, slow and natural, like I'd got all the berries I could get. And I scrammed outta there. I sure didn't want to meet him close up, nor his stumpy-toothed tribe, I can tell you."

"Don't bother them, they don't bother you," Cloudy said. "Trouble is, you might not know when you're botherin' them till it's too late."

"Anyhow," Peeler concluded, "you can be sure they ain't none of 'em livin' up to the spa. Ain't nobody could live in that place, way it is now."

"I got inside the building, too."

"Inside the building," Cloudy cried in pain.

"That's just askin' for trouble," Peeler said with a look that was as close to real anger as Ned had seen on the old man's face. "You stay away from there, hear?

"Yeah, but—"

"Never mind that. You supposed to be a friend of ours?"

"Sure."

"Okay, you do like we say."

"All right," Ned said softly.

For a while none of them spoke. Cloudy resumed his examination of the electric mixer. The motor seemed to work fine by itself, but as soon as he attached the eggbeaters the appliance made a kind of strangled, grinding noise and refused to run. He removed the beaters and again the motor hummed smoothly.

"Darndest thing," Cloudy muttered, breaking the silence. "Works fine as long as you don't try to use it."

"Junk," Peeler said scornfully,

"I know it's junk," Cloudy responded. "The problem is, it's junk on the fritz." He shook the mixer vigorously, as if expecting a coin to pop out, solving the problem and enriching him at the same time.

"Peeler."

"Hmmmn."

"Do you think there could be any ghosts or evil spirits up there in the old spa?"

"Ned, I swear you're as stubborn as all get-out sometimes. You just don't know when to let go."

Peeler got up and went into the baithouse, where he opened another beer and busied himself checking the tanks. Curiosity was a wonderful thing, he thought, but not always easy to handle. How do you tell a boy that there is magic ... and there is magic? That you had to be open to it, but that you also had to keep your distance and fear it? If you were blind to it, you missed some of life's better moments. If you ignored it, you did so at your own risk. And if you sought it out, no good would come of it. It was a kind of power, and like all power, you couldn't really hold it; you could only be held by it. The boy was like a dog, snuffling around a tricky rock; if he succeeded in rolling it over he might be sorry.

Ned appeared in the doorway and then stepped hesitantly into the baithouse. Peeler noticed him but continued what he was doing.

"Are you mad at me?" Ned asked timidly.

"Nope."

"Well ... You act like you are."

"Well, I ain't."

"Well ... What are you?"

"I just don't like you pokin' around no place where you could get nipped by a cottonmouth or copperhead and not be able to get back for help in time, that's what."

"I was careful."

"You was, huh." Peeler showed how impressed he was by hawking up a mouthful of phlegm and spitting it to the ground.

"I didn't get hurt."

"This time you didn't."

"I'm not going back there, Peeler. Honest."

"I shouldn't never've told you about it in the first place." There it was: his feeling of complicity in the matter.

"I would have found out anyway," Ned said. "Everybody knows about the spa and you can see it from lots of places in town."

"Maybe."

"I've seen it and I won't go back again." No response. "I mean it, Peeler. I don't even want to go back, I didn't like the place."

"If you say so."

"Well, I do."

Peeler stopped worrying the crayfish and looked at Ned.

"I told you how I stay away from the swamp folks, and you can be sure I stay away from Sherwood's spa. There's times when you might have to take a risk, and there's other times when there ain't no sense in it at all. Understand'?"

"Yes."

"I hope you do," Peeler said. "I hope you got that well and truly fixed in your head."

Peeler went and fished another can of beer out of the tank. Ned stood where he was, still feeling a little awkward but glad the touchy subject was now apparently closed,

"I'm goin' over to Stony Point," Peeler announced. "Want to come along?"

"Stony Point? Well … " Ned hesitated. Actually, he didn't want to go to Stony Point that evening, but in the circumstances he thought he probably should. Cloudy always managed to find something else to do, but Ned had been on several of these treks before, Peeler liked to walk to Stony Point a couple at times a week, getting there just before sunset. It was a high, bare piece of land just outside of town, and it provided a superb view in all directions. The sunsets were certainly spectacular from that vantage point, but they didn't seem to be what Peeler was looking for. Every time Ned had been there, as soon as the sun disappeared, Peeler would frown or mutter "Shit," or just turn away and stalk home. Clearly the old man expected something else and was unhappy not to find it, but no matter how many times Ned asked him, Peeler refused to talk about it. He would tell Ned to be quiet and watch, and then, when it was over and nothing unusual had taken place, Peeler would hardly say another word all the way back. It was the least enjoyable time to be with Peeler, but Ned realized it had fallen to him to be the witness to whatever it was that never happened.

"If my parents let me," Ned said. "I'm still kind of on probation with them, I think."

"Okay," Peeler said.

Ned did go to Stony Point with Peeler that evening. As usual the old man pointed to a dirty yellow cloud that dominated the sky to the northwest and said, "There's good old Washington, D.C."

The sun was deep red, easy to look at. By now Ned knew how to watch the sunset and Peeler at the same time. When the horizon had swallowed the last bead of crimson, Peeler got up to leave with a familiar expression on his face. He looked like a man who had hiked a great distance only to see a dog crap.

CHAPTER 13
GOODBYE, GRETA GARBO

Linda had bought the two books to prove something to herself, but now it seemed like a mistake. They sat on the coffee table like bricks, daring her to have another go. The newspapers and magazines were full of stories about the author, Conrad Linger, and interviews with him. He was an unqualified literary and popular success. His novel, *Anchor the Land*, and his book of short stories, *Goodbye, Greta Garbo*, were both on the bestseller list. It was either the first time an author had two books on the list simultaneously, or the first book of stories on the list in decades—Linda couldn't remember which. But the point was: Conrad Linger was the man to read.

Linda had picked up both volumes in the Reading Room, a combination book and card shop in a mall outside of Lynnhaven. Judging by the photo on the back cover, Conrad Linger looked a lot like Mr. Rogers of kiddie TV fame. Linda started with the novel, *Anchor the Land*, but put it aside after a few chapters. There was no story line, just a crowd of characters who conversed in ambiguities. Linda remembered reading in a review that one character spoke only in haikus, but to her it seemed that they all did. Hardly a page went by without the use of a "So be it," or a "Be that as it may." Perhaps I'll be more receptive to it another time, Linda thought, turning to *Goodbye, Greta Garbo*. The stories in this book were all set on a luxury liner that was on a supposedly romantic cruise to an unknown destination. The title story was about a distraught woman who eventually found relief by throwing her collection of old wine labels overboard. In another story, a man spent the entire cruise in his cabin, reciting haikus to his pet parrot. In spite of his efforts, the man failed to teach the bird a single haiku. The only thing the parrot would say was "Fuck off." The captain of the liner appeared briefly in every story. He had no name. His eyes "scoured the inner distance." He was always being given bad news about the weather ahead. "So be it," he said stoically. Linda gave up after five stories, leaving a dozen unread. She took another look at the picture of Conrad Linger. He had the kind of smile you seldom saw on the face of a serious writer.

What's wrong with me, Linda asked herself. I can't even finish a book anymore. She knew that all kinds of people read these books and found them to be witty and perceptive, enjoyable on many levels. But she had been unable to concentrate or to really get into either one. Did the "Dick Cavett Show" and the Sunday *New York Times* now mark the outermost limits of her intellectual life? A few years ago she'd had no trouble reading books or doing any number of things—whatever she wanted. How had she changed since then? Was it just another aspect of becoming ... ordinary? Dull? It wasn't simply the result of demands placed on her as a wife and mother; it was more recent than that. Or perhaps it wasn't, perhaps she was only now beginning to see what had been happening to her for some time. If that were true she could thank the move to Lynnhaven for helping to open her eyes. Thanks a lot. ...

Sitting in the living room and staring at those two slabs of culture, Linda remembered an unhappy incident that had taken place when she was nineteen and at college. Art history was her favorite subject, although not yet her major, and a well-known artist named Beverley Boulder had arrived on campus to give a series of three guest lectures. Linda attended them all, and was very impressed. Beverley Boulder was a thin, intense woman who had nearly lost her life in a freak accident a few years earlier. The pastel cigarette she was smoking had come too close to a bucket of solvent. The mini-explosion that followed had burned off her eyebrows and most of her hair, leaving scars. Beverley Boulder looked like an Auschwitz survivor who had literally been snatched from the incinerator.

There was a big party after the last lecture, given by the head of the department, Professor Bellini (known to some of his students as Art Dago). Linda managed to get in, and during the course of the evening she met Beverley Boulder. An intense conversation developed between them and they drifted away from the crowd for a few minutes. Linda was thrilled and enjoying herself immensely. Until the famous artist put a hand on Linda's hip and invited her back to Room 308 at the Ramada Inn.

Linda was shocked. It was the first time another woman had ever made a pass at her, and the fact that it was someone as prominent as Beverley Boulder only made matters worse. But as she thought about it over and over again in the days that followed, Linda was even more disturbed by her own naiveté. Before that awkward moment, Linda had put together in her mind an impossible image of Beverley Boulder: a woman damaged but toiling on, a heroic soul fiercely dedicated to Art, a priestess at the altar of Culture. Well, maybe there was some truth in that, but Beverley Boulder was also a red-wigged lesbian who propositioned coeds. Not that there was anything wrong in that—it wasn't Linda's thing, but neither did she go in for judging the way other people live their lives. No, Linda was annoyed at herself, embarrassed that it had taken such an incident, trivial in itself, for her to learn something so basic. Heroes and heroines exist in the minds of their worshippers. The great and the famous are only human (they, too, have genitals). Why had Linda needed to create such an exalted and one-sided picture of Beverley Boulder, a picture that reality could only diminish? What did that say about her?

The worst part was how long it had taken Linda to get over that evening. Whenever she saw this theme repeated in one of its million variations on television or in a story, she squirmed and felt upset all over again. It seemed that she had lived through one of life's greatest clichés and would never be allowed to forget it.

Now: Conrad Linger.

You bought those two books of his for the wrong reasons, Linda told herself. It's the same sort of mistake. You didn't really want to read them, you only thought you did. And now you've found out that you can't read them. They may be moronic or they may be the greatest thing since peanut butter, but you can't turn another page.

And so what? Did it matter at all? No. Did it make any difference to Ned whether his mother had read Conrad Linger? No. It was time for Linda to start being the person she was, to live in her own skin and feel comfortable about it. She owed that much to her husband and son—and, of course, to herself.

Now, she was pleased to find, the two books on the coffee table no longer looked important or intimidating. They were just two books.

Goodbye, Greta Garbo, indeed.

CHAPTER 14
RESISTANCE

Ned woke early, which was unusual. He was in his room every night at a proper hour for someone nine-going-on-ten, but that didn't mean he was asleep. He would sit at the window and look at nothing in particular, or he would lower the screen and try to sight Jupiter through his telescope, or read by flashlight beneath the sheets, or just lie on his bed and listen to the sounds of the night outside, letting his mind roam over a thousand strange worlds. However tired Ned might be, sleep never came fast—it hadn't, for as long as he could remember. And so he usually had to be roused in the morning. But today his eyes opened at first light.

He lay still for a while, letting thoughts form by themselves, unprompted. It was early, because the light was gray and the house perfectly quiet. It was cool, and he could feel the dew in the air, the sweet taste of it in his nose. Was it six in the morning? Maybe not even that. Ned luxuriated in the moment. This was wonderful, a delicious time of the day. The world felt rich but at peace. Your body might or might not exist; you were floating on a cloud. The mind stirring, but not yet locked into its daily patterns. Receptive, directionless, undriven.

When the feeling became too ripe to sustain, Ned flung the sheet back and sat up. He shivered, pleasantly surprised that it could be so nice and cool at any hour here in the blistering heat of July. Outside, all was brightening gray, and far out in the meadow he saw a patch of morning mist hanging low. Ned pulled on a pair of cut-off blue jeans and a T-shirt. He slipped out of his room and tiptoed along the hallway to the top of the stairs. The house felt big and empty, it was so quiet. He went down the stairs carefully, hugging the banister to avoid the spots that would creak. He didn't want to wake his parents.

The digital clock in the kitchen read 6:13. Ned drank a glass of cold orange juice and then, with nothing special in mind, went to the cellar and got one of his father's hatchets. It was a little heavy, but felt comfortable enough in his hand. Ned stood in the front foyer for a couple of moments, apparently unsure of what he was doing. The next thing he knew, he was at the back door, quietly unlocking it and stepping outside.

He wanted to drive the hatchet into something, chop, chop, chop.... And now he could see what it was. The scarecrow. No one grew anything out there anymore. The scarecrow was obsolete, an eyesore. Besides, it bothered Ned almost every night, seeming to dance in place, pointing up to his bedroom window. Ned had tried to ignore it by not looking—but how could he not look? It was impossible. Now he would solve the problem. Ned marched in a straight line across the back lawn toward the field where the offending object stood. The wet grass felt good to his bare feet.

Here I come, Mr. Scarecrow.

See me coming?

I'm going to take care of you.

For good.

The rough grass and weeds of the field scratched and pricked Ned's feet but he took no notice of it, striding determinedly onward.

You thought you were safe.

You thought I'd never leave the window.

Or dare to come down here and deal with you.

But you were wrong.

Ned stopped a yard away from the scarecrow, and now everything swirled together in his mind. The phantoms, the strange light in his room, the garbled sounds he heard in the house, the grotesque gardens at the spa, the awful presence he had felt looming behind his back there—and this scarecrow, which appeared to mock and threaten him by moonlight. ...

Chop! The hatchet was sharp and the scarecrow quickly shattered and fell apart. Yes, it was a phantom, but one which had made the mistake of lingering through the daylight hours—the time when Ned could do something more than hide beneath the sheets. It was like finding Dracula's coffin and driving a stake through his heart before the sun went down. Ned smiled grimly as he went about his task, elated now that he was finally striking back. At least this phantom could be destroyed.

Chop! It was also a way of dealing himself a new hand by cutting down the skinny ghost he had been until now, the pale child who could only huddle in fear of things around him, pulling the bedclothes tighter, afraid to look over his shoulder, nothing more than a scarecrow of a boy ever since that night he had seen his mother lying like a sack of old laundry on the bathroom floor, unable to move, unable to help, unable *to do anything*. You began to silt up then, and it has continued in all the days and nights that have followed, the Sandman working on you from the inside. But at least now you finally understand, you can say No more, you *can do something* about it.

Chop!

When Ned finished he was pleased to notice that he was sweating. Good sweat, this time, for a chore well done. The scarecrow was nothing more than bits of kindling on the ground. Ned gathered up the pieces and, one at a time, hurled them as far away as he could—zing, zing, zing—scattering them widely across the field.

All the king's horses and all the king's men, won't put you back together again. Good-bye, Mr. Scarecrow.

Ned went back to the house, put the hatchet away and flopped down on his bed. Once he rolled off to take a look out the window. There was nothing to see, and that made him happy. Just an ordinary lawn, an ordinary field and the dew steaming up as the sun began to make itself known.

Ned fell back onto the bed and tried to get to sleep once more. But his eyes wouldn't stay shut. He watched the mist, swirling and burning, writhing in the force of heat and light. Phantoms formed, one after another, but they were atomized instantly. It was a gratifying spectacle. If only those words would stop—YOU WILL BE MINE AGAIN—but they were a kind of mental tape loop, repeating endlessly in the back of his brain.

Ned stared vacantly at the spot where the scarecrow had been, wondering if he had really accomplished anything at all.

CHAPTER 15
SOUNDS

It was nothing more than an unpleasant buzz around the ear or the back of the head, and Ned would wave his hands as if to shoo away a bothersome insect. He never actually saw or felt anything, but only heard that buzz. It was enough, however, to worry him. Ned didn't know which to dread more, a bee crawling in to jab poison through his eardrum or a mosquito sucking blood from within his head. The worst thing would be an earwig, an insect that might burrow in and settle down to make a long, slow meal of his brain. Your abilities, mental and physical, disappearing one by one down the throat of a bug. Raving insanity followed by a horrible death. How could you be saved? Picture a doctor using wicked platinum pliers, fine as needles, to poke into your skull and drag out the vicious buzzing creature, tearing bits of vital jelly with it—no, that was not being saved. Even if you lived you'd be about as bright as a turnip.

A couple of times Ned's mother or father had come across him flapping his hands, his face screwed up with fear and anger, and he would suddenly feel foolish. But although they gave him funny, puzzled looks, they never asked him what on earth he was doing. The buzz went away, of course, whenever either of them appeared, gone so swiftly Ned wondered if he really had heard it in the first place. But it always returned, and hardly a day went by without Ned's being bothered at least once by the unnerving noise. It could come at any time—he might be reading a book or making a snack or watching a "Star Trek" rerun. It came when he was alone, and it usually came during the daylight hours. Ned knew it wasn't really an insect, but that was no consolation to him.

He wanted to mention it to someone, anyone—his mother or father, or Peeler and Cloudy—but how could he explain it without sounding like a silly kid? They'd probably think he was losing his marbles. That was a worry, too. Maybe there was something wrong with his head. Something real, something bad. People did go crazy; that's what they have asylums for, right? It could happen to him—as far as he knew, kids weren't exempt. This idea renewed itself whenever Ned realized he was talking out loud to the sound, out of sheer frustration and mounting anxiety. "Who is it? Who are you? What are you? Get away.... Leave me alone.... " But the only sound that came back to him was the same whispered buzzing. Perhaps he had jarred his head more than he thought in the fall at the spa. And yet he hadn't been hurt when he hit the ground, merely had the breath whumped out of him for a minute.

He had heard the sound, or something like it, once or twice before in recent weeks, and thought nothing of it. But then it was almost as if the noise had decided to get serious about Ned, and it started to come regularly, persistently. He tried to ignore it but that simply proved to be impossible. Talking back to it, whatever else that might signify, did have a certain usefulness, as the sound of his own voice provided some distraction. But it was not enough, and Ned knew that if the occurrences became much more frequent and uncomfortable he would have no choice but to tell his parents about it ... and go along with whatever they decided to do. And that might be unpleasant—doctors, tests.

The strange light that woke Ned once had not appeared again, but the nights were not empty. There were ... other sounds that reached his ears in the dark. Getting rid of the scarecrow had been a wise move, Ned thought, and for a few nights after he had done so he felt relieved and slept easily. But then the sounds began. The noise that would bother him for a minute or two during the day was one thing, but what he heard at night was something else altogether.

They never seemed to come from within his room, but rather from behind the walls and ceiling, beneath the floorboards or just outside the window screen. Ned's mind would filter out the familiar—his parents moving around elsewhere in the house, the chirp of crickets, the wings of birds and bats, a breeze riffling the trees—and create a zone of silence that would, soon enough, pick up the unfamiliar.

Ned detected several sounds in the night. Once, after his mother and father had gone to bed and he knew it couldn't be either of them, he heard someone or something moving around in the backyard. Ned crept from his bed to the window, but he saw nothing. Still the sound continued: feet walking heavily across the grass, stepping on the flagstone path, and then the protesting squeak of plastic and tubular metal as if somebody were sitting down on one of the lawn chairs. But even as he heard these sounds Ned could see that there was no one walking around out there and that all the lawn chairs were empty. He was sure the sounds were too distinct to be just the product of his imagination, but on the other hand it obviously made no sense for a prowler to stroll about or sit down on a lawn chair in the middle of the night, as casually as someone taking the afternoon sun. Perhaps he was hearing simple, routine sounds, and his mind was magnifying them into something more. But …

There were other sounds of movement outside. Some were so sharp they seemed to come from only inches below Ned's window, and some were as far away as the meadow, feet tramping through the brush, back and forth, stopping and going, like a soldier on night watch. But even on the brightest of nights Ned could see nothing that might have made the sounds he heard. It was almost enough to make him wish the scarecrow was still there, because the sound of unseen activity was proving even harder to deal with. But the scarecrow was gone, and the funny thing was that Ned couldn't remember ever hearing an unusual sound when it had been there, moving or not.

The most disturbing sounds were those that were closest to Ned's room. One night he had made a tent of the bed sheet and was curled up inside it reading a Hardy Boys adventure, *The Ghost at Skeleton Rock*, when he abruptly turned off the flashlight. Something had pinged on the window screen. It might just be an errant moth, but then again it could be something else. Another sound soon followed. It was as if someone were pressing hands along the clapboarding on the side of the house near his window. Pressing, pushing, sliding, rubbing…. And then the sound was all over, coming from beneath the floorboards, behind the walls and on the beams above the ceiling, as if these hands held Ned's whole room and were caressing it. Ned pictured his room as a little matchbox in the grip of some enormous, invisible giant who would any minute now detach it from the house and hold it hundreds of feet up in the air, inspect it, shake it perhaps, and watch Ned rattle around inside. Maybe it would crush the room like a useless toy and throw it away. Maybe ...

The next night, the sound was back in a slightly different form. Again it started around the window, and there was the softest scratching on the screen. Then a long, deeper noise, like one heavy surface being dragged across another. On and on it went, up one side of the window frame, across the top, down the other side, and then into the house itself, trailing around Ned's room, zigzagging up the back of the plaster and finally fading away somewhere overhead. It went on like that for several nights, each time assuming a new variation—and always it seemed to grow tighter, closer.

Early one morning in August Ned woke to find that he couldn't move. His body seemed to be tied to the bed with a thousand wires holding him in place, and his face felt like it was covered with stitching. It was difficult even to breathe through his nose, and he couldn't open his mouth. As he became more awake and conscious of his situation, the sense of alarm grew in him. His breathing came shorter and faster, and his heart raced like a straining motor. Was that sweat trickling down his neck—or blood oozing from his ears? Then something was on his face, wispy fine as hair-ends tip-touching his skin, walking across his cheek, his laced-up mouth, crawling over his nose so lightly but so deliberately—*a spider!*—and now it was settling atop his nose, preparing to spin a death cap for Ned's last access to air. His eyes had already been sewn shut. Ned was sure it was a spider and he tried desperately to squirm free, to wriggle loose and shake the monstrous thing from his face. But he was in an iron cocoon, one that shrank more tightly around him the more he struggled to move. It became harder to inhale as his chest was slowly being crushed beneath bands of steel. *Help me, I can't breathe,* his mind screamed. At that moment Ned heard a new sound, so near it might have come from the spider—or whatever it was—sitting on his face. It was a tiny, distorted, whir rushing of noise that somehow managed to sound plaintive and doleful, even as it labored on relentlessly. It could have been a microscopic emanation of the spider echoing its way along the network to the very center of Ned's brain. It was the sound of a dying thing, perhaps Ned's own blood, or the ghost of his breath. It was the music of sadness, broken, mangled and forced to a level of cacophony that marked nightmare's end.

Ned felt himself exploding into a shower of brilliant lights and clear air, so pure it hurt at first. Did he still exist? There was no focus, just a dizzy, spinning sensation. His brain was a hailstorm of meaningless pieces tumbling down an endless shaft of light, gradually clumping one to another. Ned dimly wondered if it could ever be put back together again, with all the pieces in the right place. *Scarecrow.*

Now he was crying with relief, gulping in air as sweet and clean as mountain spring water. His parents were lifting him up off the floor and hugging him. They sat on the bed and sheltered Ned between their bodies. The feeling of love and comfort was so overwhelming that Ned started to cry more, wanting this moment to last forever.

"My God, he's drenched, his pajamas are soaking wet."

"Bad dream, Ned?"

"Is he running a temperature?"

"No, he's all right."

"Do you think he hurt himself?"

"Kids fall out of bed all the time. He's just a little shook up, right, Ned?"

Ned nodded his head vaguely, but his mind was elsewhere. Thoughts were beginning to form again. He knew he had been through something far more serious than an ordinary nightmare.

They had come.

They had compromised the safety of his room.

And they almost got me.

"What'll it be like the next time they come?"

"What did you say, Ned?"

"He's still dreaming, poor fella."

"There's a bump on his head."

"It's just a bump, honey. It'll go away in a while."

Michael and Linda stayed, rocking Ned gently between them until his eyes finally closed and he found sleep again.

A couple of days later, when Ned visited the baithouse, he just had to tell Peeler about the sounds he had been hearing. But only the external sounds, not the buzzing around his ears, nor what happened in his bedroom. The old man listened patiently, sharpening jig hooks while Ned skated around the subject, trying to appear curious but not overly concerned.

"Ain't nothin' to it," Peeler said. "The metal frames in the lawn chairs expand as they bake in the sun all day, and then they contract when they cool down at night. Same thing with the wire mesh in your window screen. That's what you hear, take it from Mr. Wizard."

It was just what Ned had been afraid he might be told, the kind of explanation—so simple, so down-to-earth—he might have got from his father. That old moon won't hurt you, son. The only difference was that Ned's father would say it as if he meant it, while Peeler didn't convey such certainty. He had given Ned a perfunctory answer and the boy sensed it.

"What about the other sounds, behind the walls and ceiling?"

"Every house has its own bag of noises it makes," Peeler remarked. "A place as old as yours is bound to have more'n most. Goes on day and night, a house breathin' by itself, but you only notice it at night 'cause it's quieter then and you ain't got no other distractions."

Again the easy answer. Did Peeler really think that Ned wasn't aware of such things, that he had to be told about them? There had to be other, better answers, even if Peeler didn't want to go into them today. Ned felt disappointed and weak, torn between his own reluctance to talk much about what was bothering him and his yearning for a measure of real understanding.

"Why? What d'you think them noises is?"

"I don't know." Ned hadn't anticipated the question, but now that Peeler had surprised him by opening another door he couldn't let it pass. "Maybe they're phantoms, ghosts, things like that. Do you think maybe they are?"

"Ah-ha."

Ned couldn't tell if that was a response to what he had just said or merely a remark addressed to the rusty jig hook Peeler was studying at that moment.

"When I asked you once before you said you did believe in things like that," Ned continued.

"I did, did I?"

"Yeah."

"Well, maybe I do and maybe I don't."

"Do you think that's what I've been hearing?"

"Could be."

"Peeler, why won't you say?" Ned's feeling of exasperation was too much for him now. "Tell me," he demanded.

Peeler put down the hook and the carbide stone.

"I truly would, if I knew," he said. "But the fact is, I don't know, one way nor the other. Look here, Nedly, you ask me on a beautiful sunny morning like this and I'll say, Hell no, there ain't no such things like what you're talkin' about. But you ask me late on a cloudy afternoon when I've progged too far into Old Woods and I won't be so sure, And if you ask me again on a bad bad night, when it's hot but I got me a bone-shakin' chill, when I can't tell if that's a nosy skunk lookin' for my garbage outside—or something else—well, then maybe I'll say, Yeah, I think you got somethin' there. But the heck of it is. it don't make so-what neither way. Now you call 'em phantoms or what-all, but to my mind that just makes it all the more confusin' for you. I told you before a name won't get a pea out of a pod."

"What should I do then?"

"Ain't a Christ-thing you can do. Don't matter if it's magic you hear or just mice in the attic, you leave it be."

Ned didn't believe that. Later, when he thought about it, he would be startled by the fact that he had actively rejected something Peeler told him, but he couldn't stop for that now.

"Peeler, it scares me."

"Why?"

"Because I don't know what it is."

"That's what most folks'd say but they'd be wrong, and you're wrong."

"What do you mean?"

"It ain't the unknown that scares a person, even though they may think it is. You catch sight of a movement outta the corner of your eye or hear an odd sound in the night, and you feel somethin' stirrin' inside of *you*, somethin' buried so deep in the back of your head you can't put a finger on it nor give it no name, but it's there, it's *known*—and that's what'll make you brown your britches,"

Peeler held up a long stretch of blue monofilament with leaders and snelled hooks branching off on either side.

"This here is a kind of double crappie rig I fixed up," he said, smoothly changing subjects. "But I put the split shot above it, not below, and it works just fine in shallow water for bluegills. I've pulled 'em outta Baxley Mill Pond two, three and even four at a time with this contraption. Kinda looks like a TV antenna for midgets, don't it."

"It's not just my imagination," Ned asserted, pursuing the original point. "It's something more than that, I'm—" He ran out of words momentarily.

"If it is, Ned, you'll know before I do. But you can't get no answers from the likes of me, nobody else, at least not none that'll be worth a damn to you." Peeler tested the knots on the rig, to keep himself busy. "You're the one who hears them sounds and sooner or later you'll be the one who decides what they are."

Ned didn't understand. How could he decide anything about the sounds? He was just the person who happened to hear them. Or did he? Perhaps he really was so wrong about his senses, so inclined to pick up strange sights and sounds, that the whole thing was, after all, nothing more than the product of his own imagination. That's what his father had been telling him, and now he was hearing the same thing, or something very like it, from Peeler. Maybe the old man was right and the best idea was not to build up the sounds into something other than what they were—mere sounds. They were real, but how real? Peeler seemed to be saying that it wasn't all that important.

But Ned remembered something else Peeler and Cloudy had told him. You don't go wading barefoot in what looks like snapping turtle water. You might not see the beast and he might not even be down there but you'd better assume he is, otherwise you could be one toe lighter before you found out for sure. Okay, maybe the lawn chairs and the house do make those noises. Maybe the buzzing is a symptom of a minor ear ailment. But assume they're not. Assume they're something else entirely.

Assume the worst.

CHAPTER 16
THE NOEKK

"It ain't nothin' but a big overgrowed mud hole," Peeler said, wiping sweat from his face. "But there's a stream in and a stream out, so it stays alive."

"Just about," Cloudy said.

Ned took in the scene. The pond covered only a few acres.

It looked shallow, muddy and stagnant. The surface of the water was studded with the remains of dead trees; brittle, bone-gray trunks and jagged, rotting stumps. It was not a promising sight, it was simply desolate. They had hiked a long way to reach this place. They were deeper into Old Woods than Ned had ever been before.

"There's catfish in here," Peeler went on as he prepared his rod and line. "A few big ones, too. Now's a good time to fish for 'em. August is when the bass're settin' back out in deep water, where it's cooler, but the old catfish still moseys around in close to shore."

"A catfish is an awful low critter," Cloudy declared. "All he does is eat the crud on the bottom."

"Yeah, but he tastes might good hisself," Peeler argued amiably. "And they put up one helluva fight."

"That's true," Cloudy admitted. "We used to eat 'em just about every day when I was a youngster." He turned to Ned. "Say, that's a smart-lookin' outfit you got there, Mr. Tadpole."

The boy smiled proudly and held up his lightweight Zebco spin caster rod and reel. "My father gave it to me."

"Well that was pretty darn nice of him, I'd say."

"You make sure you hold onto it real tight," Peeler warned. "You don't want no grandaddy catfish pullin' it right outta your hands and swimmin' away with it."

"They're not that big," Ned said, although he wondered about it. "Aren't you going to fish, Cloudy?"

"Oh, no, not me. No, I'm gonna wait till you and Peeler start haulin' in the monsters and then I'll be here, ready to bash their heads in. I got to find me a good stick." Cloudy wandered off, searching through the brush. A few minutes later he returned, carrying a hefty piece of broken branch. "This'll do the job," he told himself, taking some practice swings.

"You really hit them with that?" Ned asked.

"Sure. You got to. Catfish'll live forever, unless you kill 'em. Peeler threw one in the garden a few years back and it stayed alive out there most of the summer, huffin' and puffin' like an engine. Ain't that right?"

Peeler nodded. "Kept the raccoons away."

Ned smiled. It was one of those stories he couldn't believe but didn't want to disbelieve either.

Peeler had cast his line out and was sitting on a rock with a can of beer in his free hand. He checked to see how the boy was doing. "Hey, put another worm or two on that line," he said. "A catfish likes a big mouthful, he ain't gonna waste his time on one dinky worm. And put some more lead on too; it'll give you better castin' range and make sure your bait stays on the bottom where the cats are."

Ned followed Peeler's instructions, then he cast out, tightened up on the slack and stood waiting. Now that he looked more closely at the water he noticed plenty of signs of life. Bugs danced across the surface, air bubbles ballooned up from the bottom and widening rings of concentric ripples formed here and there. Of course there had to be fish here, Ned thought. Peeler knew. Peeler would never come all the way out here to fish a dead pond. The boy fidgeted with impatience. Come on fish, he urged silently. He held the line taut in his fingers, the way Peeler was doing. Before long, he felt a nibble.

"Something's out there," Ned said. "I can feel it."

"Let him get it in his mouth and start to move on you," Peeler advised. "Then give a short, sharp yank on the line, and set that hook real good."

Nothing came of that nibble, but within the hour the old man had landed three good-size catfish and Ned one. Peeler showed him how to hold them without being stabbed in the hand by the fish's spiky whiskers. Cloudy whacked each one with his club and Peeler slit their throats, letting the blood drain out of the fish. He sliced open their bellies and scraped out the entrails. Then he wrapped them in wet grass and packed them in a wicker basket. Ned was startled by the fierce struggle put up by the first cat, whipping through the air in a frenzy, then the sudden splat of the branch, followed by the knife blade and the brief rush of bright red blood—it all happened so quickly. But it was exciting, not disturbing.

Ned was fascinated by the surface of the pond. It never remained the same for more than a few seconds at a time. The lightest breeze, a build-up of clouds, the shifting angle of light, all registered on the water, becoming part of its constant transformation. It was almost hypnotic, and with that and the afternoon heat, Ned began to feel drowsy. Then he saw something out in the middle of the pond. It was the kind of roll and swirl in the water caused by a top-feeding fish. But it was too big. It was huge, perhaps five feet long judging by the movement it made, and Ned thought that no fish so large could live in such a small pond.

"Look," he said, pointing. "Look at that."

Both men stood up.

"I told you there's some big ones here," Peeler said.

"*That* is a monster," Cloudy said. "Don't catch that fella, Mr. Tadpole, otherwise you gonna have real trouble on your hands."

"It can't be a fish," Ned said. "Not in here, it's too big."

"They come that big." Peeler sat down again. "Bigger, too."

"Really?" There was awe in Ned's voice.

"Big enough to make a meal outta you," Cloudy added, breaking into laughter.

"Maybe it was a noekk." Peeler's smile had turned into a mischievous grin.

"A what?"

"A noekk."

"What's that?"

"Yeah, what you talkin' about?" Cloudy asked with an exaggerated look of skepticism on his face.

Peeler jiggled his line, putting the worms through an exotic dance for the benefit of any passing fish. "I never did see one myself," he said. "But a crazy Norwegian sailor once told me about the noekk."

"Just a second," Cloudy interrupted. "Would that be Happy Hansen?"

"That's him. Happy Hansen."

Cloudy smirked. "That old fool never had his head outta the gin bottle long enough to put two sentences in a row."

"What'd he say?" Ned asked Peeler.

"Well, he told me that the noekk is a big, black, slimy critter that lives in certain rivers and ponds. Nobody knows just what it looks like because nobody never sees more 'n a glimpse of it, and then only very rarely. But they're ugly as sin, with real sad eyes, and you're supposed to be able to hear 'em cryin' and wailin' for their lost love or because they're so lonely, or some damn thing like that."

"Can they hurt you?"

Peeler shrugged. "Could be. I know they're said to play tricks on a man, like sing to him from under the water, or knock a boat over, cut a fishin' line—that sort of thing."

"Do you believe it?"

"Who knows? Like I said, I ain't never seen one in my life, but Happy Hansen, he always did say there's one around here somewhere, and that he seen it once."

"Yeah, he saw it, I'm sure of that," Cloudy said. "From the floor of the bar, lookin' up."

The movement out in the middle of the pond had ceased. Ned continued to watch but there was no further sign of it. A noekk. He didn't believe it for a minute, of course. But still, he tried to imagine what it might look like if it really did exist. Peeler had such a could-be way of delivering such stories that it was hard for Ned to dismiss them completely, no matter how improbable they were.

"Whatever become of Happy Hansen?" Cloudy asked.

"I guess the noekk finally got him," Peeler replied, laughing some more. "He was somethin' else, that guy was."

"That's for sure."

Another hour passed without a bite so they decided to begin the long walk home. Ned reeled in his line slowly, but suddenly it stopped. The harder he tried to budge it, the more his rod bent over, until it looked as though it was about to break.

"I think I snagged a rock or a log," he said.

He waved the rod back and forth, hoping to dislodge the hook, but it didn't give an inch.

"Looks like you're gonna have to cut it," Peeler said.

Just as Ned was about to give up and snip the line, it slackened a little. He wound in a foot or two, and it felt like he was pulling a very heavy weight.

"It's loose," he said, grunting from the effort.

"Nice and slow," Peeler coached. "Save the hook."

Ned's eyes widened as he gasped as something broke the surface of the water right in front of him. It was dark green, as long as his forearm and just as thick. Ned saw two black, seed-like eyes staring at him. Then the jaws opened and the hook, stripped of its worms, was spat out. The thing sank back into the water, disappearing from sight. Ned gaped, unable to speak.

Finally he heard Peeler and Cloudy, giggling like a couple of school kids.

"What was *that*?" Ned asked.

"Must of been a monster, the way you looked," Cloudy said.

"The noekk," Peeler offered. "Darn near got you."

"What was it, really?"

Peeler smiled and came over to pat Ned on the back. "That was a big old turkle," he said. "A mean old turkle."

"Biggest turkle I ever seen," Cloudy added. "Why didn't you pull him in, boy? You had him there. Oh, my, but he would make a gorgeous meal."

"That was a turtle?" Ned was astonished.

"Jesus, Mary and jockstrap." Peeler had picked up Ned's line and now held the hook in the palm of his hand. "Look at that, will you."

The steel hook, normally shaped like the letter J, had been bent back and straightened out so that it looked like a miniature harpoon.

"Gosh," Ned exclaimed. "A turtle did that?"

"You seen him do it. Snapped the barb clean off, too. You better watch out, Mr. Tadpole. I think you got that turkle so mad he just might come back lookin' for you."

Peeler cut the hook from the line and handed it to Ned.

"Show that to your dad," he said. "Now you got a real fish story of your own and the evidence to go with it."

They talked and joked all the way home, but Ned's mind was on the turtle. He kept seeing that powerful neck, the black, blank eyes and those defiant jaws spitting his hook back at him. A turtle that big and that strong—yes, maybe there were a few big fish in that little pond. He thought again of what he had seen moving out in the middle of the water—it must have been bigger than Ned himself.

When Ned went into the house and held up his catfish, his mother shrieked. His father came running, but when he saw what it was all about he laughed and insisted on taking a snapshot of the boy and his prize catch. Ned told them all about the fishing expedition and his parents listened attentively. He was pleased to see that they were both genuinely impressed by the straightened hook. Ned put it in an empty matchbox and kept it on the night table next to his bed. When he turned off the light to go to sleep he thought again about that turtle. What other unknown creatures might lurk in that pond in Old Woods? A noekk? What were they doing now? Sleeping? No, nothing so dull. They would be prowling around in the murky darkness, maybe even crawling up onto dry land to hunt. Giant catfish, giant turtles, the noekk....

Ned was glad to be home in his own bed.

CHAPTER 17
STRAIGHT LINES BREAKING, BECOMING CIRCLES

Things happen in August. The heat is deadening, paralyzing, enervating, but … things happen. From one day to the next, or even in the space of a single afternoon, whole worlds may change decisively.

Ned crossed the lawn toward the house. He carried his T-shirt, which had become so sticky he couldn't bear to have it on anymore. He also had a Skippy jar full of cloudy, stagnant water from the little frog hole out in the back meadow. It wasn't even a pond, just a pocket of still water barely ten feet across, but Ned had been keeping an eye on it ever since he had arrived in Lynnhaven. Some nights, when he wasn't distracted by other noises, Ned could hear what sounded like a large frog out there. He had never seen it, but he was sure it dwelled in that pool. In spite of the heat, the sun and the lack of rain, it hadn't dried up, and Ned wondered if some underground source bubbled up just enough fresh water to keep it going.

Linda was sunning herself on the patio and she had a portable radio tuned to a phone-in program. A woman was complaining about American tax dollars being wasted on foreign aid. "We give them money, we feed them, we build dams and things for them," she said, "and they don't even like us." "And do you know why they don't like us, madam?" asked the program host, whose job it was to be provocative. "They spit on us and they burn our flag," the woman gave as an answer. "We ought to put a stop to it, right now." Linda appeared to be dozing through this, so Ned went into the house without disturbing her.

He poured a tall glass of icy lemonade and took it upstairs. The temperature in his room was only a few degrees cooler than outside, but it still felt like a refreshing change. Ned put the Skippy jar on his desk. While the water was settling he got some clean slides and adjusted his microscope to a low-power magnification. He finished the lemonade and was ready to begin work. Using a long eyedropper, Ned carefully took samples from the top, middle and bottom layers of the water, preparing a separate slide of each. He smeared a bit of green slime on a fourth slide. Ned angled the light mirror until it provided the best illumination, and he adjusted the lens so that the focus was sharp.

As always, he was amazed at what he saw. There was no great difference in the four slides, at least none Ned could detect, but each one presented the dizzy and extraordinary kingdom of the protozoa in all its absurd beauty. Amoebas lounged lethargically. Squads of paramecia zoomed about like manic bumper cars. A stentor stood atilt, a tiny replica of the Leaning Tower of Pisa with a fringe on top. Rotifera wheeled and floated, stately as blimps. A hydra waited patiently for prey to blunder into its deadly tentacles. A euglena whipped itself in short, spasmodic movements, like a wandering penitent. And there— Ned's favorite: the volvox, which was not one creature but a vast colony of them linked together to form a whole, a perfect sphere, a shimmering green planet unto itself. All this, in a few drops of water. All this, invisible to the unaided human eye. It was a remarkable universe, and one in which Ned could easily spend hours.

The microscope was his sailing ship, his spacecraft. Ned tried to imagine what it would be like to be as small as a protozoan. He pictured himself as an explorer whose task was to chart a path from one side of the frog pond to the other, through that ocean of strange and menacing creatures. It could take a lifetime—if he survived the journey. What would he use for a weapon—a sliver of algae? Perhaps he could train a rotifer and ride it like a horse. Crossing the Pacific Ocean on a raft would be child's play in comparison.

Ned made a mental note. It probably wouldn't be like this if the water was brackish, so the pool must have a freshwater source, however small. It was an interesting thought, since the pool was so close to the sea. But then again, why not? Lynnhaven Spa was on the bay too, and it had been built because of its freshwater springs.

Ned looked up from the microscope and cocked his head to one side. *What was that?*

It might have been the buzzing noise again, but this time it was somehow different. It could almost be the sound of a human voice. It was far away, and yet there was something intimate about it. And unnerving. Ned forced himself to concentrate, to try and decipher what he was hearing. It was like listening to a distant radio station that faded in and out through static on a stormy night. It sounded like crying, or shouting, and there was an urgency to it that combined anger and sorrow in a single disturbing pitch. It *is* a voice, he thought. But is it human?

Ned shook his head violently and rushed out of the room.

He had to escape that awful sound. It seemed like a taunting, terrifying proof of his unformed fears. It was the threat which, although he couldn't define it, he knew was drawing closer to him. In his own room again. In the middle of a sunny afternoon.

Ned stopped in the kitchen. He was panting and sweating, but his head was clear. The house was as quiet and normal as on any other day. From the patio came the sounds of the Washington radio station. Callers were now discussing the high price of peanut butter. "The so-called shortage is a phony hoax," one man declared hotly. Ned went to the screen door and looked out. His mother was in the same place on the patio, stretched out and taking the sun. She had rolled over onto her stomach, but still seemed to be napping. Ned watched her for a moment and then turned away. He wondered what to do next, but he immediately knew he had no choice. He had to go back upstairs to his room.

His room.

Would these things be happening to him if he had a brother, or even a little sister, to play with? No. They never take place in front of witnesses. Could it be that he was imagining all these sounds, that his mind was creating them to make up for what was missing in his life? But you couldn't miss someone who never existed, could you? Besides, if he had conjured up an imaginary friend, that would be one thing; but vague and threatening noises—that was something else, and it didn't make sense. He had asked his parents once why he didn't have a brother or sister like other children did, but he couldn't remember what they had said. No, now that he thought about it he was sure it had nothing to do with his being an only child. It wouldn't just suddenly start bothering him now, when he was nearly ten years old. It would have developed earlier, if it was ever going to develop at all.

No, the real problem was: going crazy. Crazy meant you were sick in the head. Crazy meant there was something wrong with you that nobody could fix. Something haywire in the brain. Crazy meant being locked up for the rest of your life with other crazy people. That was the most frightening thought of all. Am I going crazy? Ned didn't even know how to begin considering that possibility; it was too overwhelming to bring into focus.

He hesitated at the threshold of his room but then walked in and went directly to his microscope. He prepared a fresh slide, extracting a drop of very cloudy water that looked promising. As he went about this, part of his mind silently counted the passing seconds, and each one made him feel a little better. Blurred shapes swam before him and he was on the verge of returning to the magic world of the protozoa when he found that he couldn't move.

Ned's eyes refused to concentrate. His fingers wouldn't turn the lens adjustment. His mind drifted without thought. He couldn't do anything. He stood up, but the effort seemed to drain away the last of his strength. He felt dizzy and his body was tired, so very tired. He thought he might fall asleep right there, on his feet, and he struggled feebly against it. That's how people drown, he knew, by giving in to it. He saw himself caught in a vast, slow whirlpool that was spinning him down, down, toward a black pit into which he would disappear forever. He remembered his mother, outside, just below his window, but now it was as if she were a million miles away. He tried to call out for help, but his voice was nothing more than a brief whimper lost in his throat. This is it, he thought, this time they're taking me.

When you destroyed the scarecrow you doomed yourself.

He could feel it now: the same sensation he had experienced in the cellar of the spa. The presence, the phantom, was there, in this room, right behind him—only this time it was worse. This time Ned was unable to move, let alone walk forward. He could feel the change as hot, lifeless air swirled around him like a shroud, and he could smell it, the foul, evil breath of the grave. It seemed to scorch the back of his neck and it curled around, over his face, stifling him. The thought came to him that he might suffocate on the spot, but still he couldn't move. It was all he could do to force a bit of air in and out of his lungs.

What is happening to me?

Hands touched his head.

No, no ...

Hands moved through his hair, brushed over his ears.

No, please, leave me alone.

Hands around his throat, coming up on the smooth features of his face. Invisible fingers pressing his eyelids shut, then allowing them to open again. The breath of the phantom roaring in his ears. One hand clamping over his mouth, the other pinching his nostrils shut. Nothing—there was nothing to see, but it was happening to him. His face felt as if it were caught in a steel press that was squeezing the life out of him. He was being taken.

Why?

The breath hesitated for a moment, then sighed softly, nauseatingly around him again. The grip tightened.

—I've missed you.

The voice was a whisper in his head, clear but anonymous. Ned could breathe again, just barely, and the hands continued to move over him. Everywhere they touched, his body felt like a thin film of jelly on a skeleton of twigs.

What?

—I've missed you.

What do you want?

—You.

Who are you?

—You.

The invisible hands clutched his sharply now, the unseen arms locked around him in a crushing embrace. Ned's breath was forced violently from his body and his eyes felt as if they were about to shoot out of his skull. The room was vanishing behind black spots that danced across his vision. The hands—those fingers, like needles, lanced his chest, reached through him to grab his heart, as if to tear it out.

Nothing, it's nothing, his mind screamed desperately. *There is nothing here. You are nothing.*

The hold relaxed, but the buzzing came back, blasting every nerve in Ned's body. He was in a cloud of furies.

—You will be mine again.

No! No! NO!

Ned broke free and ran for his life. The presence stayed with him, enveloping his body as he thrashed to get away. It was in his mouth and his nose, and it blinded his eyes. The buzzing had turned into laughter, howls of mocking laughter.

He fell against the screen door in the kitchen, smashing it open, and fell out onto the patio.

"Don't let them take me," the boy moaned before losing consciousness.

CHAPTER 18
AND/OR

"No, I don't want a drink," Linda snapped. Unable to sit still, she moved restlessly about the living room. "Michael, the boy was terrified. I've never seen anyone so frightened in my life."

"I know, I know." Michael stared at the bottle of scotch as if reconsidering, but then he poured a double. A drink wouldn't solve anything, but neither would abstaining.

"We have to do something."

"What do you have in mind?"

"I don't know, I honestly don't know." She looked at her husband pleadingly. "Can't you think of anything?"

"Yes, I can. I think it's very simple," Michael said calmly, suppressing a smile. "Make him take a rest in the afternoon."

"A rest?"

Michael nodded. "What happened today was the result of too much sun and too much heat."

Linda couldn't believe it. "You think that's all it was?"

"Of course. You know what August is like. And he's only a boy, honey. He doesn't know when to take a break. Too much running around outside in that sun and heat—and it caught up with him. We should have known better than to let it happen in the first place."

"Michael—"

"If he doesn't want to rest, at least make him sit down and read for an hour or two in the afternoon. Or watch TV. Anything, but don't let him be outside all the time, not until the weather's cooler. It's only for the next three weeks or so."

"Michael, he said there was someone in his room."

"Sure there was. In his imagination."

"You don't think it's possible?"

"Nope, and neither do you, because if you did you would have been on the phone to the police right away."

"I was taking care of Ned, and he didn't tell me until a while later, and then you got home."

"Oh, come on, Lin. He imagined it, pure and simple. If somebody goes into a house to cause trouble, he'll cause trouble. He won't sneak upstairs, say 'Boo' to a kid and then flit. That's just silly."

"But what if that's what happened? Ned and I are alone here during the day, you know."

Michael fiddled with a pipe. This was exactly what he didn't want to let happen, a small thing having a catalytic effect on Linda, escalating her natural fears out of all proportion.

"First, you're a lot safer here than you ever were living in an apartment in Washington, and you know it." His voice was firm and insistent, as it had to be. "And second, when we asked Ned what this Mr. Someone looked like, he couldn't tell us anything. Not even whether the fellow wore long sleeves or short. Nothing, not a thing."

"You can say what you like, but I think there's more to it." Linda was afraid that the incident earlier that day was the warning sign she had been dreading, the sign that Ned really was in some kind of danger. But if that's what it was, she still didn't know how to interpret it, nor did she have any idea what she could actually do about it.

"Okay, you think there's more to it," Michael allowed. "Tell me what. I'm willing to listen. Go ahead, tell me."

"I don't know," Linda admitted helplessly. "But you don't always have to know what's wrong to know that something is wrong, and that's the way I feel now. We can't simply ignore this or play it down as sunstroke."

"And, so ... ?"

It was frustrating, infuriating. What could she say? Michael was being cool and reasonable, but that was no help tonight. Still, Linda lacked the tiny, hard seed around which her diffuse anxieties could crystallize into clear thoughts.

"I think we should go away," she blurted out.

That brought a sudden look of concern to Michael's face. "Go away? What do you mean? Go where?"

"Anywhere, it doesn't matter," Linda said. "We could drive up to Buffalo and see the folks, or take a trip down south. I just think it would be a good idea if we took a couple of weeks off and got away from here. You've got the time coming to you anyhow, so why not do something with it?"

"Hey, hold on there a second, honey. We already talked about this before we moved in. We're spending our vacation here this year, remember? There's so much I have to do around the house, and besides, you know the money's going to be tight for a while. Better to put it into the house than gas and motels."

"The house won't go anywhere," Linda said. "We don't have to do everything we want to do to it all at once."

"Sure, but going away and spending money on a vacation isn't going to solve anything either. If there's a problem, as you seem to think there is—"

"Yes."

"—what makes you think we wouldn't take it with us, or that it wouldn't still be here when we got back?" It was the wrong argument, Michael knew; he had to stick to money.

"Doing something is better than doing nothing."

She was making it easier now. "Not necessarily," Michael said patiently. "One thing I've learned is that some problems will work themselves out or just cease to be problems, if you leave them alone for a while."

"Michael, we're talking about our son, not the goddamn bureaucracy·."

"Take it easy, hon. You're not being rational about this. Now, I'm not insensitive, but I won't go along with a bad idea just for the sake of doing something. It doesn't make any sense, and if you take the time to think about it I'm sure you'll come to the same conclusion."

Linda turned away and tried to blink back the tears. Michael put down his drink and went to her. He put his arms around her and for a moment they hugged each other without speaking.

"You've had a rough day," he said comfortingly. "That doesn't mean it'll happen again, or get worse, or anything like that. It just means we have to be careful, and now we know something else to watch out for. In other circumstances you would never let a small thing like this upset you so much."

Linda knew what he meant by "other circumstances." If she wasn't asthmatic, if she didn't live under the threat of a severe attack, if Ned were not their only child ... then perhaps she would agree with Michael and dismiss today's incident as sunstroke, and not worry unduly about it. But Linda *didn't* live in "other circumstances," she had to deal with things the way they were. She *did* have a troublesome medical history. Ned *was* their only child. She didn't care if this made her an overanxious and overprotective mother; it wasn't a matter of choice.

"Do you think he should see a doctor?" Linda asked.

"Sure, why not? If you want to take him in for a check-up, by all means do so. You can tell the doctor what happened today and see what he thinks. That's a good idea." Michael was happy to agree. The doctor's fee would be a small price to pay for peace in the house, and a consultation made a lot more sense than a drive to Buffalo. Besides, he was sure the doctor's opinion would be much the same as his own. Maybe then Linda would feel a little better about it.

"All right, I'll do that," Linda said. "We have to do something, Michael. I couldn't live with myself otherwise. I'll make an appointment in the morning."

"Fine, that makes sense."

"Oh, Michael, if you could have seen the look on Ned's face. He kept saying, 'Don't let them take me, don't let them take me,' over and over again when he came to. It was awful."

"I know, honey." Michael hugged her again and began to massage the back of her neck and shoulders. She was still all tensed up. "It was like a nightmare to him and he didn't know what was going on, so his mind just created all that stuff. Of course it was real to him. but ..."

"I know you think I worry too much because he's our only child, but there's another side to that. We have to remember what it's like for him. You and I have each other, but we're all Ned has. He's more alone than we are. We can't let him down, or he'll be lost."

"We won't, honey. Not ever."

"Do you know what I mean?"

"Mmm-hmm. I saw a good sign, by the way."

"What?"

"Ned didn't object to going to bed in his room. It didn't seem to bother him at all, so I guess the room doesn't hold any unpleasant or frightening associations for him. I think that's a good sign, don't you?"

Linda nodded. "I hope so."

Upstairs, Ned sat cross-legged in the middle of his bed. He might be wrong but he had the feeling that nothing would happen tonight. Not after the attack this afternoon. And what else could he call it but an attack? The funny part of it was that he now felt more sure of himself than he had before. A move had been made, all pretense dropped, and the game finally seemed to be out in the open. He stood alone against it and he knew he really had one chance, but at least he no longer had to guess about it. *It* had spoken to him. *It* had laid hands on him. Oh, yes, it was real. But what was it—a ghost, a phantom, an evil spirit, Satan?

Next to him on the bed was the book he had just finished reading, *The Ghost at Skeleton Rock*. It was a mystery involving smugglers and subversives, and at the end of it the Hardy Boys discovered that the "ghost" was nothing more than a huge balloon which had been covered with phosphorescent paint and made to look like the spirit of an ancient Indian chief.

No answer there for Ned, but then he hadn't really expected to find one. What was happening to him was not the kind of thing that could be taken care of by looking up a remedy or an explanation in a book. He was on his own. His mother and father couldn't help—what could Ned possibly tell them that they might believe? Peeler and Cloudy were at least sympathetic and seemed to understand some of what was bothering him, but they offered no way out. Perhaps because there was no way out. Hadn't Peeler said something about Ned not being able to do anything but see it through? And he had also said that Ned would be the first to know…. But, now what? That grown-ups couldn't help him. It was like that time at the spa, when Ned knew that no one was going to come and rescue him. If he was going to be saved he would have to save himself.

But could he save himself? He didn't even know what he was up against. His opponent was invisible and apparently capable of doing whatever it wanted. Ned felt that he had no hope of survival in such a one-sided confrontation. He was an insignificant mouse being toyed with by an unimaginable predator. He was in the grasp of supernatural forces which were impossible to resist. Ned thought of the protozoa in the jar of pond water on his desk. Could they influence what he did with them? Hardly. They wouldn't even realize what was happening—whether he put them on a slide under the microscope or simply flushed them down the toilet. It didn't appear to Ned that his own situation was substantially different from that of the protozoa. But he couldn't merely surrender himself to an unknown, blind fate. His instinct was to struggle, to fight back, regardless of whether that would achieve anything or not.

What could he defend himself with? Were there any weapons he could use against his foe? Ned knew from the movies that vampires were afraid of garlic and the cross, and that a wooden stake driven through the heart would destroy them. A silver bullet or blade was necessary to stop a werewolf, and zombies had to be burned. But Ned also knew that these things were completely irrelevant to his situation. A vampire would already have drained him dry by now, and werewolves and zombies were even more implausible. No, he was not being stalked by such familiar and predictable creatures. They were hard to believe in, but the supernatural was not. It was silly to think that a string of garlic could have any effect on the powers of the supernatural.

Ned tried again to understand how he had escaped this long. In his bed he had avoided confrontation and capture by staying under the sheets and blankets, and by not looking out or exposing himself to the danger around him. In the old spa he had survived by always moving forward and by refusing to give in to the great temptation to look back over his shoulder. In both situations he had known enough not to gaze into the face of hell. But today, in his room, that had not been enough. The evil presence had touched Ned, spoken to him and very nearly succeeded in taking him. His puny defenses no longer worked. Or did they? What had enabled Ned to break free at the last moment and run? Was it the fact that he had not looked at or seen the face of the enemy? Or perhaps it was that desperate burst of mental rage—*You are nothing*—which denied the phantom's existence. If so, it could mean that the terror was, after all, nothing but the product of his own imagination. He really could be going crazy, disappearing into his own nightmares. Being taken by a real phantom would be better than that.

The only other explanation Ned could come up with was that something else had disrupted the attack. Nothing suggested itself to him, but he remembered thinking about the scarecrow in that terrible moment. Why? Now that he considered it again he wondered if unintentionally he could have triggered something when he cut down the scarecrow in the back meadow. But at the time, the scarecrow had seemed to be a visible part of the problem, a dancing, taunting extension of the forces gathered around Ned. Then a picture of the scarecrow formed in his mind and he was shocked by it. Take away the tattered cloth and what was a scarecrow? A man-sized *cross*. Maybe he was getting somewhere. Ned's parents were not religious, and he was not being raised according to any faith or church, so the cross had little significance for him. It was something you saw on certain buildings and in all vampire movies. But now he found himself in a situation where the cross might well be of importance. Perhaps he had stepped over a fateful line that morning he had chopped the scarecrow to bits.

It was all too much. No matter how he tried, he couldn't begin to make sense of it. He wished he could tell Peeler everything and beg the old man for help. There was a tremendous desire in him to tell someone, and Peeler was the person most likely to understand. But Ned could imagine what he would be told. Peeler would say that Ned was wrong to try and figure it all out in his head, that it was a mistake to look for answers or explanations where there were none, or where they would do no good. He would tell Ned that he shouldn't try to work this out as if it were a jigsaw puzzle. And Peeler would probably be right, too, Ned thought. But that was no help, because he was in a situation where he really did need an answer, or at least a clue. He couldn't just do nothing and carry on, oblivious to everything that had already happened.

He wanted it to be over, one way or the other, no matter what that meant for him. It was time to stop thinking, and to start acting. No more shying away. It was time, finally, to lift up the sheets, to turn around and face whatever was there. He had tried everything else but that, and now there was nothing left to do but *seek it out*. Attack, with nothing but nerve, perhaps, but: attack.

Ned decided that he had to go back to the spa. Whatever happened would happen there. He didn't want to wait for another invasion of this room, his room, in his parents' house. The struggle was not theirs. Ned knew it was foolish to think of returning to the spa, but there were no alternatives now. He couldn't drift on from day to day, always fearing what might happen at any moment. Nor could he cling to his parents, or to Peeler and Cloudy, for protection; he wasn't a baby. It was his problem, and his alone. So he would march into the dark ruins and force the issue, once and for all.

This time, however, he would be better equipped. He would bring along candles and matches, a flashlight and batteries. He would carry rope and a knife. He would wear sensible clothes. He would have no preconceived ideas of what to expect—they would only distract him. He would expect anything, or nothing.

And, just in case, he would search around in the back field and find two sturdy sticks, which he would bind together to make a cross, and he would carry it with him.

CHAPTER 19
THE SPA (1)

He had to wait nearly a week. His mother took him to see the doctor a couple of days after the attack. The physician gave Ned a thorough examination and found him to be in fine health. But he said that as long as the current heat wave continued it would be a good idea for Ned to take it easy and not to overexert himself. Linda told Dr. Melker what had happened, and his opinion was indeed much the same as Michael's had been. The doctor added that Ned's dizzy spell might have been aggravated by hunger, since it occurred in the latter part of the afternoon and light lunches were the norm in summer. He advised Linda to make sure that Ned ate plenty of fresh fruit between meals. She felt considerably relieved after listening to the doctor. On the way home that day they stopped at a sporting goods store and bought a new baseball cap for Ned to wear to protect his head from the sun whenever he went outside. Ned was compliant but uninterested. A visit to the doctor, a baseball cap—these were things obviously of some importance to his mother and father, but Ned knew they wouldn't do him any good when the time came.

He spent those days carefully going over his plans and preparations. The list of items he was going to take with him grew until his knapsack was full. As far as possible, he was determined the expedition and the likely confrontation would be on his terms. Ned reckoned that by going to the spa he would be taking the initiative, and he hoped that would count for something. Moreover, he intended to set off immediately after breakfast so that he would have the advantage of a full day's sunlight. Ned studied the weather forecasts with great interest. Six days after the attack in his room, the heat broke. The temperature dropped into the low eighties and a steady breeze further improved conditions. Ned knew he couldn't afford to wait any longer.

He had prepared his mother and father for this in advance, telling them he would be gone all day, hiking and catching frogs and crayfish. He led them to believe he would be with Peeler and Cloudy all the time. His parents had no objections, so long as he promised to be careful and to keep his baseball cap on. It was the first time in his life that Ned had gone well beyond an innocent fib with his parents. He didn't like the feeling it gave him, but he couldn't think of any other way to handle the matter. It bothered him, too, that if he never returned from the spa the lie would stand and forever color his last hours with his mother and father. Ned thought it might be a good idea to leave a note for them. He could put it among his clothes in the bureau so that they wouldn't find it until some time later—if, and only if, the worst had come to pass. But when he tried to write the note, he ran into difficulties. He saw again how defeating the problem was, how impossible to explain. Finally he gave up and wrote simply: "Mom and Dad, I love you always. Ned." He dated the paper, put it in an envelope and slipped it in beneath some clean shirts in the second drawer of his bureau.

Ned also wanted to see Peeler and Cloudy. They were the two friends he had made since moving to Lynnhaven. His only two friends. But he was afraid that if he saw them again he would be unable to keep from telling them everything, including his plans to go back to the spa. That would upset them too much and quite possibly undermine his resolve as well. No, he could only hope that he would see them again, but first he had to go through with this other matter on his own.

As Ned walked purposefully through the streets of Lynnhaven he let his mind begin to consider what might actually happen to him that day. It was the one question he had done his best to avoid—not so much out of fear, although there was that, but more because he didn't want to confuse himself with all sorts of possibilities. He needed to concentrate on what was, and nothing else. But now that he was on his way he felt free to think about it. The assumption behind this journey to the spa was that once Ned was there again something would happen. But what? An encounter with the devil? A battle for his soul? A huge phosphorescent balloon? A phantom? Or nothing. In a way, that last was the most worrying. If Ned passed the day uneventfully at the spa, would it mean that he had been wrong, that no phantom haunted him, that the crisis was all in his head? Or rather, that his gambit had been declined? He knew it was too easy, and foolish, to dream of triumph. It was not impossible, however, that he could survive. He believed this, as he had to. The alternative was that he would be taken. That he would die. Death; it could happen. Ned was well aware of that possibility—it had prompted his note to his parents—but he kept it locked away within him. To dwell on it would be paralyzing. Besides, people always believe they will somehow live through almost anything; the human mind rejects the notion of its own imminent death, and the young mind, especially, barely conceives the idea of death.

Ned crossed the old railroad tracks and made his way to the long drive. This time he would enter the spa from the front. This approach was useful in two ways. It was far simpler and easier than scaling the back wall again, saving Ned time and strength, and it was also a psychological ploy, a kind of reversal in his favor, as he returned by the route he had taken in fleeing the spa on his previous visit.

By the time he reached the front door, any fear he felt had been overtaken by a growing sense of anticipation and excitement. He might be walking through the gates of hell, but it was an adventure! Ned knew he could be making the biggest mistake of his life, but the day was right and he was as ready as he would ever be. He reminded himself of the possible advantages on his side. Perhaps there were limits to the unknown power Ned faced. Perhaps challenging it in this way really was the smartest thing to do. As he stood outside the enormous building Ned realized that he might succeed in another way. If nothing at all happened today he would then at least have managed to conquer the old spa, defusing it and eliminating it as one of the elements in the nightmare. Yes, he told himself, he was doing the right thing. One way or the other, Ned's mission today had to be a step forward.

The cross he had made from two sticks of wood was tucked under his belt. He crawled past the loose boards in the doorway and stood up. He was inside, once more.

The first thing Ned looked for was the place on the floor where the threatening words had been scrawled in the dust. He had obliterated them with his sneaker, and now he saw that nothing had changed; the message had not been rewritten. It was a good sign.

Nor did the rest of the large entrance hall appear to be any different. Although Ned had been there only for a few minutes the last time, it seemed quite familiar to him. Not evil, but dead. Not dangerous, just … sad. Again he found it easy to imagine how splendid the spa must have been when it was alive with people and activity. A shimmering palace of wealth and beauty. But Ned knew it was important for him to remember that this place was now just a ruin, nothing more.

His plan was to climb the wide stairway directly to the top floor, explore the rooms there and then do the same on the next floor—and so make his way back down to ground level. By noon, Ned calculated, he would have covered the entire spa building, with the exception of the cellar, which he would decide about when the time came. It was not that Ned was afraid of descending into the darkness again; he carried two flashlights and extra batteries for just that purpose. But he knew that if he put the rest of the spa behind him first he would be in an even stronger position to take on the cellar.

The stairs wound up and around the central atrium. Paint or paper hung in tattered ribbons from the walls. Ned touched one strip and it crumbled to powdery flakes in his fingers. Like some strange creature that sheds its skin from the inside, he thought. After that, Ned didn't pause until he had arrived on the uppermost landing.

There, he was surprised to discover how different the visual perspectives were. The rich blue morning sky above seemed to be literally sitting on the roof of the spa, so close and tangible that Ned almost believed he would be able to grab a piece of it if only he could reach up through the broken frame of the skylight. It was a remarkable illusion. Perhaps this was how Jack felt when he climbed through the clouds to the top of the beanstalk.

Ned turned and peered down the stairwell. He gasped—it was like looking through the wrong end of a telescope. The ground floor seemed to zoom away from him as if it were the ever-receding bottom of an abyss. The whole mansion felt like it was tilting slowly around Ned, trying to push or pour him off the top floor. He gripped the marble banister tightly and shut his eyes to fight the terrible sensation that he was slipping over the edge. There was something attractive, dangerously attractive, about looking down, and Ned knew he couldn't give in to it. Could the building really spin around? No—but then, why did Ned's body feel as if it were hanging upside down? These are illusions, games, tricks, he told himself. Just the spa's way of saying hello. Use your sense, and your senses; don't let them be used against you. Gradually, he regained a measure of confidence. He felt okay, sure that he wouldn't betray himself. He opened his eyes. Vision apparently all right, and right side up. Ned backed away from the stairwell. He was here to explore the rooms, not to gape at the view.

The landing was strewn with debris that had been blowing in for years through the open skylight, mostly rotting leaves and twigs. The summer heat had pretty well dried out the place, but today the air was pleasantly cool, with a sweet, woody smell. Taking care to watch out for snakes, Ned moved toward the passage on his left. When he had examined that wing he would come back for the other. As he approached, the corridor made him think of a cave, dark and beckoning. Something was wrong. Ned knew from his observations outside that all the windows were wide open on the upper floors of the building, so the corridor should be reasonably well-lit. But no, maybe not. All the inside doors could be closed, and daylight from the open skylight wouldn't penetrate far into these corridors. Ned took one of the flashlights from his knapsack, switched it on and stepped into the gloomy tunnel.

He cried out immediately and jumped back, stumbling and losing his balance. He had dropped the flashlight, and now he scurried to retrieve it. It still worked. Cautiously, Ned inched forward again, wondering *What did I see?* Something startling ... but he didn't feel frightened by it. It was like a wall, a barrier of some sort—but more than just that. The light beam probed the darkness. There was a gauzy gray veil suspended from the ceiling to the floor, filling the hallway. Tiny shapes flitted around behind it—or rather, *in it.* Spiders, Ned realized. It was an enormous spider web, dozens, hundreds of them, built up to form a whole colony. They had taken over the corridor in this wing.

Ned went back onto the landing and found a piece of wood. He poked it into the webbing, which felt unusually firm, and tried to carve out an opening. To his amazement, the webs ran deeper than he thought possible. There was no end in sight. And as soon as Ned started damaging the structure, several spiders danced out *toward* him. He stepped back and tossed the stick aside. As far as he knew, there was only one poisonous spider in the United States, and that was the black widow. He had no idea what these spiders were but he did know they were not black widows. Nonetheless, he wasn't about to assume that they were harmless. They looked rather aggressive.

Ned went back to the landing, and this time he came up with a lump of fallen plaster. It was crumbly, but there was enough of it to hold together. He took off his knapsack and flung the piece of plaster as hard as he could into the spider web. It should have flown through the flimsy stuff and bounced along the floor. But, instead, it disappeared into the darkness and made no sound at all. Ned couldn't believe it. He got another hunk of plaster and hurled it with such force that he felt a twinge of pain in his arm muscle. But again the missile was swallowed up silently. What kind of spiders are these? he wondered.

Ned held both flashlights together and moved as close as he dared to the webs. He put his head against one wall of the corridor and directed the light along that side. The spider colony stretched back as far as the light reached. They've completely filled the passageway, Ned thought, from here to the end of the wing. His lips formed the word "wow," but the sound stayed in his dry throat.

Now he turned the light to the center, where he had torn a small opening with the stick. Spiders, in uncountable numbers, moved about in the depths. The astonishing network of webs glinted like dull silver lace. There were several small tunnels swirling through the web, reminding Ned of Swiss cheese. They keep the air moving through the colony, he thought, as well as providing a kind of internal highway system. And the larger passages would also bring insects into the interior. The whole thing must be incredibly well organized and put together.

Ned noticed a few bulky shapes hanging here and there in the spider kingdom. They were dark, wrapped in web-shrouds, and they hung like macabre Christmas-tree decorations, or shrunken heads.

Birds? Ned had never heard of spiders killing a bird, but he was beginning to believe that anything was possible in this place. It wasn't so fantastic, now that he thought about it. Sparrows flying in through the open skylight, getting caught in that mighty web, and then being bitten to death by scores of small spiders. It was the sort of thing you might imagine happening in a tropical jungle, but that didn't mean it couldn't occur here. There was no other way Ned could explain what he saw. Do spiders lay eggs? Probably, but he wasn't sure. Anyhow, those things didn't look like egg clusters-they were far too big for that. They looked like food, bagged and hung. Or ... trophies.

Ned crossed the landing to the other wing. He came up against the same thing: a massive colony of spiders. So, they ruled the entire top floor of the spa, both sides, with only the exposed central landing as a clear zone. Ned sat there for a few minutes, looking left, then right. He had seen large spider webs before, but nothing like this. At least there was nothing supernatural about it; it might be a very unusual natural phenomenon, but it was just that, a *natural* phenomenon. The sort of thing that must have a perfectly reasonable scientific explanation. Perhaps the water at the spa was bad (something to do with the scandals decades ago), and an odd mutant strain of your everyday house and garden variety spider had developed here, one that built elaborate colonies of tough webs. Why not? It might be an item for Burgess Meredith and "Those Amazing Animals" on TV, but it had nothing to do with Ned's problem.

He glanced again at the corridor closest to the top of the stairs. Something seemed to be moving there. A few spiders on the floor. But they don't hunt, Ned thought. They wait for their prey to blunder into the web and get caught. Maybe this was another aspect of the unusual phenomenon—that there were so many of them they were driven to search among the leaves on the landing for bugs. Colonies this size would certainly require a lot of food.

A lot of food ... ? No, that's crazy, Ned thought. But now he noticed that there were more spiders crawling around at the top of the stairs. What were they trying to do, cut off his only exit and trap him there? It was a silly idea. They were small spiders, probably even incapable of piercing human skin. Still, their numbers were increasing and Ned thought again of the birds, or whatever they were, hanging in the webs.

Drained and mummified. Ned began to feel uneasy. He put the flashlights away, stood up and slipped the knapsack on over his shoulders.

A second wave of spiders had gathered around the entrance to the other corridor. Ned was in the middle. Unease turned to worry, and then anger. This couldn't be what it looked like. It was ridiculous, impossible. Vaguely, he recalled the tale of Gulliver being tied down by the Lilliputians. That was not a true story, Ned knew. But what about that morning not so long ago when he had awakened early to find he couldn't move? Even his eyes had been stitched shut then, and he had felt something like a spider on his face. That had been real, and perhaps it was an omen he should have given more thought to afterwards. What if the spider, and these spiders, were but one manifestation of the phantom presence he had sensed and the voice he had heard? Wasn't it possible for a supernatural force to change itself from one shape into another—like a vampire into a bat, or a man into a werewolf?

Why are you standing here?

The spiders advanced out onto the landing in irregular surges. They formed a gray-brown carpet, rolling inexorably toward the center. When one spider came close to Ned he flicked it away with the toe of his shoe, but it was as if his foot had acted on its own. The spiders no longer worried Ned.

Move.

They were fascinating to watch. They must have attained a very high level of cooperation for colonies of this size to come about and survive. It was possible to see them all as components of the greater whole, the higher unity, not unlike the volvox, Ned's favorite microscopic creature. Yes, these spiders were truly extraordinary.

Get out of here.

Ned didn't want to move. Now the spiders reminded him of a tide, lapping gently closer. Why, it might even be nice to lie down and let it wash over him. It would feel cool, but pleasant, and somehow ... delicious. That's right. Yes, he could lie down and let it bathe him, and he could leave his mouth open and let the tide splash in, cool and sweet as the best water. Just a few drops. At first.

It's hypnotizing you. Get out while you can!

Ned's feet moved, and the movement made him feel dizzy.

He closed his eyes, hoping it would stop. With each step he took he heard terrible squishing sounds. They seemed to be trying to say something to him, but he couldn't make out what it was. The sounds were cries of agony, pleas for him to stop what he was doing. Every step crushed dozens of them, and their noise was the anguish of loss. Don't do this to us, it said. Don't murder us, don't leave us. But still Ned's body moved and the sounds grew more unbearable. Then his foot came down on a clear marble stair. His shoe slid on the spider pulp it carried and Ned wheeled through the air, crashing on hard stone and falling. Pain snapped him out of the daze he was in and he managed to stop himself after he had bumped down about a half-dozen steps. He sat up and leaned back against the inside wall on the stairway. There was a lump on his forehead and his left arm ached because he had landed on it, but apparently there were no serious injuries. Suddenly Ned yelled and grabbed his leg. It was as if a hot needle had been jabbed into his calf. He pulled his pant leg back and saw the single spider. He snatched it up and squashed it between his fingers, then quickly wiped his hand vigorously on his jeans. Gray slime, the same horrid stuff that still clung to the bottoms and sides of his shoes. Ned felt sick, and he couldn't move for several minutes.

The spiders. They had been all around him up there. It came back to him in a rush, and he shuddered at the thought of what had almost happened to him. *It* really is here today, he decided somewhat ruefully. He was in a different ballgame now. Twice already he had come close to giving in to it, surrendering himself like a lamb for the slaughter. How much longer would his strength—and luck—hold out?

The spiders. How close he had come to lying down and letting them sweep over him. Unable to penetrate human skin? Ha. They would have eaten through his eyeballs and poured down his throat. Ned pulled himself to his feet and looked back up the stairs. They were still there, waiting for him should he be so foolish as to return. Sorry, boys. I'm not your prize. Be glad I forgot to bring a flame-thrower. But behind the mental quips, Ned felt shaken. It had been that close. He scraped the spider pulp off his shoes as best he could and then went down to the next landing.

The corridors on both sides were unobstructed here. The doors in each wing stood slightly ajar, providing sufficient illumination in the hallways. Each room seemed to invite Ned to enter. On the floor above he had been unable to explore a single room; here, every room was open to him. He didn't know whether to feel glad or worried. Where to begin? At least this looked more like what you would expect of an abandoned building.

Be careful, take nothing for granted.

He moved cautiously into the first corridor. On his left, the doors opened into rooms overlooking the maze of gardens out back; to his right, the rooms ran along the front of the spa. Ned decided he would go up this wing checking the rooms on the back, and take care of the others on his return to the landing. He pushed the first door wide open. The room was neither large nor small, and it was virtually empty. A few rusty beer cans on the floor, and the remnants of a magazine. Ned bent over to look at the pages and saw the photograph of a naked woman. The colors had pretty much washed out, leaving the picture with a pale bluish tint. Ned poked the magazine with his shoe to flip over some pages, but they had hardened into a lump. He had seen pictures like this once before, last year, in the school yard in Washington. They gave him a funny feeling inside. Ned walked across the bare room to the open window and looked out on the gardens. They seemed somehow different from his previous visit—but perhaps it was just because he had a higher vantage point here. Ned left the room, slightly disappointed. Traces of teenage visitors some time ago, nothing else. Nothing sinister here.

The next room was the same size as the first. It had the same bleached, chipped walls, and the same plank floor. A few more beer cans and, this time, a pair of women's underpants, so weathered and ragged that they were almost unrecognizable. Again Ned had that funny feeling. Why would people come here, of all places, do whatever they did—and then leave without their underpants? It didn't make sense.

The third room was the same, except that it was completely empty. And the fourth. Ned began to feel annoyed as he proceeded along the corridor, kicking open the doors of one bare room after another. The spa was not living up to its promise, at least not on this floor. But as Ned approached the end of the wing he noticed something curious. The corridor seemed to narrow down around him, the farther away from the landing he walked. Was it just his imagination, another optical illusion? No, the ceiling was definitely lower here, the walls closer, the passageway tighter. Ned looked back. It was like being in a tunnel. All four sides appeared to focus down toward the point where he stood.

Ned opened the last two doors on the left side of the corridor. Nothing. He had reached the end of the wing, and now he turned to work his way back, examining the front rooms. But as he turned, the perspective hit him, and it was disturbing now. Both walls and the ceiling were so close Ned felt like he was in a box. The whole building seemed to be settling around him, resting its weight on his body. It was a frightening sensation, but what made it worse was the sudden rush of sorrow and sadness that overwhelmed Ned. He found himself crying, sobbing violently. His body shook so much he was sure he was falling to pieces. Some immense, fearful image had seized his mind. He couldn't make out exactly what it was, but he knew it had something to do with his mother. She was in trouble. She was in grave danger, maybe she was even dying at this very moment, and there was nothing Ned could do about it. He wanted to run and help her, but he couldn't move. He felt as if he were being buried alive, entombed in the spa.

Mother, take me with you.

Her face swam in and out of his mind like a fragment of a lost dream. Her eyes were wide with terror, and her lips—they were a shocking bluish-purple—moved frantically but silently. Then her face was spinning away into the distance like a pale coin. Ned wailed and ran after it.

Don't leave me! Mommy!

As he ran his body seemed to grow lighter and faster, as if he were disappearing, transmuting into a single, final subatomic particle flying nowhere at the speed of light. Ned shot out of the corridor onto the wide landing and stopped sharply. The vision of the mother was gone, the image vanished. He was a boy again, in his own body. Pain knifed through his side and he doubled over, gasping loudly to catch his breath. He sat down heavily, unceremoniously, on the floor. Moisture streaked his face, but he didn't know whether it was sweat or tears. Not that it made any difference. The important thing was that he was coming out of it now. Ned was still trembling, but he managed to smile faintly. *It* had tried again, and failed. Surprise, surprise, another inning gone by and the underdog kept the lead. The phantom presence had even tried to use Ned's mother against him, but it hadn't worked. I'm going to make it, Ned thought. I may get bumped and bruised, and it may take every ounce of strength I have in me, but I am going to make it. For sure.

When Ned's breathing returned to normal and he felt ready to move on, he stood up and adjusted the knapsack on his back. The wooden cross was still hooked through his belt loop, but Ned noticed that it had been bent slightly out of shape. The fall on the stairs had done it, probably. He fixed it.

Now to the other wing on this floor. The first couple of rooms on either side were empty. As Ned came back into the corridor, he caught a glimpse of something moving at the far end of the wing. A brief shadow, and then it was gone. Into one of the last rooms. Maybe it was nothing, but there was only one way to find out. Ned couldn't take the risk of wandering in and out of all the intervening rooms while something might be sneaking up on him. Slowly, but with determination, he walked down the middle of the long corridor toward the point where he thought he had seen the movement. He unsheathed his small hunting knife and held it ready at his right side.

Ned thought of his mother again. What if she really were in trouble—like that night years ago in the Washington apartment? She could be sick now, lying on the floor, and this time she'd be alone. Ned's father was at work. There was no one else at the house to help her or to call the doctor. Ned had heard of people having premonitions, or telepathic flashes in emergencies, and he wondered if he had experienced something like that. He tried to dismiss it as just another trick, but it continued to prey on his mind. What if she had cried out to him in a moment of crisis? Perhaps this trip to the spa was the real trick, the point of which was to get Ned out of the house and away so that his mother would be left alone and vulnerable.

No, please, no.

And if that were the case, then he would be playing a direct part in his mother's—

No, no, no!

Ned reached the end of the corridor, but he was hardly aware of the fact. Visions of his mother filled his head once more. She had fallen, in the kitchen maybe, or the living room, or on the cold bathroom tiles. Absurd voices came from the radio, competing with the steady whirr of the air conditioners. She was on the floor. She was rigid. Her teeth were locked together and a few beads of saliva gathered on her lips— her lips, which were a bright, hideous purple. Her face was white, turning pale blue, a blanched photograph of a person. Her eyelids here half shut and all that could be seen of her eyes was a blind, glassy sheen. She was not breathing.

Mommy!

Ned could see it all with alarming clarity, but there was nothing he could do. He had been removed, drawn away by the demon to a safe, useless distance. He walked leadenly into the last room. He went to the open window overlooking the back gardens. His mother was dead now. He knew it. He had lost her. He had given her away. He had let her be taken without a struggle.

Ned stepped onto the wide window ledge. The wrought-iron grille sagged a fraction of an inch as it took his weight. There was nowhere else to go, nothing else to do. His mother was dead. He looked at the knife in his hand. The blade gleamed in the sunlight. It was a beautiful day. But his mother was dead. The wild foliage of the gardens, a brilliant metallic green, rolled gently in the breeze like rippling water, cool and inviting. Ned looked at the knife again. The sun was harsh and the glare off the blade pained his eyes, but it was irresistible. There was something in it. His mother's face, ringed by a dazzling corona.

Mommy!

He held the knife out and up at eye level, and it was as if he held a bar of living fire in his hand. But now the image of his mother was pulling away from him, drifting down toward the green depths of the gardens.

Don't leave me, take me with you.

Anguish and loss battered him, but in that instant Ned knew he could still be with his mother forever. He had one last chance. He could fly—yes—he would swoop down from this perch and dive into that wonderful water garden after her. He had failed her, let her go, and now this was the only way he could put things right. Dead but together. The only way. Infinity.

Mommy, here I am....

The grille lurched another inch or two on the right side, enough to throw Ned against the window frame. The knife fell from his outstretched hand and tumbled down through the air like a miniature jet in flame-out. It clattered noisily on the wrought iron, dropped through and plummeted to the ground far below. Ned jumped back into the room. It was an act of sheer body instinct, an organism recoiling from danger.

He retreated another step. The blue of sky and the green of garden that filled the window were changing. As he stood there, watching, they became darker, merging together until they seemed to turn into a deep black cloud. The sun was gone; there was nothing but inky blackness. Now it came right to the window, and the first wispy tendrils snaked into the room, licking across the walls and floor.

Ned backed out of the room and slammed the door shut as he left. Okay, it's okay, he told himself. There's nothing for me here. He hurried along the corridor and came back out into the welcome daylight on the landing.

Ned found it difficult to think at all about what had happened. What had saved him? Not a guardian angel, not the cross in his belt, and definitely not any display of self-control on his part. Luck, if anything. He felt subdued now, and yet he wanted to believe that this escape was one more sign that he was destined to survive. He wanted to believe—but how could he? How could any person overcome a force, a power so great that it was able to toy with the mind and senses? Maybe that's exactly what it is, he considered. I'm being toyed with, directed, steered, haunted, brought to the brink, and then pushed back for a temporary stay of execution. *It* can take me any time it wants. Well, get as much sport out of me as you can, Ned thought bitterly. He was filled with anger and hatred, and the dreadful frustration of having nothing to strike back at. Don't let me be taken meek and mild, frozen like a scarecrow.

Ned descended the stairs to the next landing. He was tired, but now he was only one floor above ground level. At least if he went out a window here he had a little less chance of killing himself. Good news, he thought. Ha ha. The rooms he had seen above had looked very much like living quarters for the spa's guests. Here, perhaps, he would find offices, consulting rooms, work rooms, a dining area—and whatever else.

He entered one of the corridors, but stopped after he had gone only a few paces. He heard a noise. It was vague and distant, and yet there was something decidedly familiar about it. Ned walked on a short distance and then stopped again. It was growing—a humming, droning sound. He looked around but saw nothing. The noise wasn't coming from this corridor, nor from the landing. It was farther away. The corridor on the other side, the opposite wing. Ned wondered if he should go there at once, or carry on in the direction he was going and try to ignore the sound. But how could you ignore anything in this place? Before he could make up his mind, a number of tiny black specks floated into his field of vision. At first he thought he was seeing things, that it was yet another trick of the eyes, but then he knew they were real. Their number increased rapidly. The buzzing was louder, ugly and insistent. They were flying out of the other corridor and into the open space of the landing. Bees, hornets, wasps—Ned didn't have to know which to know that he was in trouble. They sounded mean and angry. He fought back the impulse to run for the stairs. It was already too late for that; they would catch him for sure. There were too many on the landing, and dozens more joining them every second. It was not a thick, dense swarm, but a loose, swirling cloud. A giant squadron of unguided missiles, circling, cruising, looking for a target.

This was the awful buzzing noise he had heard those many times at home, but now it had taken on a new, more frightening dimension. Now it could be fatal. No question of poisonous or nonpoisonous; bees killed, pure and simple.

Ned moved gingerly, but it had the effect of a galvanic shock. The bees responded at once and started pouring into the corridor, right at Ned. Even as he ran he had the terrible feeling that he had finally made the one mistake he wouldn't be able to put right. They would have him trapped in this wing. He glanced back over his shoulder just once—the bees, like a hot, expanding gas, billowed towards him. The noise drowned out his thoughts now. The end of the corridor was in sight—what would he do there?—but seemed to get no closer. The air turned into a heavy soup, and then into a kind of jelly, even more resistant to his body. The harder Ned struggled to run against it, the slower his progress. The bees were almost on him.

Never mind running.

Get out of the corridor!

Ned flung himself against a door, crashing it open. In the room he spun around quickly and banged the door shut. He saw some old rags on the floor—something about them bothered him, but there was no time to think. He grabbed a long piece of cloth and crammed it into the space beneath the door. He poked and pushed until the crack was tightly blocked up.

Now the smell hit him. It was sweet, too sweet. There shouldn't be much of any smell here, Ned thought, not with a wide open window. The sound of the bees distracted him again. There were tiny patting noises on the other side of the door, as if the insects were actually hurling themselves against the wood. The buzz was fierce, and as relentless as a tornado. Ned checked the latch and the cloth again, to make sure there was no way the bees could get into the room.

He turned to look again at that pile of rags. They had obviously been there for years. Old blankets. Army green once, now just dingy and ratty. There were a few other things on the floor too, objects that Ned was aware of but couldn't focus on. They were not important. He was drawn to those green rags. They were important.

Ned peeled back the top layer of blanket.

Beneath it was a corpse, thin as a pressed flower.

The skin was translucent yellowing leather, stretched taut over delicate skeletal bones.

Ned reeled back, screaming, gagging as vomit burned his throat. The room spun around him like a demented carousel. The buzzing snarl cut jaggedly into his brain, and the floor jumped up to kiss him as he blacked out.

The corpse was his mother.

CHAPTER 20
THE SPA (2)

—Child.

A voice out of darkness.

—Child.

An echo of a whisper.

—Come with me now.

Urgent, but fading. A flurry of leaves lost on a nightwind.

Fear woke Ned. His eyes fluttered open anxiously. The side of his face was on a grimy floor. His head throbbed painfully. He remembered: the bees … the room … the rags … and the corpse. The noise of the bees had not gone away. Ned wondered how he could still be there and still be alive. Why hadn't he been taken? A moment ago he had heard a voice. Not so much heard, exactly, as felt, inside his head. But now it was gone. A dream? Just end it all, please, Ned wished in despair. The reason I came here was to get it over with one way or another. So take me now.

Maybe it was ending. Maybe the resolution was that he would survive. He had escaped everything so far. By this time, however, it was impossible to boost his morale with such thoughts. Much as he would like to, Ned couldn't think himself into believing that he had a chance to win. Not on his own, and probably not at all. This was no phosphorescent balloon, to be punctured by an enterprising junior sleuth. I live because *it* lets me live. No other reason. He was caught in the rhythm of some titanic force from another world or dimension. No amount of will or effort on Ned's part would influence it or overcome it. He was a leaf on a vast river, going whichever way it took him.

Stop thinking like that, Ned chastised himself. This place will tie your mind in knots if you let it. Concentrate: one step at a time. You're still alive, that's all that counts. He sat up. The throbbing in his head got worse. He fished the little first aid kit out of his knapsack and took two aspirin, washed down with a large gulp of water from his canteen. The water was good, it had a cold, metallic flavor, but it left an aftertaste in his mouth that became unpleasant. No, it wasn't the water—Ned remembered now that he had almost thrown up earlier. He tried to spit out the bad taste, but that was only a slight improvement. The smell in the air was what made it worse, he realized. That terrible, lingering death-stink. Ned spun around and saw the ragged blankets and the corpse again. Still there. No trick. Very real.

His mind struggled to keep control of itself. No matter how bad it gets, Ned reminded himself, you have to try to see it through and make sense of it. He was afraid to stand up and take a close look at the corpse, but he forced rational arguments on himself. That couldn't be his mother. Even if she were in trouble, even if she had died (no, no!), she wouldn't be here and in this condition. It cannot be. So: it must be someone else. Also: it couldn't harm him. The dead are dead. They don't hurt people (do they?). Maybe that wasn't a proven point, but it was buttressed by something else: surely, if the corpse were going to do anything to Ned it would have done so already. It didn't occur to the boy that he was dealing with the situation in the natural, logical way that would have pleased his father. He drove himself to keep thinking, to come up with a reasonable explanation.

Those other things on the floor. Food cans. A blackened Sterno container. A canvas bag. Now it began to add up. Someone had taken shelter here, perhaps even lived here for a while, and then that person had died here, undiscovered until now. A hobo or a lone gypsy or an outcast of the swamp people. That's all. It was bad enough to stumble across the remains of a dead person, but at least Ned knew it couldn't be his mother, and it certainly wasn't some vampire waiting to devour him.

Shaky, praying that he was right, Ned got up off the floor. Sight of the skull made him shiver. But this was followed by a feeling of relief as he saw that it definitely was not his mother. Just ... someone. The spa and Ned's imagination had conspired against him before. Now he could see that there wasn't any flesh or skin left either. Death had come to this person some time ago, leaving nothing but moldering bones and that unmistakable smell. Who were you, Ned wondered, that you had to come here, of all places, to die alone and unfound. My bones will be here too, he thought grimly, if I don't take care and get out. It was time to go.

Ned knew the bees were still in the corridor, but he went to the door and listened carefully. Their sound was a low roar, like a mighty engine straining impatiently in neutral. If Ned tried to leave that way he'd never even get close to the landing. The bees were real, like the spiders above. Not supernatural, just deadly. Everything Ned had run into so far had been natural, of this earth. The visions, the optical illusions and mind games—his own brain must have been responsible for those. Peeler had been right; this spa was a very dangerous place, whether phantoms dwelled here or not. But it does the condemned man no good to understand how dangerous the guillotine is, unless he escapes the prison. The problem at hand was how to get out of this room safely.

Ned went to the window. He was one floor above the building's ground level, but at this end of the wing the back garden was actually about two floors away, below him. And if he went down here he would still be within the confines of those labyrinthine gardens. The jungle would swallow him. The clear area around the terrace ended about ten yards away. This side of the spa was rather different from the other side, where Ned had fallen during his previous visit. He hadn't noticed then that the gardens came right up to the building at the end of this wing. The thicket below looked uninviting. Would he be able to make his way out of it? He would have to get to one of the walls and climb up on top of it. He could make a pile of some of the brush, to stand on. It might take a lot of hard work and time—he no longer had his knife to cut the stuff with—but it could be done. Besides, there was no alternative.

Ned tested the wrought-iron grille set in the window casing. It seemed sturdy enough. He put all his weight on it and bounced lightly. This one didn't budge. From his knapsack Ned got a fifty-foot roll of K-mart nylon rope. It would hold him-it had to. He tore off the cellophane wrapper and unwound the rope. He looped one end around the wrought iron and tied a slip knot, just as Peeler had taught him. Ned had no idea if it was a good knot for this kind of job, but it seemed a better bet than the only other one he knew—a conventional shoelace knot. He held the rope out and let it fall. It reached the ground below with plenty to spare.

Now the question was: Would he be able to hold his own weight as he lowered himself to the ground? Ned decided against using a safety harness and kicking his way down the side of the building because that would involve too much swinging and bouncing, and he wasn't even sure how to rig such a harness. He would simply have to rely on his hands and feet. He tied knots along the length of the rope, every three or four feet. It was tedious work, but at least it gave him "steps" to climb down on.

Ned checked the slip knot once more to make sure it was good and snug. Then he stepped over the grille. He was nervous as he took the rope in his hands. He stood one foot on the other, with the rope pressed between his shoes. There was a brief moment of panic when he moved away from the grille and had a sudden urge to leap back to the security of the building, but he clung to his lifeline and breathed deeply to settle himself. The rope was too thin and it felt like cord cutting into Ned's palms, but he didn't dare relax his grip. Hand over hand, a few inches at a time, he descended. The rope slid obligingly through his feet, and Ned had done a good job of spacing the knots conveniently. But it still took a great deal of effort to hold himself up. His breath quickened, coming in short, sharp grunts. Sweat soaked his clothes. His hands really hurt now, and the moisture made it harder for him to keep from slipping.

A cramp was forming in his thigh muscles, but Ned was close enough to the ground to know that he would make it. He let go of the rope and dropped the last six feet, landing on his butt in a bed of ferns. His body was sore, but he smiled with pleasure as he looked back up at the building. Beat you again, he thought. It occurred to Ned that this was probably the most daring thing he had ever done in his life. He felt a measure of pride as he examined the red welts on the palms of his hands.

Ned rested where he sat. He ate an apple, a chocolate bar, and he took another drink of water from the canteen. The effort of coming down the rope had made his headache worse, but it was letting up now as the aspirin took effect. The loss of the knife still annoyed him. Other than that, however, he hadn't done badly. He was still alive.

Ready to move on, Ned turned his attention to the garden he was in. It looked different, now that he was down here and actually in it. From above, even from as close as the top of the walls, it had appeared to be an impenetrable snarl of briars and weedy brush, a jungle choking on itself. But that had been deceptive. At ground level, in this area of the garden anyway, there were occasional thin spots. Beneath the taller, sprawling, bent-over bushes, there were low, tunnel-like passages through which a small body might move. It would be slow going and difficult, but if all parts of the garden were like this Ned thought he would be able to reach the clearing and terrace without having to find a way up one of the high walls.

He went the route of least resistance, always trying to keep an eye on the walls, looking for the doorway into the next section of the garden. In some places he could almost stand upright, but most of the time he had to stay low or even crawl on his hands and knees. The knapsack on his back snagged constantly, but there was nothing he could do about it except to struggle on. Fortunately, it was cool and shady in the garden, as the tall, leafy foliage screened out a good deal of the afternoon sun.

After about twenty minutes Ned came to a door in the wall. It wouldn't budge at first, but he kicked it several times until it scraped across the stone sill enough to let him slip through. Was there a doorway in every wall, or just one in each section of the garden? Ned tried to remember what he had observed on his previous visit, but he wasn't sure.

He wanted to move to the left, toward the center, but he was unable to get very far that way. The dense growth shunted him more or less forward, and after a while he came to another doorway, this one already open. Ned was pushing out, away from the spa building, when he needed to be circling around and back toward the clear ground. An hour later he stopped and tried to get his bearings. He could see enough of the building to get a rough fix on where he was: perhaps halfway between the spa and the back wall, virtually in the middle of the garden and still somewhat off center. Too far, he thought. He had to cut across and back. In spite of the shade he was hot and sweaty and beginning to tire now. He sat down for five minutes to rest again. The bugs were a nuisance—tiny gnats getting in his eyes, and the unnerving buzz of ugly fat flies always around him. But Ned reminded himself that they were much better than bees. So far, no bees, no spiders and no snakes. Think of the good points.

Funny … These gardens had always seemed to be the worst possible place Ned could get stuck in, more frightening and dangerous even than the black cellar. Ned had imagined all kinds of strange beasts and deadly creatures lurking in this jungle, waiting to tear apart any hapless intruder. But that fear had vanished—in fact, he hadn't given it a thought—as soon as he had actually landed in the garden. Now it appeared to be no more or less threatening than any other piece of wild ground. Thicker and heavier, maybe, but aside from that Ned could just as well be hiking through part of Old Woods. If this was the devil's playground, there wasn't much to it, he thought. Not yet, anyway; he wasn't safe until he was out—and maybe not even then.

A little further on, Ned was finally able to break left. He couldn't count the number of bramble scratches on his hands, and he knew there were some on his face, but this turn in the right direction tapped a fresh reserve of energy and enthusiasm in him. Ducking low, brushing away the raspy weeds and saw grass, he crossed the central ground of the gardens. Now: back to the clearing and the terrace. By then he would have seen and done enough for one day. The light would be fading. He would get out of the spa through the front door and head for home. If he felt it was necessary, he could come back another day to finish the ground floor and the cellar—but right now there was no longer any sense of urgency or importance to the idea. The crazy spa and the crazy gardens had deflated a little on their own. It was a place of natural hazards, and one that lent itself to a lively imagination, but Ned hadn't really encountered anything he could honestly call supernatural. He had to smile. He could see now that he had, in a way, done what his father had always advised. He had faced the nightmare, the weird phenomena, the unexplained and unknown—and he was working his way through it, literally, and coming to certain explanations and an understanding. In the end, there would be no phantom.

Ned located the spa building. He should be moving toward it. In that direction would be a wall and a door, he knew, followed by another wall and another door, and so on, until the clearing and the terrace. But the way was barred by an immense tangle of briars, thick as cables with vicious, inch long thorns. Jump in there and you'd bleed to death in a few minutes. Once again, Ned was steered off on a tangent, unable to complete the arc. He went the only way he could.

When he came to the wall, he didn't recognize it, but as he edged along, looking for a doorway, it dawned on him. This was the circular garden. The one Peeler and Cloudy said probably had a hot spring or something of the sort in it. Ned had to see this. He tried to recall how the layout had looked from atop the walls. If he went into the circular garden he might lose a little time, but there was still plenty of daylight left and his course was so unpredictable anyway that it probably wouldn't make much difference. But even if it did, Ned knew he had to enter; instinct told him this was not to be passed by. He stayed close to the wall, afraid to lose sight of it. The mass of vegetation was so dense it almost seemed to push him back. The knapsack was more of a hindrance than ever now, but Ned wouldn't consider ditching it as he climbed and crawled along the base of the wall.

The entrance itself was also a circle. No hinges, no holes. Never was a door here, Ned thought as his eyes took in the sweep of unbroken brickwork. Just inside, however, there was a kind of door. A tight cluster of twisted saplings had reared up against the inside wall. Holding his knapsack in one hand, Ned slid easily past this natural barrier and into the circular garden.

The differences were immediately obvious. He could stand up here. The plant growth was tall, reaching the full height of the surrounding wall, but the heavy leaves were banded there at the top, forming a spiky green ceiling. The trunks, or stalks really, were thin and deformed-looking, like spun vines marred by grotesque knotty eruptions. There was hardly any ground cover or scrub—just a bare, hard clay. It was so different from any other part of the spa gardens he had been through that Ned stood for several minutes, looking around in astonishment. He wondered if a bamboo grove might be anything like this. Then he thought, Yeah, in a bad dream.

He had been aware of the smell from the moment he had come to the entrance. It was not overpowering, but it was acrid and pervasive. Ned had performed enough experiments with his chemistry set to know it was the stink of burning sulfur. It was hard to imagine people wanting to spend time here, breathing this air, much less thinking it was somehow good for their health. Even the insects stayed out of this area; there wasn't a fly or a gnat or a bug of any kind to be seen. It was the quietest part of the spa Ned had come across yet.

The peculiar nature of the plant life here made it easy for Ned to move around. The last time he had been at this place, looking down from above, the greenery had reminded him of a giant wreath that filled the circular garden but for an open spot in the center. He would get there shortly, but first he wanted to complete one circuit of the inside wall. No doubt he could go to the library and find a book that would tell him what these plants were, but he came up with his own name for them: pipe-cleaner trees. They were sticky to touch, glistening with some kind of sap or resin. Ned moved carefully between them, and soon arrived back at the entrance.

Now to the center, where the smoke or steam had emanated from. He wanted to see what was really there: the mouth of a fire-beast, the gate to hell, or nothing at all?

The clearing was a small circle, perhaps twenty feet in diameter. It was ringed by the pipe-cleaner trees, which grew much more closely together at this spot. Ned squeezed through them and stood at the edge of a gradual depression in the ground. Only a few inches from his feet the clay became a deep black pudding, from which a light mist rose. The air was very warm and the smell of sulfur was quite sharp. Peeler was right again, Ned thought. This was the bizarre mud bath the old man had mentioned. In the center of the pit the steam was thicker and the mud was at low boil. Hot bubbles the size of baseballs forced their way up from below and broke the surface with a gruesome, gurgling sound. Ned wondered what the temperature was there. He bent over and tested the mud near his feet with one finger. It had a surprisingly smooth, creamy texture, not at all gritty like ordinary mud. And while it was hot, it wasn't too hot; about like ... well, a nice bath. Of course, it would be much hotter, unbearable, at the center, but there was obviously plenty of usable space. Quite a few people could slide their bodies into this muck at any given time, if that's what they wanted to do.

Ned thought about it. Did people really come here to wallow like pigs, as Peeler and Cloudy had said? Naked? Men and women together? What a thing to do, and what a strange sight it must have been. Were they young or old, or of all ages? Children too? And what did they look like when they came out-black, coated with mud from the neck down? There must have been showers nearby, perhaps in one of the adjacent gardens. Or maybe they hosed down right here, where all the pipe-cleaner trees now grew.

Looking at the pit, watching the mud bubble and the mist swirl slowly, Ned could almost see what it had been like. Human heads, male and female, dotting the black cream all around like beads on a necklace. So many of them, so close together their unseen bodies must be touching beneath the surface. It gave Ned a bad feeling, in a way he didn't understand. There was something disturbing about it. His mind kept going back to that room in the spa, to the picture of the young and beautiful woman he had seen in the magazine. Now he could see her walking into this garden, taking off her clothes and getting into the mud with the other people. The thought of it repelled him, and yet at the same time he couldn't help but be fascinated by it. It seemed to be a part of the whole basic feel of the spa—a kind of beauty that had gone a step too far, so as to be itself and something else, something off, something wrong.

The mud sucked and gurgled. The steam danced on the fetid air. Was there a small breeze here? The pipe-cleaner trees swayed one to another ever so gently, their leaves whisper-hissing overhead. They looked different, as if they had undergone a subtle transformation in the last few minutes. Now they had a flat, two-dimensional quality, like a very detailed and complex line drawing with contrived perspectives. It was a monochromatic scene, a gray-on-gray variant, every line shading off obscurely. Like one of those puzzle pictures for kids, Ned thought. "How many animals can you count in this picture?" Or, "Can you find all the people hidden in this picture? (Clue: There are 27!)." But now the puzzle was life-size, and Ned was in the middle of it. The picture was entrancing. Faces formed everywhere, fingers curled and flexed. But if Ned tried to focus on anyone spot the image disappeared-a face became another gnarled knot on a pipe-cleaner tree, and fingers were just a spray of twigs. The trick was not to focus but to let his gaze wander slowly, taking in the whole panorama around him. When Ned did that, the effect was dramatic. The grove of weird trees was suddenly full of implicit life, as faces and hands and bodies insinuated themselves into the scene with short, stop-start movements, like clouds on a weather satellite film loop.

Don't play into it.

Ned backed away a step but the trees held him comfortingly. He stretched his right arm out to one side and it seemed to blend in as part of the picture. Neat! When Ned was younger he had sometimes thought that it would be great to be able to step through the television set into cartoon land, that magical world. Now, being here was almost like that; not quite, but close. He felt giddy, as if he had just discovered the key that would give him that special ability. No one else in the world would have it. He stood at the gateway to a land that knew only a child's happiness, a land of mystery and adventure and high excitement, a land of fun and eternal play, free from fear, free from pain, a land that went on forever. It was a gateway you could pass through only once. Ned knew dimly that if he turned around and went home, he would never again be able to find his way back to this wondrous threshold. It was too fantastic to lose, but ...

From the center of the clearing a woman beckoned to him. She seemed to be wearing only a filmy veil of mist. She had a most beautiful smile, and her arms were an open embrace.

—Child.

She spoke without sound, directly into his mind. Who are you, he wanted to ask. The woman in the magazine? Yes. No—his mother? Ned's heart ached with uncertainty.

—Child of mine.

The thought-words, a sweetness, a light that glowed within him. Just run to her, a few steps only, and lose yourself in her love and goodness for all time in the magic realm beyond the gateway.

—Child, child, come to me.

Now and this once, never to know fear or pain again. This is what you have been looking for, this is what you came to find. Ned moved forward hesitantly, his feet sinking into the hot mud.

—Child, you will be mine again this day.

The words detonated like depth charges in his brain. Ned froze, eyes widening in terror. You will be mine again—he knew those words. They had been written in the dust on the floor of the spa. They meant he had to get out of here, fast. He stepped back, but the trees seemed to jostle him and press him on toward the woman.

Her smile was gone now, replaced by a look of anguish and rage. A face that had been beautiful but was now torn by elemental conflict. Again Ned pushed himself back, but the trees were a puzzle picture of hands and faces and bodies gathering around him, a phantom army that would not let him go. Steam bellowed up from the center of the pit, a scalding rush that engulfed the woman. The boiling mud roared at her feet. The leaves above, rippling from the force of the blast, made a noise like a crowd laughing obscenely. Ned couldn't turn away from the woman's eyes. They were burning with sorrow and loss, and they cut into the boy accusingly. It's my fault, he thought. I'm the one to blame for this, I'm doing it to her.

The spring vented. A searing jet of steam shot fifteen feet into the air. Ned was spattered with gobs of hot mud and sulfurous water, but he hardly noticed it. The woman was turning bright red before his eyes, and then her skin began to peel away as her flesh sizzled and popped.

—Child, why?

Ned screamed.

—Child, why are you doing this to me?

Ned turned, tore his way through the ring of pipe-cleaner trees and ran.

—Child, why are you leaving me again?

Her words, a weeping in his brain, a cry of emotions so great and unexpected that it reduced the boy to raw confusion. He had no defenses left, no final pocket of sense or understanding to draw on. All he could do was run, full of shame and self-hatred. When he came to the way out he didn't stop to think, but instantly scrambled up the ramp of saplings, pulling himself like a frenzied monkey.

Suddenly he was standing there, in darkness. Everything had changed. He had reached the top of the wall and it was a thin, luminous ribbon at his feet. The wall fell away a million miles below into endless space. All was blackness around him, utter night. The pale, glowing strip he stood on was his only foothold. He ran as fast as he could, never missing a step, following the line as it unrolled in front of him. Tears streamed down his face, tears for the woman he had left behind. She had burned and died, and he had done nothing. Nor had she died alone. More, so much more, had gone with her. A chance he would never have again. A secret, a truth he would never know. The feeling was beyond words for Ned. All he had left were useless tears and a vacuum within.

The ribbon ran out and Ned was flying before he realized it. Then: whump! Stunned, blinking, he rolled on his side and looked around. He was in the clearing. There was the terrace and the spa building. He was lying on soft field grass. The wall was just behind him. He had jumped out of the void and back into daylight.

He cried bitterly.

CHAPTER 21
MOTHER AND CHILD

Two days later Ned still didn't know what had happened to him at the spa. Had he really survived the final encounter he had sought, or was it merely a hallucination? Had he stood at the door to heaven, or hell? Was the woman in any way real, or was she just a fantasy? But the most important question was whether it was over at last, the haunting he believed he had been going through? Somehow it still felt unresolved, but he had no way of knowing whether there was anything even to resolve. How good it would be if he could write it all off as the fearsome antics of a boy's imagination, but Ned knew that you cannot willfully take shelter in ignorance or innocence.

He was not apprehensive, but subdued. His body felt as if all strength and energy had been drained out of it. He had spent the two days sitting around the house listlessly. He couldn't get past one page of any book he looked at. He watched television, napped, said little to his parents. Mostly he brooded over the incidents at the spa. Some things continued to amaze him. He couldn't remember climbing up the saplings, for instance, and yet he must have done it. And then being able to run along the top of the wall—*run*—in a moment of crisis when it seemed as if he hap been transported to the black reaches of deepest space. His guardian angel was that part of the brain which had kept control and functioned automatically, delivering him from ... whatever.

The second night, Ned went to bed after staring without interest at the television for a couple of hours. He put on his light pajamas and sat by the window. The sky was dark enough, and very clear. Ned pushed the screen up and brought his telescope to the open window. It was not an expensive or sophisticated instrument, like some in the Edmund Scientific catalogue, but it could bring him a reasonable glimpse of

Saturn on a good night. He had seen planets, the moons of Jupiter and plenty of stars, but one of these days he would have to get a book that would enable him to properly identify other objects in the night sky. Like pulsars, or those baffling quasars. In a school magazine there had been an article about quasars; it said that astronomers didn't know exactly what they were—and that pleased Ned. There were some things grown-ups could see and study, but not explain.

Ned found the Pleiades. Distance was such a tricky business. To look at this star group you would think they were all bunched closely together. But Ned knew they were actually separated by hundreds of millions of miles, vast gulfs of space. The sizes and distances involved were almost more than the mind could comprehend.

And what if this whole universe were nothing but a speck on a microscope slide, being examined by a boy in another universe, the same being true of his universe, and so on, and on.... Talk about giants! Hello, up there. Was there any way a phantom could fit into this scheme of things? Ned had to admit that it seemed silly. But, who knows—maybe one of those boys in another universe had a similar problem. Size and distance would mean nothing, when it came to that. Hope he's doing better than I am, Ned thought.

He heard someone in the hall. As he turned to look around, his mother's face appeared in the doorway.

"Ned?"

"Hi, Mom."

Linda came into the room.

"Can't sleep?"

"In a few minutes. There's a good sky tonight."

"Are all the stars where they're supposed to be?"

Ned smiled. "I think so."

Linda sat down on his bed and leaned back against the wall.

"Come on over here with me for a minute," she said.

Ned pulled the telescope in and lowered the window screen.

He started to get up onto the bed.

"Oh—want me to turn the light on?"

"Don't bother. Just get close to me."

Ned sat next to his mother. It was a very bright night, and they looked like ghostly figures in the dark. Linda put her arm around the boy and hugged him, resting her head on his. Ned snuggled closer, luxuriating in her warmth, the clean smell of her and the feeling of love she always gave him.

"Are you okay, Ned?"

"Sure."

"Anything bothering you?"

"No...."

"Anything at all, you just tell me about it."

"Uh-huh."

"The reason I mention it is, you've been in a funny mood lately. Know what I mean?"

"Well ... " Ned let the word fade away and gave a small shrug.

"It seems that way to me," Linda went on. "Just a little."

"Mom?"

"Yes?"

"How old do you think you'll be when you die?"

"I don't know, hon. Nobody knows that about themselves. Why? Is that what's bothering you?"

Another shrug. "I don't know."

"Well, if it is, don't waste your time thinking about it. The important thing is to live a good, happy life, with as much love as possible. That's all. That's everything."

"But, Mom ..."

"Hmmmn?"

"I don't want to lose you."

"Oh, Ned." He sounded so sad and helpless, Linda suddenly felt herself about to cry. "You're not going to lose me, honey. No, you're not. Please don't worry about that." She gave him another long hug, then brushed his hair back off his forehead and kissed him several times. "No, no, no," she whispered.

"But, Mommy—" Now that Ned had started, he couldn't stop. His voice trembled. "I'll be gone and I won't ever see you again."

"No, no, no." Softly, soothingly, but firm.

"But I will, I'll be gone and—"

"No, Ned. Where?"

"I don't know…. They'll take me somewhere way far away."

"Who?"

" … Somebody …"

"No, that's not—"

"*Yes.*" Surprisingly insistent. "I know, Mommy, I *know.*"

Linda found her son's eyes in the dark and she could see the fear running loose in them.

"Ned, is it those two old men? Are they—"

"No, they're my friends."

"Well, have you seen somebody else? Has someone followed you home or threatened you, or anything like that?"

After a long pause, a tiny voice: "No…."

"Okay. Now you listen to me, sweetheart. You don't have to be afraid. Nobody's going to take you away from Daddy and me."

"Yes, they will."

Once more Linda was surprised at how certain Ned sounded.

What was it? Not paranoia, not in one so young. Then she remembered something from her own childhood. How old had she been at the time—five? Anyhow, it was the first time someone explained the word kidnapping to her. For weeks after that Linda had lived in sheer terror, convinced that at any moment she was going to be snatched and murdered and buried in a swamp and never found again. Finally she had gotten over it, but she still recalled the fear. Vividly. Ned was nearly ten, but ten was still very much a child. He could get a notion into his head and it could grow out of all proportion.

"My poor baby." It had to be something like that, some irrational childhood fear. Linda rocked him in her arms. "Do you think Daddy or I would ever let anybody take you away from us? Of course not."

"But what if you couldn't stop them?"

"That'll never happen, Ned. Never, never, never."

"Mommy, I love you."

"I love you."

"And Daddy."

"And Daddy loves you. We both love you so much."

"I don't want it to happen to me."

"Nothing bad is going to happen to you, Ned. Only good things. And no one is ever, ever going to take you away from us."

"Oh, Mommy ..."

"We love you too much, and nothing can beat that."

"Will you stay here with me in the dark, Mommy?"

"Of course, I will."

"Really all night?"

"Sure."

"Because, well, I really want you to stay and hold me."

Little-boy talk. Regression? He sounded more like an Oedipal five or six. This thing tonight, Linda thought, it's set him back. But at least he's brought it out and told me about it. With lots of love and a bit of luck it'll be over with in a day or two. Please.

"I'll stay here as long as you want, Ned."

"Mommy, Mommy ..."

His whole body shook, and then Linda could feel his hot tears soaking through her blouse. For a few minutes she couldn't keep from crying along with him. She hugged and rocked him some more. She sang gently to him and hummed any soft tune that came into her head. Ned cried himself to sleep in her arms, but whenever she tried to move, his fingers grabbed her tightly. At some point Michael looked into the room, but Linda waved him away, afraid that Ned would wake up.

Later, much later, she managed to slip out of Ned's room. Her arms and legs were stiff, and her breathing was a little irritated. She took two puffs of Becotide from the inhaler. Michael was asleep.

After a while, so was she.

CHAPTER 22
THE FARLEY PLACE (2)

"Lady of Spain I adore you. Pull down your pants I'll explore you...."

As Ned entered the baithouse, Cloudy was singing to himself. He was perched on a stool at the small zinc table that served as a workbench in the back corner of the shed, where he was fiddling with a dozen or more flashlights. Peeler sat in his armchair, thumbing through an old catalogue of fishing and trapping gear. Both men glanced up at the boy.

"I told you he didn't run off to join the Navy," Cloudy said.

Peeler grunted.

It was a drizzly morning, fit for doing nothing, and Ned had been sure he'd find either or both of his friends at the baithouse. He shook the moisture off his baseball cap and made his way past the tables of tanks and wooden boxes.

"Where did you get all the flashlights?"

Cloudy nodded toward Peeler. "That old fool had these lyin' around for years, and there ain't a one of 'em works. Now I brung one good set of batteries so we can see what's what." He pushed the switch to try the flashlight in his hand. Nothing happened. "Okay, now, this one here needs a new bulb, see?"

Ned nodded.

"So far, every dang one I tried needs a new bulb." Cloudy took the batteries out and put the flashlight with a group of four others to one side. He resumed humming the same schoolyard song as he took up the next flashlight.

Ned moved away a few feet, to a tray of baby crayfish. He teased them with his finger, sending them scurrying through the water.

"So watcha been doin'?" Peeler asked after a few moments.

"Oh … nothing much."

"Another one needs a new bulb," Cloudy announced. "You sure need a lot of new bulbs."

Peeler harumphed. "You gotta check the connection," he said. "It don't matter if you got good bulbs and batteries if they don't make the connection.'"

"I know, I know."

"Some of them things been kicked around so much they don't connect no more. That's what needs fixin'."

"Yeah, yeah."

"Don't need but one anyhow," Peeler added in a mutter.

Ned waited until he was sure this exchange was over before speaking. "Something did happen to me a few days ago," he said. "I thought I was in real trouble for a while there."

"How's that?" Peeler looked at the boy over the top of the catalogue.

"Oh, I was just out walking. Near the old railroad tracks, you know." Ned kept his eyes on the crayfish as he spoke. He wouldn't come right out and say he was in the spa again, but he didn't think he would have to tell a blatant lie either. "And suddenly these bees came up, a whole mess of them. Boy, did they chase me. I never ran so hard in my life."

"They'll do that," Peeler said. His eyes dropped back to the catalogue page.

"Was they yellow jackets?" Cloudy asked.

"I didn't stick around to find out."

"You musta come on a hive of 'em, to stir 'em all up like that," Peeler said. "Did it myself once."

"It was scary."

"They can hurt you, yes, they can," Cloudy said. "I used to know a fella—Peeler, you remember old Billy LeBeau?—he'd get sick real bad from bees."

"Yeah," Peeler replied.

"Just one or two bee stings and his face'd get all swole up like a big pink marshmallow, and he'd have trouble breathin' and all."

"Really? That bad?"

"Oh, yeah, sure. They had to give him oxygen once, and he had to carry a little jar of pills around with him all the time, in case he got stung."

"Billy didn't have to see a bee," Peeler said. "If he just heard a buzzin' around him, he'd drop his load and head for the hills. Hey, whatever become of Billy, anyhow?"

Cloudy considered for a moment, then shook his head. "I don't know. He's gone somewhere. Ain't seen nor heard of him in years now. Maybe he's out in the desert, or up with the Eskimos. Any place where there ain't no bees."

"I think we have a nest in our house," Ned said. "I've heard them buzzing around."

But the subject of bees was apparently finished, for this brought no response from the two old men. Peeler scanned the pages of the catalogue as if looking for something he had lost, and Cloudy was humming again as he worked on another flashlight.

"When are you going fishing again?" Ned asked.

Peeler shrugged. "Tomorrow, maybe. If it's not too wet out. I got red wigglers to spare, so we could go over to Baxley Mill Pond and get us a bunch of sunfish, if nothin' else."

"You gotta catch so many of them," Cloudy protested. "And then they're a pain in the butt to clean."

"They ain't so bad," Peeler said. "We can all pitch in. Ned'll cut up a few punkinseeds, won't you?"

"Sure."

"See? I think it's a good idea. I been feelin' so bone-lazy this past week, that's about as much work as I can stir myself to do."

"And you wouldn't do that if you couldn't get the boy to do most of the work for you, ain't that right, Mr. Tadpole?"

Ned laughed. "I don't mind. I like to go fishing."

"Okay, okay." Cloudy gave up. "I'll watch the shop, you guys bring home the food." Then, to himself: "Dinky little sunfish ..."

Peeler threw the catalogue over his shoulder, stretched and gave a mighty yawn. He slumped back in the armchair, his eyes a little watery. "Darned if I ain't like a watch that's all wound down," he said. "Must be the weather."

"Yeah, and we been havin' this damn weather for thirty years now," Cloudy remarked, with a sly wink at Ned.

"Peeler."

"Hmmmn?"

Ned sat on a wooden crate near the old man. "Tell me about my house," he requested.

"Your house?"

"Yes."

"What about it?"

"Well—everybody calls it the Farley place, don't they?"

"Sure do."

"How come?"

"Folks name of Farley used to live in it, a long time ago. They built the place."

"But why do people still call it that, if it was so long ago?"

"Ah, that don't mean nothin'. Somethin' gets a name, it sticks, that's all."

"What happened?"

"What d'ya mean?"

"Something happened at the house—to the Farleys—didn't it?"

Peeler smiled, but Ned noticed that the old man was chewing his lower lip. Cloudy had turned around on his stool, a flashlight. lying neglected in his hand.

"You're guessin' now, Nedly."

"But it did, didn't it?"

"Why? What makes you think so?"

"There's something about it—the house. I don't know what it is, but I get a funny feeling sometimes."

"He still thinks it's haunted," Cloudy said with a laugh that was just a trifle forced.

"Maybe," Ned allowed quickly. He sensed that he had the initiative and he enjoyed the feeling. He pressed on. "So tell me what happened."

Peeler yawned again. He seemed so bored that Ned suddenly wondered if he might not be wrong after all about the Farley past.

"There ain't an old house in the country that don't have some kind of story or other about it," Peeler said in a tone of complete dismissal.

"I want to know about the Farley place," Ned insisted. "I live there now, Peeler. Please tell me."

Ned was glad to hear that the light drizzle outside had grown into a steady rain. It drummed on the metal roof of the baithouse, and a few drops leaked through in places. He had Peeler and Cloudy cornered, at least until the rain let up. Ned leaned forward on his seat, propping his elbows on his knees. Undisguised expectation showed on his face.

"There ain't a whole lot to tell," Peeler began reluctantly. "It was before my time, really. Well, I mighta been a little kid then, I don't know. Anyhow, the thing is, the Farleys had some kind of family trouble, that's all. I believe one of the sons worked on the fishin' boats, and a storm come up real quick, like they can sometimes, and blowed him over the side and they never did get him back. He was lost at sea. That sort of thing used to happen all the time in those days, you know. It was a lot worse than it is now. And probably nobody'd remember it except that not long afterwards the mother got killed too. Now, I don't know the ins and outs of what done her in, whether it was an accident or natural causes, or what. But comin' so soon after the death of the son, well … it made a little more impression on folks."

Ned didn't speak. All he could think was, *That's it, that has to be it.*

"There was some trouble about that time with the Sherwoods too, wasn't there?" Cloudy asked. "Didn't they own the boats?"

Peeler nodded. "Yeah, they owned the boats, they ran the fishin' fleets hereabouts. Made a lot of money too. I guess some said it was their fault about the Farley boy, but that's just stuff. I don't see how it could be their fault if somebody gets blowed away in a storm."

"Seems like more people died young in them days," Cloudy said. "You had big families—eight, ten, twelve kids—so it wasn't unusual for some of 'em not to make it. More folks died from accidents while they was workin' too. And sickness—they didn't have all the medicines they got now. So, all in all, you had a lot more of that kind of thing goin' on…."

"Yeah, that's right." Peeler took up where Cloudy trailed off. "There wasn't nothin' special about it."

"What happened to the rest of the family?" Ned asked.

"You got me there," Peeler said. "Nothin' I know of. I guess the other kids just growed up and went their ways. The old man never married again, that I'm aware of. He musta packed up too, somewhere along the line. Anyhow, I ain't never heard no more about any of 'em."

"Seems to me the house sat empty for a while," Cloudy said. "I can't swear, but I got a vague recollection it was some time after the father was gone before somebody else moved in."

"Yeah," Peeler agreed. "I think you're right about that, but the main thing about the Farleys is that it was just one of them things that happens now and again. Tragedy strikes, a family drifts away, finally the last one pulls up stakes and that's the last you see. They settle down elsewhere and start over again, that's the way it is, but because folks don't hear about that they only remember the unhappy part."

It didn't escape Ned that Peeler and Cloudy had seemed wary of this subject at first, but then had teamed up to sketch it out as a very ordinary, down-to-earth matter. They were making a great effort to convince Ned that the Farley story was in no way remarkable or unusual, that it was "just one of those things." But they were wasting their time with that; Ned knew he was on to something. In some way, the Farleys *had* to be a part of what he had been experiencing. Tragic deaths. A son and his mother. Ned's parents, and Peeler and Cloudy too, probably. would explain it away as a coincidence of local history and a young boy's imagination. But Ned couldn't. He had been through too much. He wondered about the Farleys all the way back home.

"What'd you go and tell him all that for?" Cloudy asked, after Ned had left.

"I dunno," Peeler admitted. "I wasn't gonna say nothin' at all, and then it just kinda eased out." He rubbed the side of his jaw, and then looked up. "You did a pretty good job of beatin' your chops too."

"Once you got goin' I had to help out."

"Yeah. sure."

"Keep it from gettin' outta hand."

"Outta hand—how?"

"He's just a boy, Peeler. That sort of story could get him all scared now, afraid to sleep in his own bed. That ain't right, it just ain't right."

"He was scared already. Didn't you see that?"

"I know, I know." Cloudy looked miserable. "But all we go and do is make it worse for him. Probably got him scared stiff now."

"Maybe," Peeler said. "Maybe that's a good thing, too."

Cloudy said sternly, "Ain't nothin' never happened to nobody in that house all these years, and that's the gospel truth and you know it."

"Ain't never been a boy child livin' there since the Farleys," Peeler said. "Till now."

CHAPTER 23
ON THE STREET WHERE YOU LIVE

"He was scared," Linda stated flatly. "Really scared. It took the longest time before he was asleep enough so that I could leave the room. He wouldn't let go."

She scraped the plates clean of chicken bones and unfinished food. Michael sat at the table, sipping the last of the white wine and listening patiently. They had eaten dinner a little while ago. The skies had cleared late in the afternoon and Ned was out in the backyard stalking night crawlers, figuring that the day's rain would bring them out early. He was eager to go fishing with Peeler the next day and night crawlers were easier to put on a hook than red wrigglers. The kitchen radio played an instrumental medley of show tunes.

"*I* was scared too," Linda went on. "I didn't know what to do or what to say to him. He was quite beside himself, almost hysterical. And then he just burst into tears."

"It's happened before," Michael said quietly.

"Before, yes, but—"

"He's been like that when he's had nightmares."

"But he wasn't sleeping, Michael. I told you that. He was wide awake, sitting at the window with his telescope when I went in. Then we sat and talked for a few minutes and it all came out. It was like something he'd been holding back, keeping inside of himself, and it finally broke loose."

Michael was nodding his head rapidly, as if prompting Linda to finish. "Okay, I know," he said. "It wasn't a nightmare. All I said was that it was like a nightmare. Like the last time."

Linda emptied the garbage into a large green plastic bag under the sink and then she put the platter into the dishwasher.

"He's convinced someone is going to take him away from us. He is absolutely terrified of it."

"Yes, and we've been through that before, too. When he had the sunstroke he said something like that."

"It's not just an idle thought he dreamed, Michael."

"What is it, then?"

"It means something."

"Ha!" Michael exclaimed, unable to restrain himself. "I'm not laughing, honey," he added quickly, "but do you really believe that stuff?"

Linda's face clouded with uncertainty. "A week, two weeks ago, I would have said no. But now ... I'm not so sure. I don't know what to think. I feel so stupid and helpless."

Michael watched his wife nearly drop the carton of milk as she went to put it in the refrigerator. Her expression was a worried, distracted frown and her movements, wiping the tabletop, were jerky and nervous. He thought she looked like an actress laboring to achieve a certain effect but not completely succeeding. She was being too dramatic about it, letting it get to her this way. It was impossible for Michael to accept all that his wife was telling him. The real problem was how to calm her down and make her see sense.

"That's a mistake," he said. "You can't keep blaming yourself—and for what? If something is bothering Ned, we'll deal with it one way or another. But I don't want it to get out of hand with you."

"Out of hand?" Linda's voice wavered upward. "Michael, he's my son. What do you want me to do—act as if nothing has happened?"

"No," he answered loudly. Then he softened his tone. "It's· just that I have to worry about you, too, as well as Ned, and the last thing I want to see happen is for you to work yourself into such a state of anxiety and nerves that you ... well, bring on another bad asthma attack. You know that tension and stress are big contributing factors."

"I used to be afraid of that," Linda said. "But now I'm afraid for Ned. He's the most important thing right now."

Was it just a good try at bravado, or was she serious? Michael couldn't tell, but it was hard to believe that his wife could pull off such an about-face as far as asthma was concerned. For the last five years she had feared nothing in the world more than a repeat of that terribly severe attack.

"It doesn't matter how you feel about it," Michael argued reasonably. "The fact is, you're still susceptible to it. You're in the high-risk bracket, and to me it looks like you're pushing yourself closer and closer to the edge. Now tell me something: How are you going to help Ned if you get to the point where your own health breaks down and you wind up in bed for a few weeks, or maybe even the hospital? How will that help Ned, or any of us?"

"E-Z listening from E-Z Radio," a syrupy voice announced. "Coming up next, the One Thousand and One Strings and their interpretation of 'On The Street Where You Live' from *My Fair Lady*, followed by ..."

"I understand," Linda said. "I know what you're saying, and you're right."

"Okay, now we're getting somewhere."

"No, we are not," Linda went on hastily. "We're not getting anywhere by talking about my health at a time when we should be doing something about Ned. His problem is real, it's very, very real, at least to him. And it's going on right now, it's not something that might or might not happen, like an asthma attack. It's here. Now. Do *you* understand?"

Michael tapped the tabletop with one finger. "All right, Linda, I'll ask around tomorrow and get the name of a good child psychiatrist, and we'll take Ned in to see him. Or her." He said it with an air of resignation, thinking that this unpalatable alternative might force his wife to back off. The change on her face suggested the tactic was working.

"Wait a minute. No," Linda said. "I didn't mean that."

"Why not?" Michael followed up promptly. "He's been to the doctor, and he got a clean bill of health. So if there's a problem, it must be a mental problem, and he should see a shrink. Right?" Michael had lowered his voice and looked out the kitchen window. He was relieved to see that Ned was safely out of earshot in the backyard. Christ, the boy'd really have a problem if he heard his parents talking about him like this, Michael thought. He had to put a stop to this nonsense, once and for all.

"No," Linda repeated. "I don't like that idea."

How could she possibly admit that her son, not yet ten years old, might need a psychiatrist? No way.

"What then?"

"You don't think there's any chance he could be right?" she asked hesitantly. It was too much to expect that Michael would agree, but she could think of nothing else.

"About somebody taking him away?"

Linda nodded, staring at the table.

"Honey, we've been through all that before," Michael said. "If I thought there was any chance, any chance at all that Ned was right, I'd have to hire armed bodyguards to follow him around from the time he got up in the morning until the time he went to bed at night and put padlocks on his bedroom door and bars on the window. Is that what you want me to do? Because if it is, we'll have to start thinking of ways to come up with all that money, and—"

He let it go. Linda's shoulders sagged, and he could tell she was giving up on that angle. Michael took another sip of wine and smiled to himself. Nothing like a little *reductio ad absurdum* to shake out a situation.

"Michael ... Help us...."

Her voice was striving to sound disconsolate and little-girl-lost. Again Michael had the sensation that she was purposefully dramatizing. How much longer could he indulge it without leaving the way open for real trouble? To move to Lynnhaven was proving more difficult for Linda than he had expected. Much more difficult, it seemed, than for Ned even. Maybe the boy was bothered by something, but it would pass. Let a plant grow, and ninety-nine times out of a hundred it'll grow. The conditions are right. If Linda refused to take Ned to see a counselor or a specialist of some sort (and Michael really didn't want that either), then there was nothing more to be said. It was time to be firm.

"All kids have fears, Linda," he said. "Big, vivid, bone-freezing fears. They see things in the dark, and then they think they begin to see them during the day too. *Things that aren't really there.* But what you're doing is taking Ned's natural childhood fears and blowing them up into your own, and then Ned gets them back from you, worse than they were before. The two of you are feeding each other's fears, in bigger and bigger doses. Can't you see what's happening? It's a vicious circle, round and round, back and forth between the two of you. Something terrible is being created out of nothing. Linda, you can't let yourself get into Ned's fantasies and perpetuate them by acting as if you believe them too. It's got to stop."

Linda reached for the wine bottle, found it was empty. She grabbed the sherry decanter and poured herself a large measure.

"I mean it, honey," Michael continued. "Fact: our son is perfectly healthy. Fact: our son is not, repeat not, being shadowed by kidnappers or a child molester or a ghoul or anything else. Fact: you ..."

Linda kept her back to him as he rattled on. He's right, her mind said, but that was no help. She hated it when Michael got off on one of his fact-this and fact-that routines. The annoying thing was that he even had her doing it sometimes. Take all your facts and stick them under your pillow, she wanted to tell her husband. Maybe the tooth fairy can make use of them. I can't. What did it always come down to in the end? Talk, talk and more talk. That's all.

Linda couldn't even hear him now, although he was only a few feet away, talking to her. She couldn't hear, and that was worrying. Were they beginning to drift away from each other? It had always seemed that they were deeply attuned to one another, locked on the same wavelength, body and soul. But you have to wonder if that can last forever. How many marriages do? If they were so far apart on something so vital as their only son ... Had they run the course to its end?

Something he had said still rankled—what was it? Talking about if Ned was right, that someone was going to take him ... Michael had said that he would "have to hire armed bodyguards" to protect the boy. Not what you would expect, the automatic I *would* hire, but the grudging I *would have to hire*. Bodyguards were out of the question, of course, but Linda felt her husband had betrayed himself, as well as her and Ned, in that choice of words.

"Ned worries about whatever it is he worries about," Michael was saying. "You worry about Ned and I worry about you. It's ridiculous."

Once, up until a short time ago, Linda might have responded to that with a smile and said, "Cheer up, dear. I know for a fact that your mother still worries about you," or some remark like that. Now she couldn't manage it. She felt alone, and bitter that they should be put in this position at a time when they should have everything going for them.

She hammered the start button on the dishwasher with a white-knuckled fist.

CHAPTER 24
STONY POINT

Peeler was in a better mood the next day. It was clear and crisp, with late August hints that autumn was just around the corner. When Ned showed Peeler the night crawlers he had caught, the old man laughed and said, "You don't need worms that big to get sunfish. Hell, you can cut up one of them things into three or four pieces, it'll do the trick. You use 'em if you want to, but it's like tryin' to feed a roast buffalo to a cocker spaniel; he'll have a go at it, but a lump of baloney'd do just as well."

Baxley Mill Pond was outside of Lynnhaven, but on the same side of town as Peeler's baithouse, so they didn't have a long walk to get there. Ned had seen the place before, although he hadn't fished it. As they approached, he noticed again the complete absence of any shoreline development. It was lightly wooded, with occasional clear patches along the edge of the water, but not a single cottage. It looked more like a pocket lake than a mill pond.

"Why is it called Baxley Mill Pond?" Ned asked.

"Come to think of it, I don't know. Must go back a long ways, because that's what it always was, to my knowledge. And it always looked the same as it does now," Peeler said, gesturing around him. "Just a punk lake, clean but shallow. Ain't nobody never had no use for it, at least none to speak of."

"Maybe a hundred years ago it was different," Ned speculated. "Or maybe back around the time of the Civil War."

"Maybe," Peeler said doubtfully.

They found a clear spot on the shore that was big enough so they could fish without getting in each other's way. The ground was covered with tall field grass and a sprinkling of cool water; Ned knew it contained a supply of beer. The old man set about his preparations as if they were a sacred ritual. Ned, who could have his line baited and ready in under a minute, stood watching. Peeler was never in any rush to get to the casting stage.

First, he carefully untied the faded cloth wrapper and took out the two sections of his fishing rod. Next, he rolled the inside tip of the second section along the side of his nose, so the skin oils would provide that tiny bit of lubrication to ensure a smooth fit. Then he lined up the guides and put the rod together. A last, small twist of the flange might be necessary for perfect alignment. Peeler would whip the rod through the air several times, until he was satisfied with the action. After clamping on the reel and threading the line, he sat down with the rod across his legs and brought out his battered folder of hooks. He chose one of the smallest and tied it on, snipping off two or three inches of excess line. Then he caught the hook in the first guide and cranked the reel until the rod arced obligingly. Now he was almost ready. He attached a small bobber to the line about a foot and a half above the hook. Peeler glanced up and saw Ned watching him.

"What're you lookin' at?" he asked good-naturedly.

Ned smiled. "Nothing."

The old man peered closely at the boy's rig. "What're you tryin' to do, catch a shark?"

"What's the matter with it?"

"Bobber's too big, for one thing," Peeler said. "Use the littlest one you got, so it don't drag like an anchor when the fish wants to turn and run with your bait."

"Oh. Okay."

"And what're you usin' for bait anyhow?"

"A night crawler."

"A whole one?"

"Yes."

Peeler shook his head in amazement. "Damn thing looks like an Italian meatball," he said. "Fish'll have a feast on that without even gettin' the hook in their mouth. What size hook you got there?"

"I'm not sure."

"Well ... See what happens."

Peeler was still smiling to himself as he slid a tiny pink angle worm on his hook. They cast out, and within a couple of minutes they each pulled in a red-breasted sunfish less than five inches in length.

"Junk," Peeler muttered, tossing his fish into the brush. He walked over to Ned. "Let's see now…. Yeah, look at that. Ain't nothin' left of your worm. This guy and all his kin just nibbled it away, and you were lucky to hook one. If you're gonna use night crawlers, just use a piece about an inch long—all you need to do is cover the hook, no more." Peeler deftly unhooked Ned's fish and flung it toward the trees. "I'd put a smaller hook on too, if I was you."

"How come you don't put the fish back in the water, if they're too small?" Ned asked.

"Too many of 'em in there as it is," Peeler answered. "They need thinnin' out. Gives the others a better chance of growin' to a decent size."

Ned changed hooks and tried Peeler's suggestion of using a small section of night crawler. It worked fine. An hour later they had caught about a half-dozen sunnies each, a couple of which were large enough to keep. Peeler set his rod down and popped open another can of beer. He took a gulp and some of the cold brew slopped over his lips, trickling down his chin and neck. It felt good.

"Hey, Peeler."

"Yeah?"

"You don't ever watch TV, do you?"

"Nope."

"Why not?"

"I used to." Peeler broke a piece of tall grass and chewed on the stem.

"You did? What did you watch?"

"I used to go down to Rudy's Bar and watch the baseball games. It was quite a while ago. Then I give up, and I ain't never seen a bit of television since."

"How come?"

"Well … because some pissant son of a biscuit went and moved the Washington Senators to Minnesota and they weren't on the TV no more."

Ned almost laughed. "That's why you gave up TV?"

"Sure. Only thing I ever did was watch Senators' games."

"But ..."

"I heard a story once," Peeler said. "Don't know if it's true or not, but I like to think it is. They say there was this young fella, maybe twenty or so, and he was in love with a beautiful young girl. And he courted her and courted her, till finally they got engaged to be married. He was the happiest fella in the world then, but a little while later she changed her mind and called it off. Now, you know what that poor boy went and did?"

"What?"

"He stopped goin' to work, just give up his job. And he stopped talkin' too, and he went into the poorhouse. They say he spent the rest of his life there, forty-four years, I believe, without sayin' a single word to anybody."

"Not even one word?" Ned didn't believe it. Nobody could do that for four years, let alone forty-four.

"Nope," Peeler said. "Not even one word."

"That's—silly."

"Maybe." Peeler spat out the last of the grass stem and smiled. "To tell you the truth, I sometimes do listen in on a game, on the radio in my car at night. It's better'n seein' it on TV too, but don't ask me why."

"I don't like baseball much," Ned admitted.

"Nobody's perfect."

Peeler finished his beer and stood up to resume fishing. Suddenly be froze, looking like a cartoon character who has just been struck with a bright idea.

"What's the matter?" Ned asked.

"Ssssh."

Peeler bent low and then snatched at something with his hand. "Got him," he announced, straightening up. "Yessir, he's a real beauty."

Ned put down his rod and went over to take a look. Peeler delicately held a black-winged grasshopper by its long legs.

"Are you going to use that for bait?" the boy asked.

"Sure am. Watch how I do it now, and you'll learn something." Peeler brought the barb of the hook to a spot just under the hopper's head. "Right down his throat … all the way … nice and easy … like so."

The hopper's jaws worked futilely on the shaft of the hook. Its legs kicked and its wings flapped, but it was well hooked, with the barb curling out low to its belly. The hopper's weight gave Peeler better distance on his cast. He and Ned watched the insect make a fuss on the surface of the water for a few seconds, and then there was a large splash. Peeler gave a short, quick tug to set the hook, and the tip of his rod bent pleasingly. The fish ran briefly, then gave up. Peeler had no trouble horsing it out of the water.

"Hey, what is it?" Ned was excited because he had never seen this kind of fish before. It was about seven inches long and shaped like a sunfish. But its sides sparkled with iridescent blue and purple coloring, and the dark spot on its gill flap was less pronounced.

"Rock bass," Peeler said. "Good size, too. They don't come much more'n eight inches or so, except at the liar's club."

"That's a bass?"

"Rock bass, that's his name," Peeler said. "But freshwater fish names are kinda screwy. Try to remember this: a white perch is not a true perch, it's a bass, a member of the bass family; and a rock bass is not a true bass, it's in the sunfish family. One of the bigger ones, and good eatin' too."

Ned put one hand on his hip. "Why do they call a bass a perch, and a sunfish a bass, if they aren't?"

"That's their names, is all I know." Peeler grinned. "Like I told you, names ain't a whole lot of use when you come right down to it. All you got to know is which one is worth cookin' and which one ain't." Peeler put the rock bass on the stringer.

"Pretty fish."

"Sure is," the old man agreed. "Tell you what. Where there's one of these guys there's usually a whole tribe of 'em. Put a couple of split shot on your line, halfway between the bobber and the hook. That'll get your cast out farther, where I caught this one."

Peeler went back to using worms, but Ned spent a quarter of an hour trying to catch one of those black grasshoppers. Whenever he got close to one and started to reach out, it flew away. Finally he quit, and cut up another night crawler.

"Got to get 'em early," Peeler said. "When they're still half asleep and heavy with dew. I was lucky with the one I grabbed."

By mid-afternoon they had thirteen worthy rock bass, gill to gill on the stringer, and they had thrown away more than two dozen small sunnies.

"I guess we got enough," Peeler said, dismantling his gear and packing it away. "The raccoons'll have a party tonight with all we left in the bushes."

They had set out on this fishing trip with brisk, eager strides, but now Peeler and Ned ambled lazily back toward the baithouse. Peeler let Ned carry the fish, and they slapped rhythmically against the boy's leg as he walked. There was a good feeling between them that came from going out to do something enjoyable and then having enjoyed doing it. No hitches, no bother about it, just a good day that was going the way it was supposed to. The mood was so right that Ned didn't think twice about bringing up the subject.

"You know what you were telling me yesterday about the old Farley family?"

"Yeah."

"Well ... The Sherwoods, who owned the boats ..."

"Yeah, what about 'em?"

"Didn't they own the spa too?"

"Oh, later, yeah. They built the spa, but it wasn't till many years later that they got around to that. When the Farley boy was lost, the Sherwoods was just in the fishin' business, I believe. So, their children, or grandchildren, I don't know who, was the ones who built the spa."

Ned was nodding to himself as he listened. "That's what I thought. I just wanted to make sure." It felt so much easier to talk about it today, perhaps because they were walking side by side, faces forward.

"Why?" Peeler asked casually.

"I think the ghost of that Farley woman is still hanging around our house." The way it came out sounding so inconsequential it nearly made Ned laugh at himself, but then he added earnestly: "I do, I really do."

Peeler surprised them both. "I been thinkin' about that too," he said. Well, why not? He hadn't slept easy the night before, and maybe it was time to be a little more frank with the boy.

"Really?" Ned kept walking, staring straight ahead, but his pulse quickened.

"Yeah, the thing is, there's always been a kind of local story about her, you see. A lot of nonsense—her supposed to be waitin' eternally for her lost boy to come back, or be found, or what have you."

"Do you think she is?"

"Nah," Peeler scoffed. "Folks just make up stuff like that to give 'em somethin' to talk about, that's all."

"But you said you were thinking about it too."

"Yeah…. Yeah, I was. And maybe I even began to take it serious, just a smidgen. Shows you how stupid an old fool can get. Don't help if he has another stupid old fool for a partner too."

"You're not stupid, Peeler," Ned argued. "I think you're the smartest person I ever met."

Peeler kept walking and didn't speak. Of course the boy was wrong, and he'd grow up to learn better. But his sincerity, his utter lack of guile, touched the old man deeply.

"Sometimes, when I think of that Farley woman," Ned went on, "I get scared."

"Only natural. She was kinda worryin' me too. Ain't that the darndest thing? A woman dead and buried eighty or a hundred years. But that's the beauty part of fishin', y'see."

"What?" Ned couldn't follow the apparent leap in Peeler's thinking.

"Fishin' has a way of clearin' the head," Peeler continued.

"Even one as thick as mine. What I'm sayin' is, she's dead, and it don't make pig-sense to worry about the dead."

"Then why do I feel scared sometimes—and you too?"

Peeler stopped and turned to face Ned. His eyes were warm and assuring, but there was also a look of seriousness in them that Ned had never seen before. He held a finger under the boy's chin.

"You don't have to be scared, Nedly."

That was all. They started walking again.

"You mean you don't really believe in ghosts," Ned said after a few moments. "Or anything like that?"

Peeler smiled.

"I'll tell you a funny thing about ghosts. When you're a youngster, you can't help but believe in 'em. Then you get a little older, and it seems like you can't help but not believe in 'em. And when you get to the point where you're an old fart like me, why, son of a gun if you don't start wonderin' about 'em all over again, and maybe you even want to believe."

"Like a second childhood?"

Peeler stopped again. His body began to shake and then he broke up and roared with laughter.

"You're right, Nedly, so help me, you're right."

They walked on.

"Well, then, you do believe."

"No. To be honest, I don't. There's a part of me that'd like to, I guess, a part of most folks. Then we'd know somethin' about the other side, or at least that there is an other side. But that ain't good enough, so the answer is: no."

Ned didn't say anything for a while.

"What about you?" Peeler asked.

"No.... I guess not," Ned replied, although his voice still sounded uncertain.

"Just remember what I told you. You don't have to be ascared of anything. Y'understand? There ain't no Farley woman no more."

When they got back, they found Cloudy dozing in the cool of the baithouse. They cleaned the rock bass and buried the scraps in the garden: Cloudy built a fire out in the yard and then sizzled up the small strips of fish meat with butter in a large frying pan. Ned thought it was delicious. Not a morsel was left at the end of the meal.

"I think he liked it."

"Looked that way to me."

They sat around and relaxed for an hour or so, talking about fish and fishing. Peeler and Cloudy competed with each other to see which one could come up with the most outlandish anecdote. Cloudy won. He told about a young man he had known many years ago, in the Deep South. This person used to tie a dead eel to his leg, under his pants, before he went to the ice-cream parlor every Saturday night. But on one occasion the eel wasn't quite dead and it actually started twitching and jumping in the fellow's pants as he stood around socializing in the crowded ice-cream parlor. It caused quite a stir. The man dashed out of the place and was never seen again. Ned couldn't understand why anyone would want to tie an eel to his leg in the first place, but Peeler and Cloudy laughed longest and hardest at that story.

Peeler pulled himself up out of the armchair. He turned to a small wooden cabinet, took a few things from it and put them in his canvas sack.

"Come on, let's go."

"Where?"

"Stony Point."

"I'm too tired," Ned protested.

"Me too," Cloudy said.

Peeler stared at his partner. "How can you be tired? You ain't done nothin' all day." Then, to Ned: "And as for you, I guess if I can make it on my old bones, then a young man like you will have no trouble."

"Aw, Peeler;' Ned pleaded. But he started to get to his feet. After such a good day, it seemed ungrateful not to go along with the old man.

"It's perfect out," Peeler said. "Come on now."

"Perfect here too," Cloudy groused. "Don't know how perfect it is out at Stony Point." But he fell into stride with the other two and wisecracked all the way.

When they reached the high ground at Stony Point they sat down wearily. The air was quite clear and the western horizon unusually sharp. Peeler produced a can of beer for himself, and a soda for Ned.

"Lemme have one of them beers too," Cloudy said. When he saw the astonished looks this caused, he explained: "I must be out of my mind already just to be here, so a little beer can't make it any worse."

Peeler handed him a can without comment. And they sat and waited.

"Ooh, that tastes strange," Cloudy said, studying the beer can as if it were some curious new invention. "Would you mind tellin' me just what it is I'm supposed to be lookin' for?"

"Yeah, come on, Peeler," Ned joined in. "We've been coming here enough so you should tell us."

Peeler wouldn't budge. "Just keep lookin'," he said quietly.

"At what?"

"The sunset."

"I seen enough of them," Cloudy said, but he watched dutifully. "Bet he thinks he might see a flyin' saucer someday, that's what."

The sun was easy to look at, an immense bead of blood lowering itself behind the black rim of the earth. Its movement was so slow as to be stately, but its diminishing surface grew a deeper, more explosive red. The sun's exit was powerful and humbling, the only way it could be. When there was nothing left but a curl of brilliance, Peeler jumped forward in a low crouch.

"Now, now," he whispered. "Watch it now."

The. fierce red vanished from sight, replaced instantly by a diffuse orange-yellow glow. Then it happened. An awesome shaft of rich, vibrant green shot up from the horizon, high into the sky, feathered there, lingered for a long second or two, then scattered like smoke. Gone.

They didn't move.

They could scarcely believe what they had just seen. Or even that they had, really, seen it. The green flash. They knew they had been privileged to witness one of nature's rare and most beautiful phenomena, and yet it was almost too amazing to accept. Peeler was the first to come out of the spell.

"That's it," he said, as if telling himself. Then he leapt up, thrust a fist in the air and screamed joyously as loud as he could.

Then the three of them were dancing around in a circle, all jabbering excitedly at the same time. Ned saw tears shining in Peeler's eyes, but he looked like the happiest man in the world, and he exclaimed several times: "I never thought I'd see it, I heard of it but never thought I'd see it." He rummaged around in the canvas sack and came up with a pint bottle of sour mash.

"I had a feelin' it was tonight," he said. "That's why I brung this along."

Peeler unscrewed the cap and took a long drink, his head right back, his face to the sky. Then he passed the bottle to Cloudy, who winced when the fiery whiskey hit his throat but swallowed a mouthful. Peeler was about to put the cap back on, but Ned stopped him and took the bottle. The two old men didn't speak, but their eyes were saying, Just a taste. Ned put the bottle to his lips and tilted his head back, but he only let a little liquor come into his mouth. He swallowed it quickly and handed the bottle back to Peeler. Ned's cheeks flushed, his mouth burned, his stomach felt as if molten lead had fallen into it, and the sprinkler system in his eyes was turned on. But he was grinning proudly. Then Peeler and Cloudy cheered and slapped him on the back. They set off for home.

"You better get in the middle, Mr. Tadpole," Cloudy joshed.

"In case we got to hold you up."

"Yessir," Peeler said. "I'm gonna sleep like a baby tonight."

They all did.

For the last time.

CHAPTER 25
THE VIGIL BEGINS

Linda was making a pitcher of lemonade when she heard the sound. It was a small thump, not particularly disturbing but odd. Not heavy enough to be Ned, who was in the living room, reading. That was it. He had been looking through the large *Wilderness U.S.A.* book Michael had ordered from National Geographic a while ago. The sound she heard must have been Ned tossing the volume onto the coffee table.

"Want a glass of lemonade?" she called to her son.

No answer. Linda put the pitcher in the refrigerator and went to the living room. The book was on the floor. Ned was lying on the sofa with one arm dangling over the edge. He fell asleep, Linda thought as she crossed the room to check him. He had lazed around the house all morning, kind of dopey and lifeless, and it seemed like it had taken him forever to finish one tuna sandwich at lunch. Linda thought Ned was still tired from his outing the day before. A day of relaxation and napping would do him good.

She picked up the book and set it on the table. Ned's hair was shiny and soft from being washed in the shower last night. Linda stroked it and brushed it back off his face. Wait a minute. Was his forehead a little warm, or was it just her imagination? She pressed her cheek lightly to his. Yes, he was warm. At the same time, she heard his breathing. It had the regular, autonomous rhythm that came with sleep, but there was a faint, reedy note to it. Ned's lips had formed a pout and he was breathing through his teeth. Nothing necessarily wrong with that, Linda told herself, but she wondered if it was usual for Ned. Dear God, how can you raise a child for nearly ten years and not be sure how he breathes when he's sleeping?

Linda fetched the fever strip from the medicine cabinet in the downstairs bathroom and held it to Ned's forehead. The crystals encased in plastic glowed a dull blue: ninety-nine, shading toward a hundred. A slight temperature but enough to start Linda worrying. She poured a little glass of orange juice, boosted it with vitamin drops and made Ned sit up to drink it. His eyes opened only a little.

"Ned."

"Mommy, I don't feel good."

"Where does it hurt, honey?"

"All over."

"Is it a sharp pain or more like an aching soreness?"

"Aches."

"Okay, honey, you've got a wee bit of a temperature. Nothing to worry about, but I'm going to put you in bed where you can get a proper rest. Okay?"

"Okay."

"Can you get up? Here, I'm right here. Lean on me."

He moved groggily, as if his bones had turned to rubber, and Linda had to help him up every step. At the top of the stairs, Ned stopped.

"Mommy, I want to rest in your bed."

"Sure thing."

It was actually a good idea, Linda thought. Their room was well equipped, with an air conditioner, an air purifier, an ionizer, a humidifier and an emergency bottle of oxygen, whereas Ned's room had nothing of the kind. She helped him up onto the big bed, and then went to get his pajamas. Ned was incapable of undoing a single button. He was like a floppy doll in her arms, but she finally got him changed. His limbs were clammy, she noticed. Poor Ned. He looked so tiny and frail in the middle of the bed, with the covers tucked up under his chin. Linda went downstairs to phone Michael.

"Ned's sick."

"What's the matter?"

She described what had happened.

"Sounds like he's caught a bug," Michael said.

"Do you think it could be something he ate yesterday—the fish they cooked? Maybe it was bad."

"I doubt it. Those two old-timers ought to know better than anybody when fish is okay to eat and when it isn't, which ponds are safe and which are polluted. And they ate it within a couple of hours of catching it, so it couldn't have spoiled."

"What do you think I should do?"

"Just what you have done."

"Should I call the doctor?"

"If it'll make you feel better."

Linda ignored the tone of that remark.

"Call me back if you have any news," Michael said. "Otherwise, I'll be home at the usual time. ".

"Try to come early, if you can."

"Sure. Bye."

Linda dialed Dr. Melker's number. The doctor was busy, his nurse said, and would call back. Linda made a cup of hot tea and waited. Forty minutes later the phone rang.

"Sounds like a bug," the doctor said after listening to Linda.

She gritted her teeth.

"What should I do?"

"Plenty of fluids, plenty of rest, and keep him warm. Give him some aspirin, too."

"All right. Anything else?"

"That mild temperature should stay where it is, or even drop. But call me if it should happen to go up."

"I hope I won't have to bother you again, doctor."

"That's all right, Mrs. Covington. I'll have my nurse phone you tomorrow to find out how the boy is doing."

"Oh—doctor?"

"Yes?"

Now that she had Dr. Melker on the line she had very nearly forgotten to tell him about Ned's catching and eating fish the day before.

"The symptoms you've described don't fit food poisoning," the physician said, in response to her explanation. "He'd have felt it much sooner, probably in the middle of last night. Very strong, sharp stomach pains."

"No, he hasn't had that."

"Okay. But he could have picked up a bug while he was out there yesterday. That's the most likely thing."

Linda was working up quite a hatred for that word, but what the doctor said did make her feel a little better. She crushed some aspirin in a tablespoon, stirred it into another glass of juice and took it up to Ned. He fell right back onto the pillow after finishing the drink. Linda checked his temperature again; it hadn't moved. She pulled her vanity chair next to the bed and sat there, holding Ned's hand. She was still there when Michael got home a couple of hours later.

"How is he?"

"The same."

"Nothing to it." Michael hung up his jacket and took off his necktie. "How are you?"

"Okay."

"Good. What's for supper?"

"Make yourself a couple of sandwiches or something," Linda said. "I'm going to stay here."

Michael gave her one of his don't-be-silly looks, but then decided not to argue about it. He went downstairs, made a drink and sat back to watch the evening news. Later, he found some cold chicken legs in the refrigerator to munch on.

A little before eight, Linda appeared in the living room. She looked more worried.

"His temperature is up to a hundred and one," she said.

"It is?"

At last some concern, Linda thought. "He's started moaning in his sleep, tossing and turning."

"You want to call the doctor again?"

"I already did."

"And?"

"He'll be here in a few minutes."

Michael gaped. "You're kidding. A doctor who makes house calls? I don't believe it."

Linda nodded. "We're lucky. Small town doc."

Lucky, yes, Michael thought, but there wouldn't be anything small about the bill, when it came. He tucked his shirt in and went to the bathroom to gargle a capful of mouthwash.

Dr. Melker was tall and well dressed. He had a wreath of Grecian Formula hair around a shiny bald spot that looked as if it had been hotwaxed. He might have been a middle-aged insurance executive, a lawyer or an accountant, Michael thought. He didn't look the part, but he tried to be a local family doctor in a way that had passed out of fashion years ago. Perhaps that explained the reliable but somewhat doleful air the man projected. House calls—imagine! Dr. Melker spent about fifteen minutes with Ned and directed a few questions to Linda.

"I don't think it's anything serious, but you're going to have to watch him carefully tonight. Especially the temperature. Check that every quarter of an hour or so, if you can. It's one-oh-one point six now and may rise some more. Don't be alarmed if it even reaches one-oh-three, but phone me immediately, regardless of what time it is, if the temperature edges past one-oh-four. Meanwhile, keep giving him fluids, as much as he can take, and I hope the fever will break during the night."

"Doctor, what is it?" Linda asked.

"The main thing is, it's *not* scarlet fever or rheumatic fever," the physician said. "And that's good news. As to what it is, I'd say a flu of some sort. There are so many strains going around these days, it's hard to keep up with them. With any luck, that's all it is, and he'll be over it in a day or two, when it runs its course."

"Aren't some flu strains very dangerous, though? Even—?"

Dr. Melker smiled comfortingly. He had dealt with more than a few frantic mothers over the years. "Yes, but a flu is likely to be a real threat only in special cases—old folks with no one to take care of them, for instance, or persons with complicating conditions. A healthy young fellow like your son should weather it with no trouble. If the fever hasn't broken by morning we'll put him on antibiotics right away. But it may not even come to that."

"It was good of you to come, doctor," Linda said at the door.

"Perfectly all right, Mrs. Covington."

To Michael, Dr. Melker's smile all but confirmed that a double-time fee would follow. Just to find out that their son "probably" had the flu. The price of small assurance—nothing you could do about it but pay.

Dr. Melker left and Michael went downstairs to watch television. Ned, who had never woken up during the doctor's visit, was locked again in a deep sleep. Linda settled down to keep watch over her son. She was going to read, but then, on a sudden impulse, she picked up the bedside telephone and dialed Washington. Janice answered after the first ring.

"I hope I'm interrupting something hot and heavy," Linda said.

"Not tonight." Janice laughed. "Tonight is hair-washing and-setting night. How're you? What's new?"

"Oh, nothing much. Ned is pretty sick, though."

"Oh, no, what is it?"

"Just a flu, I guess. I *hope*."

"Ah, well, he'll be over it in a day or two."

"Carry a black bag and you can get paid for saying things like that."

They talked for almost thirty minutes, and it was the easiest, closest talk they'd had in some time. Linda felt much better, and just before they finished she said: "I'm not going to get in to Washington in the near future, so you have to come out and see us here. You have to, that's all there is to it. Now, what I want to hear from you is: when?"

"Okay.... Let's see ... not next Saturday, but ... how about the one after that?"

"You're on."

Linda smiled as she hung up the telephone. I still have a friend out there, she thought.

Ned's temperature nudged one hundred and two, and held steady for the next few hours. Shortly before midnight Michael went upstairs again. Linda was on her seat by the side of the bed, leafing through a pile of old magazines.

"Any change?"

"No."

"Want me to take over?"

"No, that's okay. You sleep in Ned's room tonight."

"I'll spell you, honey, I don't mind. Get some rest."

"You have to work in the morning. Besides, I wouldn't be able to sleep."

"You can't stay up all night, Lin."

"I'll catnap on and off. Anyway, the doctor said the fever might peak and start to go down."

Michael hugged his wife. "Well…. If you get too tired and find yourself nodding off all the time, don't be afraid to wake me."

Linda nodded.

"I mean it," Michael said. "I can always take tomorrow off, if necessary."

"Michael?"

"Yes?"

"Do you think I've been silly?"

"No, of course not. You worry too much, but most mothers do. I'll tell you if it gets out of hand, have no fear."

Linda forced herself to cheer up and smile. "Was there anything good on TV tonight?"

"Mom … 'The Battle of the Las Vegas Showgirls.'"

"Lucky you." "Jiggle, jiggle."

"And now you have to sleep alone in Ned's room, poor guy."

Michael grinned.

"I hope it's just for one night. I'll live."

CHAPTER 26
INTO THE NIGHT

"We drank all the sour mash last night," Peeler said. "What'll you have—beer, or beer?"

"Maybe I shouldn't have nothin' at all."

"Bullticky. Here, have a beer."

"Oh … " Cloudy accepted the can. "Hey, you hear about what Jake Hinman went and did?"

While Ned's father was watching "The Battle of the Las Vegas Showgirls," Peeler and Cloudy were in the baithouse. Outside, the night was still. The shed was illuminated by a single 60-watt bulb, hanging on an extension cord over the zinc workbench. Aside from the voices of the two old men, the only sound was the trickle of water in the tanks.

"Bein' in town, you hear all the news before I do," Peeler said. "What's Jake done now-got hisself killed at last?"

"Nope. His wife up and left him."

"Is that all? I've only been expectin' that for twenty years or so."

"Yeah, me too. Well, now she finally went and done it."

"I mean," Peeler went on, "Nellie ain't no bundle of brains neither, but you always did see them bite marks on her. They don't call Jake old Nip 'n' Fuck for nothin'."

"Wasn't his bites she minded, way I heard it," Cloudy said.

"She got fed up with them snakes of his?"

"Right you are. I guess he says to her one day, 'Don't you go usin' the garage no more.' And she says, 'What d'you mean, my car goes in the garage. I got to use it.' And Jake says, 'No you don't, not no more. I got some new rattlers in there. Son of a gun, he'd gone off and brung back another dozen snakes—big ones—and he just let 'em go in the garage."

Peeler laughed and shook his head. "How many's he got now?"

"Must be close to a hundred. He probably lost count a long time ago. They're in the cellar, the barn, under the porch, all over the place. Anyhow, Nellie, she wouldn't take no more, so she throws her stuff in the car and drives away."

"Took her long enough."

"She wouldn't mind, but every one of them snakes is poisonous."

"Oh, yeah," Peeler agreed. "Copperheads, rattlers and water moccasins. You give Jake a garter snake, somethin' harmless, hell, that guy'll just throw it away."

"Good-bye, out the door, and gone." Cloudy sipped his beer. "Took the car and all."

"Can't blame her. He's a looney tune, like his father was."

"Yeah, he loves them snakes. Talks to 'em all the time."

"He'll be happy now," Peeler said. "Just him and his snakes, with no wife to get in the way or bother him any. I expect he'll let the snakes have the run of the house too."

"A wonder he ain't got killed."

"Oh, he's probably got so much snake bite poison in him now that it don't do no harm no more. He's immune—that's what he is."

"Yeah, I guess," Cloudy said. "He's sure been bit enough times. You know, once I run into him outside the barber shop in town, and his hand was all red and puffed up to twice its regular size. I says, 'Oh, boy,' and Jake says, 'Yep, went and got bit again.' I asked him if he didn't have to get hisself to the hospital, and he says, 'Yeah, that's why I'm goin' to get a haircut.'"

Peeler cackled. "Had time to get a haircut."

"Yeah, that's right," Cloudy continued. "I says to him, 'Man, you're gonna die.' But he just looks at his watch, real calm like, and he says, 'No, I got time.'"

"Jake don't know a whole helluva lot, but I guess he sure does know his snakes."

"That he does. I wonder what Nellie's up to."

"Long's she don't come around here," Peeler said.

"Oh, listen to that," Cloudy joked. "You're safe, don't you worry, boy. She ain't gonna leave one old no-good to go runnin' off to another."

"She was handsome once," Peeler allowed.

"Everybody was."

"How would you know?"

"I remember, I remember," Cloudy insisted. "I used to have me a red-hot mama when I was in New York City."

Peeler, who was fishing another can of beer out of the cooler, raised his eyebrows in disbelief. "You ain't even never been to New York City, what're you talkin' about."

"Sure I was. Way back when I was just outta the service."

"Oh, Lord, we need a shovel here."

"I don't care if you don't believe me," Cloudy said with a mock-hurt look on his face. "I'm tellin' you, I know. Goodness me, I ought to know."

"Off your rocker."

"Hey, I was all over the country, out west, up north, down south. I had a full youth before I got stuck here and had to settle down to the quiet life."

"The quiet life, ha." Peeler hawked a gob of spit on the dirt floor to show what he thought.

"What was you doin' back then?"

"Same as always—not a damn thing."

"You shoulda had your own boat, Peeler, you know? You knew how to be a good fisherman."

"The hell with that."

"A good woman to take care of you. Not one of them skinny ones, but a good fat mama with plenty of meat and potatoes to keep you warm and—"

"Oh, shut up, for Jesus' sake," Peeler said, but without anger. Then he added, "I had enough women without havin' too much of anyone of 'em, and I don't reckon you can do better than that."

"You mean nobody never put a ring through your nose."

"Damn right."

They drank some more and talked on. Later, about the time Michael Covington was going upstairs to sleep in his son's room, the two old men went outside for a breath of fresh air. The night sky was dark and featureless.

"Overcast," Peeler observed. "Maybe we'll get some rain."

"There's a hurricane down south. They say it's comin' up the coast, this way."

"Could be, this is the season for 'em and we ain't had one yet this year."

"But it could blowout to sea before it gets here. I hope it does that. We don't need no hurricane. The one in 'Fifty-five was bad enough."

"Real quiet out, ain't it?"

"Bugs' night off, I guess," Cloudy said.

They sat down on the front end of the old Studebaker.

"You ever know Snuffy Hagstrom?"

"Snuffy Hagstrom." Cloudy gave the name some thought. "No, I don't believe I ever did."

"Now there was a real funny bird. He used to sing all the time."

"Lotsa folks do."

"No, no," Peeler said. "I mean he used to sing *all* the time. You ask him how he was, he'd answer you by singing—I'm very well today, I wouldn't have it any other way—just like that."

"All the time?"

"All the time." Peeler nodded, smiling at the memory. "If he got mad at somebody he'd sing, son of a *bitch*. Like funeral music: da da da *dummm*."

"That's the silliest thing I ever heard," Cloudy declared.

"It's the truth, so help me. And I don't know of nobody that heard him talk normal. All he ever did was sing."

"Yeah, so what happened to him, anyway?"

"Beats me. I was gonna ask you that." Peeler looked around, and then shouted at the night sky, "Snuffy! Where are ya?"

"Ain't here," Cloudy said. "Thank God for that."

The air began to chill them, so they moved back into the baithouse to carry on drinking.

"I'm gettin' into the swing of this again," Cloudy said as he opened another can of beer.

"Might as well, now that you ain't got no red-hot mama no more," Peeler said sarcastically.

"Yeah, but this is bad for me." Cloudy drained the can, then belched. "Real bad." He reached for another.

It may have been the recollection of Snuffy Hagstrom, or simply the beer. Peeler suddenly began to sing in a loud voice.

"Won't you go home, Bill Butler, won't you go home...."

"Hey, hey, cut that out," Cloudy protested. "Anyway, I think it was Bill Bailey."

"I didn't know no Bill Bailey, but I did know Bill Butler."

"Yeah, well ... Leave him alone. These here are mighty fragile ears I got."

"Bill Butler," Peeler mused. "Talk about watery eyes. You look at him, you'd swear you was watchin' Slide Creek go by. He was never too steady on his pins, but he was okay...."

"Spare the bull and pass the brew."

"Hey!"

"What?"

"Let's make a night of it."

"I thought we was."

"Okay, good."

But as the night wore on they sank lower and lower in their seats and the talk wound down. Finally, Peeler stopped in the middle of a sentence, having lost his train of thought. He closed his eyes to concentrate, but he didn't open them again. A moment later, he was snoring. That didn't bother Cloudy, who had stretched out on the junked car seat and fallen asleep already.

At about the same time, Linda Covington dozed off as well, a copy of *Glamour* open on her lap.

CHAPTER 27
4:47 A.M.

The magazine slid off Linda's knees and landed on the throw rug at her feet. Her eyes opened briefly, then fell shut again. A few seconds later, she sat bolt upright and looked around anxiously. There was a painful crick in her neck and a sudden hammering behind her forehead. She had been asleep for a little over two hours.

Ned's face was covered with a ghostly sheen of perspiration. It had formed a line of tiny beads along his upper lip. His hair was smeared to his head and the pillowcase was dark with moisture. When Linda touched the boy's arm it felt wet, but very hot. He's burning up, she thought. Her hands trembled as she took his temperature; the plastic strip registered one hundred and three degrees exactly. That's the limit, no more please, she prayed. This has to be the fever's crisis point. It has to break here, and soon. She felt guilty for having slept, but grateful that she had not awakened any later. A line from an old song flashed through her mind—*the darkest hour is just before dawn*. This was the hour.

Linda hurried downstairs to get a fresh glass of cold juice, but when she returned she couldn't get Ned to drink. He moaned and whimpered in his troubled sleep as she tried to raise his head. She forced the rim of the glass between his lips, but he wouldn't swallow. Juice ran out of the sides and trickled down his chin. She would try again in a few minutes.

There was something else about this hour of the day. Something that was trying to worm its way into Linda's conscious mind. A fact. An item of information. No, forget it. But she couldn't push it away. It was a space-filler, one of those morbid tidbits of useless knowledge that newspapers put in to take care of a two-line gap in a column. *Doctors report that most deaths occur in the hour before dawn.*

Linda had to do something to keep from thinking. She went to the bathroom and let the faucet run until the water was good and cold. She soaked a face cloth, wrung it out and went back into the bedroom to wipe down Ned's face, neck and arms. Even after she had done that, however, her son's skin still felt very hot. The fever was raging in him. What else could she do for him? She found a bottle of rubbing alcohol and applied it to his arms and chest. Such frail little bones, she thought as her fingers worked. He seemed to be all ribs, thin and pliable. A sparrow of a child. She buttoned up his pajama top when she finished.

Something else. Linda remembered being told once that a person's blood sugar level dropped to its twenty-four-hour low at this time of the day. The human body was at its weakest. The bottom of the pit of night. The deepest sleep, from which some never came back. Blood sugar level—that had been a contributing factor in the massive asthma attack she had suffered a few years ago. Or so the doctors said, but what did they know? After all those tests they had given her, not one of a half-dozen specialists had been able to say what had caused such an unusual attack. You believe in doctors, you had faith in them because you had no choice—but sometimes it seemed that they were just guessing too. Blood sugar ... Linda tried once more to get Ned to swallow some juice. Maybe a little went down, but not much.

Perhaps Dr. Melker was wrong, for all his good intentions and his air of confidence. Perhaps it wasn't a flu or a viral infection. It could be something more serious, something the doctor had failed to recognize. Would a small-town doctor read all the journals and keep himself up-to-date? No one had known Legionnaire's Disease until all those people died a few years ago....

Linda held Ned's hand and sat watching. "I'm here, honey," she whispered softly. "I'm right here with you."

It was as if the words had triggered something. Ned's face tightened into a grimace and his hand turned sharply this way and that on the pillow. It looked as if he was trying to avoid something in his sleep. Perhaps he was running or looking away, in a bad dream. Linda leaned over, close to his ear.

"It's all right, Ned," she told him. "It's all right, I'm here. Mommy's here with you."

Ned mewed pitifully, like a frightened kitten, and his face was bathed in sweat again. Linda checked his temperature. It was creeping toward one hundred and four. She began to feel panicky. Should she call the doctor now, or wait a few minutes and take one more reading? Melker had said to phone if the temperature went over that point. Nervous, struggling to impose calm on herself, Linda decided to hold on just a little longer. She wondered if she should wake Michael before doing anything else. No, not unless it became necessary to rush Ned to the hospital. Otherwise, this was in her hands. Besides, what was happening to the temperature now might be the last outburst before the fever simmered down. If only she could believe that.

The house was so still at this early (or late) hour. To Linda the silence, freighted with expectancy, was disturbing, almost threatening. The only sound raised against it was the slight whistle of Ned's shallow breathing. Linda busied herself by wiping away the boy's sweat and giving him another rubdown with alcohol. Useless gestures perhaps, she thought, but better than doing nothing. She tried to convince herself that the most important thing was simply to be there, touching Ned, holding his hand, always in contact, whispering to him, so he would know, if only on a subconscious level, that he was not alone.

Ned was anything but alone.

Out of the tumultuous black storm in his mind, a figure was taking shape. The suggestion of a woman's body, a woman's face, darkly shrouded in a swirl of darker clouds. A pale apparition glimpsed in a confusing play of shadows. She was distant, elusive, but unmistakably there. Ned was adrift on a sea and the night was a hurricane of chaos all around him. The only fixed point was that woman, drawing closer. He had no control, but part of his mind knew what was happening. The games were over now. The cross was no help; it was nothing more than a wish, an idea of a defense when there really was no defense. Vampires and werewolves were unreal, myths people had created to give form and limits to what they feared most. Which was this woman, bearing down on him. She was real. A phantom, a lost soul, trapped between one world and another. All those years she had been unable to find peace.... But now she would, by taking Ned with her. This time, he knew, she would not be denied.

Linda stared at her son. Feelings of fear, anger and helplessness warred within her, and yet she concentrated on keeping Ned at the center of her mental focus. If sheer force of will were sufficient, she would have extinguished his fever in an instant. But all her psychic energy was funneling away, apparently into nothingness. Her instinct was to fight, but the lack of a target completely undermined her.

Ned's breathing became more labored. Linda took his temperature. How many minutes had elapsed? It didn't matter. The fever was on the verge of one hundred and four. Break, break, break, she prayed. Or even advance a little—that would at least set her on a definite course of action. But for the temperature to stay lodged at that terrible point-that was the worst thing.

Ned began to wheeze, his throat muscles contracting visibly, his breath coming in pronounced but seemingly airless spasms. At the same moment, Linda noticed the reaction in herself. It was as if her own lungs were being winched taut. The pressure of a very heavy weight was building up on her chest.

"No, not now," she said aloud, fumbling for the right inhaler. Becotide wouldn't do now, she needed the Alupent, which was a bronchial dilator and which might hold off an attack. She found it, clicked the device firmly and sucked in the mist as deeply as she could.

"Mommy ..."

Ned's eyes were screwed shut, and his face was contorted with fear and pain. His lips were turning purple-blue, set off against the rest of his face, which was incredibly white. Linda jumped to the closet and pulled out the small metal oxygen bottle.

"Don't—let—her—take—me," Ned pleaded haltingly.

His head twisted and turned, as if trying to bury itself in the pillow. It had taken considerable effort to force the words out, and even then they were as weak as bubbles, gone as soon as they surfaced.

Linda gave herself the first short blast of oxygen. It helped, and the equipment worked. She tried to hold the mask to Ned's face, but that only made him struggle more. He shook and rocked his head furiously, and then his hands flew up, swinging wildly, trying to fend the thing off.

"Ned, please, this will help you."

The boy rose up from the pillow, almost into a sitting position. His eyes opened and fixed on Linda. In the split second when their eyes met, she thought she saw pain, wonder, love and terror. The look pierced her soul. Then there was nothing to see but terror and hysteria. But before Linda could react, everything vanished from Ned's eyes. It seemed as if an invisible cord attached to his body had been violently yanked out. Ned collapsed like an unstrung marionette.

Was he breathing? Was this what it had been like the night of her big attack? Was she witnessing it from the outside now?

Linda clamped the oxygen mask over Ned's nose and mouth. She could hear the familiar, low hiss, but the boy's body wasn't moving at all. Frantic, Linda pulled the mask away and pressed her ear to his lips. Nothing.

"Michael," she called. Just one word, but her voice had gone all over the place, like a seismograph charting an earthquake.

She put the mask back over Ned's face, and with her other hand she ripped open his pajama top. She put her ear on his chest and was shocked at how cold and clammy his skin felt. She listened for something, anything, in what seemed an eternity of silence.

It was 4:47 A.M.

Ned's heart had stopped beating.

CHAPTER 28
THE DANCE OF DEATH

—Child.

Ned thought his insides had been vacuumed out of him. His body was somehow unfamiliar, and it felt as light as balsa wood. But there was neither pain nor fear.

—Child.

He was lying on the ground, which was hard, like rock, but covered with a thin layer of very fine black sand. The light, which came from no visible source, was dull red and diffuse.

Where am I?

—With me now.

She was standing over him. Ned got up and faced her. He wasn't afraid, only curious. He saw her clearly for the first time. She was truly beautiful, her features remarkably like those of his mother, but with subtle differences. She might have been his mother years before, when she had been younger and not yet married.

Who are you?

She smiled. That was all, but it was enough.

What is this place?

—The end of time.

Am I alive or dead?

—Alive with me forever.

I'm dead.

She smiled again.

No! I want to go back, let me go!

The impulse was brief and hollow. An echo from a dead past. As soon as the thought formed, Ned knew it was useless. Somewhere, in another world or another universe, his other body was lifeless on his parents' bed. And they—but as soon as sorrow approached, the woman erased it.

—Child.

She had only to communicate that single thought-word to restore Ned to a kind of airy, neutral state of being. He looked closely at her again, and her eyes held him. There was peace in them, a peace he had never known before, and now that he had experienced it he didn't want to lose it. But the woman turned and moved away.

—Come.

Ned found himself going along with her, like an object in the tow of a magnetic field. He was keeping up with her, but he could no longer see her eyes.

Where are we going?

—To the top of the mountain.

Ned looked around. They appeared to be out in the middle of a vast rocky plain. There wasn't a mountain to be seen. The entire panorama was alien, like the scorched sun-side of Mercury.

Where is the mountain?

—Come.

What will we do when we get there?

—Stay.

Are you—but he didn't get a chance to finish the thought.

—Child.

The view was deceptive, perhaps because of the strange light. Gradually, they were descending. Their path took them through a long, shallow gully and brought them to a bizarre sight. They had reached what Ned could only think of as a forest. But the trees were nothing more than bare, black trunks, ten or twelve feet tall and about a foot in diameter. The top of each tree was a fused, glassy knob, shiny, but otherwise as black as the trunks and the sand. No trees had more than two branches, and they had the same stunted, or amputated look.

The woman led Ned through the forest, not in a straight line, but by a zigzag route, as if she were following an invisible trail. They came out into a small clearing. Just ahead was a natural rock wall and a cave leading into it. The woman swept on, without hesitating. The utter darkness was spooky at first, but they moved through it easily.

The cave proved to be a short tunnel. The first thing Ned noticed when they emerged from it on the other side was the red disk on the horizon. It was not much bigger than the head of a pin.

What is that?

—The sun.

The sun?!

—Yes, what's left of it.

Then, this is the planet Earth.

—Of course.

When?

—At the end of the sun, at the end of time.

Why are we here, now?

—Child.

They came to a small city, or at least what had once been a small city. Now it was a charred ruin. The outline of streets was still clear, although blanketed with black sand and littered with debris. The buildings were mere shells, with blasted walls and beds of rubble. But new colors introduced themselves to the scene—shades of blue and green in the form of odd, coral like encrustations that rose from the ground here and there. They were anemic, spindly creations. Diseased flowers—that was all Ned could think of them as. He wondered if they were what "life" had been reduced to here, mindless chemical or crystalline growth, a kind of hideous postscript to the past. How long ago was the past?

What year is this?

The woman's laughter filled his mind. As they passed along the street, Ned kicked one of the "plants." It disintegrated in a shower of dust. The thing had felt so flimsy and insubstantial that Ned wondered how they could exist at all; a little gust of wind would blow them all away. But, he noticed, there wasn't even the slightest hint of a breeze in this place. Then he was startled to discover that he wasn't breathing at all. Of course—why should he? The dead don't breathe.

As they moved from the outskirts toward the center of the city, the old roadway narrowed, at times becoming little more than an irregular lane through mounds of rubble and the tangle of weird growth.

—Stay close.

The woman needn't have bothered. Ned couldn't leave even if he'd wanted to, and in this place he had no desire to lose the woman. What would he do here on his own, where would he go? Only the world and the life he had left behind might attract him now, but that was a million miles and a million years away—and already it was taking on the aspect of an ancient memory. It was distant, detached, and it hardly seemed to have anything to do with Ned. Were his parents mourning him? The thought seemed unreal, and the boy let it slip out of his mind.

They turned a corner and the woman stopped for the first time since they had set out on this journey. She looked at Ned and her eyes completely relaxed him.

—It will be all right.

Why? What is it?

—You will see things now, but it will be all right.

The way ahead was a narrow path down the middle of a long street crammed full of tall, thin tubes that reared up about eight feet from the ground. They were blood red and they clicked against each other, sounding like plastic. Ned saw that they were rooted to the black earth in dense clusters. As he and the woman entered the street, the tubes bristled, as if reacting to a static charge. They leaned and swayed like a field of nightmare corn in a wind. The clicking noise grew louder, but what was more disturbing was the sight of the tubes so close. Their hard casing was transparent, and they were filled with organs in a red liquid that Ned realized must be blood. These things were living creatures—Ned could see the blood pulsating now. Suddenly he looked up. At the top of each tube a fist-size head could be seen. Some of them protruded, while others lurked just inside the casing, or moved in and out. Ned felt dizzy and sick-the faces were almost human. Tiny, wizened, they looked piteously on the two people moving through their midst. Their mouths moved silently and their eyes seemed to cry out for some unknown meaning. They're trapped here forever, Ned thought, and he began to understand the terrible expression on all their faces. They were harmless, but to move among them was to be subjected to a powerful emotional and psychic assault. Ned wanted to shut his eyes and block his ears, but something in him rejected that idea. It would be too much like walking away from a paralyzed infant in need of help. But what could Ned do for these tube creatures with the haunting faces? Nothing.

Who—what—

—Dead.

They're not dead. Look at them.

—Still, they are dead.

What will happen? Do they just stay like this?

—This is their place.

But why?

—Child.

The woman soothed his mind and they walked on, but after a while the clicking mounted again. Ned tried to keep his eyes on the woman alone, but it was impossible to ignore the virtual wall of pumping blood and tightly packed organs that surrounded them. There was no end in sight. It seemed to Ned that they must have passed tens of thousands or even hundreds of thousands of the wretched things. Finally, he was numb to their plight. They were a nuisance, an irritation that wouldn't go away. For a moment Ned wished he had an ax, so that he could chop them all down. The woman, knowing his thoughts, turned and stared at him, but this time there was no love or comfort in her eyes. Ned suddenly felt ashamed and confused.

—You still have that in you.

Ned remembered chopping down the scarecrow; perhaps that had been wrong. He remembered flinging chunks of plaster into the spider webs at the spa, when perhaps he should have left them alone. Small actions, arising out of small impulses—or were they? What, if anything, was the woman trying to make him see?

—You.

Now she let the boy feel the cold touch of fear. The thought came to Ned that he had been brought here to be rooted in place and transformed into one of these tube creatures. It was the fate in store for everyone after death, and he was no different. His skin and his muscles would be peeled away, his arms and legs severed, and he would be poured into a plaster tube and anchored there. His head would shrink to a mockery of itself. He would be just one more in the meaningless, forgotten throng, a prospect that was as humbling as it was terrifying.

—Come.

Somewhat relieved, Ned followed the woman. He couldn't imagine anything worse than to be one of those tube creatures. Were they really, or had they once been, people? Immobile in a wasteland, unable even to speak. It would be better to be dead—but then Ned remembered that this was death: in this place you couldn't die again. Welcome to eternity.

After what seemed like hours of walking, they emerged on a large square, bordered by more of the shattered remains of old buildings. They continued on, across the open ground. Maybe there had been a park here once, Ned thought. Now it was just a barren expanse of black sand, petrified stumps and a few of those strange "plants." They had not gone far when a band of animals appeared thirty yards away. It was a pack of dogs, Ned saw, as they drew closer. The woman stopped, and the boy stayed near her. The dogs numbered about twenty, and they approached cautiously. They moved in single file and skirted around the two people. Now Ned could see that these were not ordinary dogs. His mouth opened in astonishment. These beasts, too, had faces that were almost human. The canine snout was absent. They walked on four legs and were covered with hair, but that didn't obscure the uncanny similarity of features, particularly the intelligence in their eyes. The most obvious and menacing part of their makeup was the single fang or saber tooth that curled down from the center of the upper jaw. It must be four or five inches long, Ned thought.

The procession passed by. Ned turned to watch the grotesque animals, almost certain that he had just seen the results of another monstrous human transformation. The dogs went straight to the tube creatures, and most of them disappeared into the mass. But at least one dog stayed in sight at the outer edge. This animal walked back and forth, as if studying the scene. Then, apparently having chosen, it punctured one tube creature with its prominent fang and stood rigidly, attached. It was revolting to see, but Ned couldn't look away.

They eat them?

—No, merely drink of them.

Through that tooth?

—It is their way.

Do they kill the tube creatures?

The question was absurd, as the woman's laugh told Ned. There had to be other bands of dogs that came here to drink, perhaps thousands of them. What was the point of it, here, where nothing could die? It is their way, the woman had said. It was probably a ritual, and one that could exist and continue in this place only as a final irrelevancy. The original point of the act, survival, now rendered pointless by its inevitability.

—Come.

Are they, or were they, human beings?

—Do you know them?

Ned wasn't sure if the woman was making fun of him or not. He thought he had recognized something in both the dogs and the tubes, but perhaps he had been wrong. No, in each case his reaction had been strong and immediate. They were related to him, in some way. It was a terrifying thought, and this time the woman did nothing to banish it from Ned's mind. Those dogs, he reflected, were like a combination of the werewolf and the vampire. Both human and not human.

Ned tried to stop, but he couldn't. In spite of himself, he kept pace with the woman. But, like someone who has only just fully awakened, his mind was beginning to make connections. A subtle change had come over the aura between the two of them. The woman had made him feel fear once. The fact that she had broken her promise cracked the illusion of her benevolence. It had taken Ned a while to realize this: that he was not her equal on this new plane of existence, that he was being led, taken, protected and preserved. But for what? He could no longer avoid wondering what he would be brought to at the end of the journey. The top of the mountain—but why? What awaited him there? A demonic laboratory, where he would be made over into a tube creature or a vampire dog—or something worse? The fact that he could even think this way now told him something else. The woman was giving him back his mind, bit by bit. Why—so that nothing of his destiny would be lost on him?

What will happen to me?

—You will be with me.

Be what?

—What you are.

What am I?

—Come.

Before, the word had seemed like an invitation, a fond beckoning of one mind to another, but now it was a quiet order, which Ned could not disobey. Helplessness, which he had known so many times while being haunted or stalked in the other world, came back to nest in him again. One more fateful connection.

Ned looked around and was surprised to find that they had left the city. It might not have been a city after all, he thought. Just ruins and old roadbeds. If he had to guess, he would say they had been walking for the better part of a day. But time meant nothing here. The light scarcely changed at all and the sun remained a dying ember, always roughly the same distance from the horizon. Only the twists and turns in their route moved the tiny red disk slightly.

Eventually, they came up onto a small plateau, and the woman promptly made Ned look back. The view was devastating. As far as he could see, the earth was strewn with the relics of catastrophe. It's beyond deciphering, Ned thought. If a team of scientists from another planet landed here, they would be unable to reconstruct anything from this. It's too far gone, all lost. Then another thought hit him and he scanned the sky above. No stars, nothing. Nothing but the ghost of the sun.

Was it war, or a nova ... ?

The woman laughed again, this time as if to say, Nothing so paltry. It made Ned think of something she had said earlier. The end of time. How nonchalantly he had accepted those words at first. Now he understood that they might well be the last words, after which no others were necessary. Was this what death, one human death, amounted to—the end of the universe? Does it happen all the time, with each human death, the universe dying billions of times? Ned was losing himself in a maze of implications and possibilities. The woman rescued him.

—Child.

He turned around. And saw the mountain.

They were still some distance from it, but the mountain dominated the landscape, so much so that Ned couldn't understand how he had failed to notice it sooner. It was huge, awesome, impossible to overlook.

The weak red sunlight must play tricks on the eyes, and disguise things, he decided. The mountain towered above the earth, and yet it was unlike any mountain Ned had ever seen. There were no sharp planes, jagged ridges of rocky faces. It looked more like an enormous matte-black lump, a mound that had grown to extraordinary dimensions over a period of time that defied reckoning. Geography no longer applied here. Nothing like this mountain had existed in that part of the country where Ned had once lived, and probably not on the entire planet. But that was the other world, a time and a place that had ceased to be.

The woman led the boy across the stark plateau toward the mountain. It rose out of sight, blotting out most of the horizon ahead of them, its upper reaches disappearing into the blackness of sky and space. It seemed appropriate, in a macabre fashion, that this mountain should be their destination. To Ned it could be nothing but the end of the line. It looked like an accumulation of all the evil and death that had ever been experienced, gathered in one place, given mass and substance. Next to it, Everest would be a mere pimple.

Ned took slight comfort from the fact that they would have a very long climb before they reached the top. He thought about trying to escape. Would the woman let him? Hardly. Was there any way in which he might foil her? Unlikely. Even as he considered this, he was trailing along beside her, one step back, as if he were on an invisible leash. Anyhow, what would he do, where would he go, if he did manage to flee? This world was the place you came out in when you broke through the bottom of the final nightmare, death. There was no "going on" from here. His only company, if they could be called that, would be vampire dogs and forests of tube creatures. For the first time, Ned confronted the feeling of being alone, utterly alone in the universe, and without hope. It was a mind-stunning, heart-withering reality, and with it came a sudden desire as shocking as it was new to him. He wanted to die. He was already dead, but death was proving to be not what he had expected. Some kids he had known thought you went to heaven or hell, or to a pit-stop called purgatory, or some place that was limbo. Ned had never been taught one thing or another, and so death, to him, had always been simply the end of life. He had never given it much thought. Now he longed for death, but not this death. He wanted the sweet sleep of oblivion, an endless, dreamless peace, the obliteration of consciousness on every level. Not even heaven or any other world, but only to be reduced to scattered, empty atoms. This is how people feel when they decide to kill themselves, Ned realized. But he knew, too, that he didn't have the option of suicide. He had no options at all. That was why the woman could let him think like this. He could change nothing.

Why does it have to be this way?

—This is the way.

But why?

—There is no other way.

Why are you letting me feel fear and pain? You said I would never know them again.

—They are echoes dying within you, and soon they will completely disappear. No fear or pain will come to you from outside.

And when we get to the top of the mountain—not even then?

—Child.

The incantation worked again, but Ned was aware of the woman's evasion. She went to the brink with her assurances, but she always stopped short of giving him anything explicit to hold onto. A loophole, a loose end—something was being left unsaid. Ned was in a cruel situation. The woman was his only hope, she was all he had in this place. He wanted to trust her, because he had no alternative. But he couldn't; not yet, not wholeheartedly. Maybe that trust would be found at the top of the mountain. And maybe I'll find cartoon land there, too, he thought in a spasm of self-contempt.

The ground began to slope gradually upward. They were in the foothills, if you could call them that. The ascent had started. Ned glanced up once, but the mountain was so alarmingly close and massive that he quickly looked down again. There was a small change in the way the ground felt to his feet, he noticed. The same black sand was everywhere, but up to this point it had been like a gritty dust on a hard surface. Now there was a barely perceptible give to the earth's crust with each step the boy took. It was like walking on heavy, thick egg cartons that had almost but not thoroughly hardened into rock.

The woman stopped, and Ned with her. She turned her eyes to him and the force of her gaze touched him deeply, as if she were trying to transfer some of her strength to him. It was not love, nor even warmth, but a kind of willed concern that fed his mental stamina. At the same time as he was being given this apparent boost, he could feel the leash tighten and pull him a little closer to the woman.

—It will be all right.

What will?

The woman looked ahead and pointed.

Then Ned saw it.

Or rather, them.

People. Crowds of people, everywhere around the bottom of the mountain. There must be millions of them, he thought dizzily as his eyes swept the scene. Tens of millions. Where had they come from, who were they, what were they doing here? Well, they could ask him the same questions. The sight was so startling Ned could accept it only in terms of manic humor. This had to be the biggest mob in history, the longest waiting line, the largest convention.... The woman kept her word: in spite of their incalculable numbers, these people didn't frighten Ned. It went far beyond that. They constituted a kind of crushing mental blow that sent his mind reeling numbly. Only a little while ago he had considered himself utterly alone, singled out for his own special fate—and with that thought he had unwittingly conferred on himself a tacit but spurious importance. Now, this vast horde of human beings showed up the lie. Their mere presence exploded any notion of uniqueness. He was alone—with the rest of mankind—at the mountain of common destiny.

As the woman led him toward the crowd, and then into it, Ned couldn't keep himself from gawking. The people were naked and hairless, and their skin was like burnished garnet. They ignored the woman and boy. Their eyes were open but apparently unseeing, as if they could focus only on some inner preoccupation. They were silent, and this absence of a single voice in an ocean of people was perhaps the most chilling aspect of the scene.

But as he looked closer, Ned saw something else. The people stood around in groups made up of from two or three to a dozen or more individuals. They moved, but their movements were short and halting, without purpose. They were like odd human sculptures; still in the process of turning rigid. Two men tottered nearby, shifting slightly on their feet—that was when Ned saw it. The two men were connected—fused together along the length of their right arms. It took a few seconds to sink in, but then Ned realized it was true of everyone. The individuals in each group seemed to be bonded to one another. Three women were joined together at the back of their heads. A larger group consisted of men and women whose arms were a chain of interlocking loops. Some were cemented chest to chest, facing each other blindly. They all struggled to move by themselves, as if they had no understanding of their true situation. Thus, they constantly bumped, and nudged and stumbled against each other, often falling to the ground, only to rise awkwardly and resume their mindless ritual efforts. Ned passed within a foot or two of some of these groups, and he could see clearly that no cement or glue or stitching held them to each other; every join was flesh to flesh, seamless and unbroken, as if they had simply grown that way. From the beginning.

Again the question presented itself: What were all these people doing here? But this time Ned wasn't eager to hear the answer. He had a feeling that he already knew it. They were here because they were here because they were here ... and this is the way it is, forever. Everything is forever here, he thought gravely. What a contrast with the world he had left behind, where "forever" carried little weight. The harder Ned tried to come to terms with the word, the more it defeated him. It was no longer a mere abstraction, it was a bruising reality in the form of all these doomed souls acting out their meaningless pantomime. Ned couldn't accept it, but neither could he avoid it. Then a terrible thought crossed his mind.

Are my parents here, somewhere?

—Child.

Tell me!

—Child, be still.

The mental leash tightened. Ned's anxiety was diffused temporarily, but not eradicated. The woman seemed to be moving faster now, dragging Ned along with her. They threaded their way through the massive tangle of people with surprising ease. The boy's eyes were open, but he was unable to focus clearly. Tens of thousands of bodies and blank faces flew past, a hellish tapestry unraveling at a frantic pace. Dimly, Ned perceived that he was about to become one more drop in the anonymous ocean. He would go blind, the woman would abandon him and, sooner or later, his body would graft onto another and ... forget the rest. As long as I don't know, Ned prayed. Please don't let me know. It all became a blur.

Finally, his vision cleared. They were on the mountain. It loomed over them like a dark moon about to fall onto the Earth. The woman was watching Ned, but now he avoided her eyes. He felt weak, and he was depressed at having been hauled back into a state of self-awareness. He looked down and away from the woman, the mountain. The view below was no better. Ned saw the people again, and they truly were an ocean, stretching to the horizon on all sides and probably far beyond sight. Their numbers no longer amazed him, nor did the fact that he had passed through that mass of bodies. Nothing amazed him anymore. You see, he told himself, your brain is shutting down. The last stage in the process. Well, maybe that was all right too. It will be all right, that's what the woman was always saying, and maybe she was speaking the truth. Stranger things have happened.

It suddenly came back to Ned in a flash of pain: his parents. Were they down there, in that gigantic collection of twitching statues? He couldn't bear the thought, and as the pain dug deeper into him he knew with certainty that he had to go back and take his place, to be with them. If that was their fate, it would be his as well. But the woman held him where he was until his pain turned into anger.

—You did that to yourself.

Why don't you answer me?

—It isn't necessary, when you answer yourself.

Then my mother and father are down there?

—Still the wrong question.

It's not wrong as far as I'm concerned.

—But it is. Exactly.

I want you to—

—Come.

The woman turned and resumed her ascent. Ned went with her because he had no choice. Her power held him as surely as the stringer had held those rock bass flopping against his leg the day he and Peeler had walked back from Baxley Mill Pond. The irony didn't escape him. The rock bass at least had no idea of what was happening to them, since they don't have ideas at all. But Ned could think, and it was a curse to him now.

The woman. He hated her. He—

She spun around and her eyes seized Ned. The woman radiated warmth and affection. Her beauty was dazzling. Ned felt as if he were dissolving in her love, and he knew that he loved her. He always had, he always would. Even in this place the end would be perfect and happy, because they would be together. Ned rushed to bury himself in her embrace.

In that instant her smile changed. It was the barest of movements, but with it she turned off the illusion. Ned stopped short, stunned with cold. Her smile was not quite a sneer, but it said: "You see what I've just done to you?" Ned felt betrayed and manipulated, but more than that he was ashamed of himself. What a puny fool he was that she could toy with him so easily. She had rubbed his nose in hopelessness.

They continued on their way. Lesson over, Ned thought. And lesson it was, for he had begun to realize that there was something to be learned from that little episode. She knew his thoughts. She had always known his thoughts, and she was undoubtedly taking them in right now. The mistake was to let thoughts form in the first place. He would have to rely on whatever was to be found below the surface of his mind. He would have to cultivate it and get it ready, but he would also have to keep it down there, unspoken, unthought, until the time was right. And at once Ned knew what it would be, but he quickly pushed it back into his subconscious before it could take shape. She can't reach that far—can she?

Don't keep the mountain waiting, don't keep the mountain waiting, he thought like a moron singing some inane anthem.

The woman yanked the leash sharply, and hooks of pain caught in his mind. Now, that's pain that comes from the outside, he thought loudly. The woman didn't respond, but Ned didn't expect her to. His wince worked itself into a determined smile.

Ned looked around. They were so high on the mountainside that it was no longer possible to see the people far below. The ocean of burnished skin and the desert of black sand had merged into a featureless expanse that disappeared without the benefit of a horizon. It was as if only that speck of sun and this mountain existed in space. The rest of the planet might as well have fallen away, Ned thought. No going back; it wouldn't be there.

Don't keep the mountain waiting....

He was learning how to keep his mind active, preoccupied. Thoughts were like ice skaters on a frozen pond. You had to keep them busy doing figure eights and toe stands while the real work went on below the ice.

The group was still changing, Ned observed. Slowly, but unmistakably. At this altitude the black sand had pretty much vanished. The mountainside was dark and bare. It looked like solid rock, but it gave slightly underfoot, with that feeling of matted egg cartons. In places it was almost springy. It amused Ned to think that the mountain might actually be hollow, a colossal papier-mâché prop. He and the woman would be ants on a stage set for space giants. Was the curtain up or down?

Then Ned noticed lines in the ground. There were only a few at first, but they increased steadily. The lines were both straight and curved, mostly short, and they seemed to be scattered naturally at random. A little further along, Ned saw that the whole face of the mountain was tattooed with these curious lines. There was something familiar about them. Ned wondered if he had seen them in another place, a long time ago.

A sudden impulse made him look up. There it was. The top of the mountain.

The ground was softer. It seemed to be composed of some kind of caked dust and broken shells. The lines were lost now, but they had pointed to this. Ned wanted to ignore it, but part of his brain told him it was important. He tried to think, to connect what he was seeing to something in his memory. The woman was tugging, but she couldn't distract him. The realization hit him, and it was a tidal wave of horror. For the first time, he stopped the woman. He dug his hands into the ground and then held them up.

These are bones! his mind screamed.

—Come.

Bones and skulls! This whole mountain is a burial mound.

—Come now.

The woman pulled Ned along as if he were a troublesome puppy, but she didn't bother to shut him up. He could babble all he wanted now. They were at the top of the mountain.

Everyone who ever lived must be here, billions and billions of them. Piled up to make—a mountain.

Steps carved into the mountaintop provided the only access to the peak itself, which was a flat, circular area. Ned was snatched up onto it and let loose. The woman stood by the top step, watching him. Now that he was here, he looked around. He walked the circumference. The drop, at every point, was sheer. How many miles below was the rest of the planet? Fifty, perhaps. Or none, for the planet was no longer there. Just the top of the mountain of death, and the void. It doesn't matter, Ned thought, and that's why there are no answers. He came back to the woman.

Her eyes burned, but with a cold, lifeless fire. The smile on her face belonged to her alone; it shared nothing with Ned. She still looked beautiful—in fact, more beautiful by far than she had at any time before this moment. Ned was almost tempted to give up and throw himself into her arms, but he knew it would be a mistake. And useless. Forget all that eternal love and peace stuff. It was time to stop looking for mirages.

Are you Mrs. Farley?

The woman laughed. Then she kicked a skull with her foot.

—That is Mrs. Farley.

She laughed again and kicked another skull.

—Or that is. Pick anyone you like and that is Mrs. Farley.

The woman's amused laughter echoed unpleasantly in Ned's mind. He got down on his knees before her and looked at the ground. He brushed the dust and bones with the palm of his hand, as if he were choosing a place for himself. But something was pushing in his mind, trying to surface and break out. Ned stared at the ground, waiting for it to come. Please. Anything. The woman caught that and laughed.

Then, without looking, Ned knew she was bending down, reaching for him. His fingers traced two bones in the dust. They were lying at a certain angle to each other. Ned recognized it. He picked up one of the bones and turned to meet the woman.

Are you Death?

—Your very own.

Remember my scarecrow?

The bone had a sharp, jagged end where it had broken. Ned rammed it into the woman, driving the full length of it up under her ribs toward her heart. No blood. Ned backed off several steps. The woman's eyes were shut, but she didn't move. Nothing happened. Can you kill Death? Ned didn't think so, but the bones had reminded him of the scarecrow and part of his brain had roared the order to stab the woman....

Her eyelids opened, revealing empty sockets. Her mouth opened in a wide, cavernous smile. She started walking towards Ned, and as she came closer, spiders crawled out of her dark eye sockets. More of them poured out of her mouth. They streamed over her face and down the front of her robe. Hundreds of spiders gushed out of her, and still the woman came, smiling. Her laughter boomed deafeningly.

Ned was incapable of thinking anymore. He turned and ran as fast as he could. When he reached the edge he didn't stop, but hurled himself off the peak and into the void. He tumbled through space, terrified of only one thing: that when he got to the bottom, she would be it.

The mountain was still there. Ned plummeted past what looked like an endless wall of grinning human skulls—it snaked nightmarishly around him but after a while it didn't bother him. Falling is a kind of peace in itself, and it can be so exquisite that great velocity is transformed into a long, gentle glide. The best thing is to have no place to land and to keep falling. Ned thought he could stay this way forever. That word again. Maybe it was valid at last. Maybe he was finally becoming that single free atom he wanted to be, falling aimlessly through the universe.

But now Ned saw something. He was flying toward a point of light. It was streaking up to meet him. When he recognized it, he knew he was about to die. It made him think again of something the woman had said. The phantom in his room, the woman—they were one and the same. Who are you? Ned had asked. *You*, had been the answer. Death is the phantom you meet up with, and it looks like you.

So did the point of light Ned flew into.

CHAPTER 29
4:50 A.M.

No! You can't have him!

Linda put her mouth over Ned's, pinching his nose at the same time, and tried to force her breath into him. His teeth were locked shut. There was no take.

She clutched her hands together and slammed them down on his chest as hard as she dared. She did it again, half expecting to hear her son's bones crack. Broken bones didn't matter. Nothing mattered anymore but the life of her child. If it were possible, she would have tom open his chest, seized his heart and squeezed the life back into it.

Take me instead. Oh, please....

Linda put the oxygen mask back on Ned's face, hooking the loops behind his ears. She turned the valve on full and then went back to pounding his chest desperately. Was it too late? How much time was there—minutes, seconds—before he was beyond reach? The ghastly details of death howled in her mind. First, irreversible brain damage would set in. Then the brain would liquefy.

Dear God, let him live!

How had it happened? In a swift, devastating moment, less than the span of a single day, everything she had dreaded for years had come to pass. In a way, her husband had been right. All that worrying had been silly, irrelevant. For now that *it* was on her, and Ned, nothing she could do had any significance. Just two more lives ground to bits in the blind, inexorable march of nature. Coming from nowhere, going nowhere, two infinitesimal blips on the face of darkness. There, then gone.

Take me with him.

Linda rocked on her feet. She was dizzy and the room was a blur drifting around her. Only the bed was still, like a raft inexplicably anchored in a turbulent sea. She climbed onto it and sat by Ned. Her breath rattled alarmingly, and the germ of a new desire began to grow within her. The desire to surrender now, to have it all end.

Her arms continued to rise and fall mechanically, her double fist making a dull splatting sound when it hit Ned's chest. But her strength was running out fast. There was no force left in her efforts. How could she bear to go on living if she failed Ned? She had to die, for him or with him. Michael would survive, but not Linda. She knew herself too well. This was it.

NO! Linda screamed. She fell forward onto Ned, her body covering him like a blanket. Black spots appeared, quickly filling her vision.

Take me....

It took Michael a few moments to realize that he was sitting up. The bed felt strange, and the pattern of darkness around him was unfamiliar. Then he remembered: he was sleeping in Ned's room. Why was he awake? He thought he had heard someone call out, but the recollection of it was dim and distant, like the wing light of an airplane flying away into the night. Maybe he had heard something, maybe not.

Linda. Ned. Better check.

He moved, and winced. Michael's mouth was sticky and foul, his head felt like a wad of steel wool. Christ, I only had a couple of drinks, he thought. I was fine when I went to bed. Scotch, that was it. Scotch always did this to him, and yet he persisted in drinking the stuff. Not for the first time, Michael vowed to switch to white liquor. Vodka, that's the ticket.

What was he doing? Oh, yeah. He stood up, groped his way to the door and shuffled down the hallway toward the patch of illumination that spilled from the master bedroom. Something came back to him. "Your lovecraft ebbing," or something like that. It was the punch line to one of Bill Kinloch's punishing jokes. But Michael couldn't remember what came before it.

The scene was weird. A magazine on the floor. Linda sprawled on the bed beside Ned, one arm flung across the boy protectively. Ned's pajama shirt was open and there were bruises on his body. What the hell had gone on here? Linda's emergency bottle of oxygen was on the bed too, its mask hissing uselessly at the side of Ned's face. Michael was puzzled but not immediately worried, because the most curious aspect of this curious tableau was that his wife and son appeared to be sleeping peacefully. Well, Ned did look pale. Michael put the back of his hand to the boy's forehead. The temperature was down, no doubt about it. Ned looked very still, though.... Too still? Michael took Ned's hand and tried to find a pulse. Come on. It has to be here somewhere. Was Ned breathing? Just for a second, Michael wasn't sure. But then Ned jumped slightly in bed and sighed deeply. The digital clock-radio on the night table read 4:50 and blinked to 4:51.

Michael shut the valve on the oxygen; that stuff costs money. Wife okay, son okay. It was almost dawn. So, what's it all about, Alfie? He would ask Linda in the morning—later. There would be plenty of time to talk—later. Right now, Michael asked himself again: Why am I awake? He straightened out the sheet and pulled it up to cover Linda and Ned. Gently, he removed the oxygen mask and bottle, setting them down on the floor by the bed.

There was enough room if he slept on the side, with Ned in the middle and Linda on the other side. Your regular family sandwich. Michael turned off the lamp and slipped into bed. It occurred to him that the alarm probably wasn't set, but he couldn't be bothered to do anything about it. If he was late, he was late; so what. He had to slide Ned over a few inches. The boy stirred briefly in his sleep, exhaling three whispery words.

"Dad—the moon...."

Michael smiled. Not tonight, son.

SUMMER'S END

Ned borrowed his mother's gardening gloves without telling her. He put them on and sat down at his desk. Before him was an ordinary tablet of ruled paper, the kind you could buy in thousands of stores across the country. He tore off a sheet from the middle of the pad. Ned didn't really believe they would check for fingerprints, but maybe they would have nothing better to do. Maybe they would decide to make a big case out of this. Why take a chance? He had to do it right: no traces, no clues. He picked up a number 2 pencil and began to print large block letters.

> **Dear Sir**
> **A few days ago I was in the old Lynnhaven spa on**
> **the hill. There is a body of a dead person in one of the**
> **rooms there. I thought somebody should know about**
> **it and take care of it. Whoever it was must have died a**
> **long time ago because it is just a skeleton really.**
> **Somebody Who Saw It**

Ned stared at the message for a few moments, decided it was all right and folded the piece of paper. He took the envelope, which he had extracted from the packet on his parents' writing desk downstairs, and addressed it to the Police Department, Lynnhaven. Ned knew they might think it was just a prank, but he thought they would probably go to the spa and take a look anyhow. A dead body is too serious to ignore. Besides the problem had nagged Ned ever since the day he had been at the spa. He couldn't come up with a better idea than this anonymous note. He put the message in the envelope and sealed it.

This was the first time he was being let out of the house since he had been sick. For five whole days he had felt fine, but he had been restricted to either his bed or the living-room sofa. His mother and father had insisted. They weren't taking any chances and they had to be convinced that Ned was fully recovered. Ned didn't like it, but he guessed he could understand it. He knew he had been sick — really sick. He couldn't remember much about it. There was a day missing from his life.

His parents unintentionally told him how serious it had been. At some point during the illness, he woke up in the big bed and heard them talking. They obviously thought he was asleep and it sounded like they were standing just outside the bedroom door, in the hallway. Their voices were hushed, but it was clear to Ned that they were having more than just a casual conversation. He didn't catch all of it, but he heard enough.

His mother kept saying his heart had stopped! It was astounding, and yet Ned believed it because she said it without the slightest hint of doubt. His father thought she had imagined it or else had simply not noticed Ned's pulse in her excitement. He told her she had probably been on the verge of hysteria and wouldn't have heard a bomb go off. Ned could tell his father was losing this argument, and he smiled when they dropped it, agreeing not to mention a word of it to the boy.

It was amusing and fascinating. Ned had no feeling that they were talking about him. Strangely, it was as if they were discussing some other person. He was the star, but he had missed the whole show! To think that his heart had stopped dead. And he was still here, still alive. It was a little scary, but it also gave him an undefined feeling of accomplishment—he knew he had done something without knowing what it was.

They also spoke of how his mother had punched his chest in an effort to revive his heart, and then she had "blacked out." Ned had been sore for a couple of days and he had seen the bruises on his body, but he couldn't remember the incident. His mother beating him. To save his life. She had, too. Ned could think of no other way to explain the fact that he was still alive. The other part, however, was not so good. He didn't like to hear of his mother blacking out. He couldn't bear the thought of anything bad happening to her.

Ned's father was cool. He wanted to play it all down. He told Ned's mother that the boy had suffered a hard case of summer flu and that she had overreacted "quite naturally." When Ned's fever was at its worst, she had, according to her husband, brought a "mini-attack" on herself. What it amounted to, as far as he was concerned, was a long, rough night, a nasty experience, but not the matter of life and death she thought it was. Ned had an inkling of something then: that it was important in some way for each of his parents to have their own versions of what had happened, with neither seriously challenging or being challenged by the other.

Dr. Melker came to visit Ned again, the day after the big night. He was not wonderful, but okay. The way his hair was arranged around the bald spot on the top of his head reminded Ned of how the circular garden looked from the top of the wall. He half expected to see steam rise up from the physician's scalp. Dr. Melker went through his routine of talking, asking, poking and listening. Then he patted the boy on the head, said something and went downstairs to confer with Ned's mother and father. Then followed five boring days of "recuperation."

Ned wondered about the missing day. What had happened to him? Where had he gone? Was he just sick? Or had the phantom come to take him, plunging icy hands into his heart, freezing the life in him until, somehow, perhaps through his mother's efforts, the spell was shattered? He would have to live with the riddle. Without knowing the answer, he knew he had it within him, buried deep in his own memory. And he was sure there was more to it than just a short history of the life cycle of the twenty-four-hour flu. Much more. Perhaps someday it would begin to surface, a little at a time. Or perhaps it never would.

But one thing was certain: the fear was gone. It wasn't a question of ignoring it or burying it. The fear was gone, and that's all there was to it. At some point during the illness, it had fallen away like dead skin. Ned didn't disbelieve in the phantom; if anything, he believed now more than ever. But there was also a fresh feeling within him. It was as if he had crossed a threshold and reached a point where he could know for sure that he was safe, that he could protect himself. The phantom was still there, right behind him—but in some way he knew the phantom now, and the compelling urge to look back over his shoulder had ceased to exist. The way from here was forward.

The sounds, the spa, the illness—everything he had gone through was now past experience. It was over and done with. It was a part of him, something he had absorbed in the same way that the body takes certain elements from the food that passes through it. Ned would think about it again, and often, his sense of wonder undiminished. But a kind of distance was setting in, bringing with it a crucial redefinition. The participant was becoming the spectator, the situation was becoming the memory, closed and intact. Ned knew it only as a feeling, unaware that it would inform his being for the rest of his life.

Ned slipped the envelope into his shirt pocket and then he put on a light sweater. He put his mother's gloves back where they belonged.

Linda told him not to be out too long, and to be sure to come straight home if he should begin to feel the least bit tired. She stood at the front door and watched her son walk down the street until he was out of sight. He will be all right, she told herself. Fear was the daily goblin, love the daily miracle.

It was great to be outdoors!

Summer's heat was spent. The air had a fine edge to it now and the breeze was spry enough to herald autumn. The first week of September. Time to have another go at the deeper waters.

It wasn't a long walk from his house to the post office in the center of town. Ned covered the distance in a few minutes. He was careful to touch the envelope only on its thin edges, not the flat sides. He dropped it in the LOCAL slot without bothering to put a stamp on it. As soon as he turned to walk away, he had second thoughts. Had anybody seen him, anybody who would remember the unstamped envelope and the youngster with the red sweater? Ned didn't want the police to come looking for him. As far as he knew, he hadn't done anything wrong (was there a law against anonymous letters?), but his parents would be upset. Well, it was too late now. He had done it. The letter was gone. He told himself again that he had done the right thing. It would have bothered him more to remain silent about that lonely corpse in the spa.

As Ned was going along Polidori Street, he stopped suddenly. He saw Cloudy up ahead some distance and on the other side of the street. He was walking in the same direction as Ned, and the boy hurried to catch up. Ned broke into a trot, keeping the black man in view while at the same time watching for a gap in traffic so he could get across the road. Ned knew that Cloudy had a room at the Capitol Hotel, which was somewhere around here, but he had never seen it, for he seldom had any reason to be in this part of town.

Cloudy turned down a side street and disappeared. Lost him, Ned thought. It didn't matter; they'd probably see each other at the baithouse later. But he jogged on, crossed the street and reached the corner where he had last seen Cloudy. Ned was curious to get a glimpse of this other side of his friend's life.

The street was short and narrow. Ned had almost walked past the place before he noticed the sign, a darkly tarnished metal plate that identified the Capitol Hotel. It looked more like a house than a hotel, and it was as run-down and weather-beaten as Ned might have expected if he had ever given it any thought.

He went through the front door, into a hallway. A young man with a blemished face and oil on his hair sat at a small desk. He wore a T-shirt that said SWORN TO FUN LOYAL TO NONE.

"Excuse me. I'd like to see Cloudy."

The man stared at Ned.

"What?"

"I'd like to see Cloudy."

The man worked his stare again, but then it got to be too much trouble. It was wasted on a kid, anyway. Come to think of it, what's a white kid doing visiting an old coon? Come to think of it, who gives a shit? He pointed.

"Down the end, down the stairs, down the end, last door."

Ned found the stairs at the back of the hallway. The steps were bare cement, winding down to the low cellar passageway lit by a fluorescent bulb. He passed three doors. The fourth was the last. Ned knocked.

"Yeah?"

It was Cloudy's voice. Ned opened the door and stepped into a small, plain room. The floor was covered with old linoleum and the only items of furniture were a painted bureau, an armchair and a camp bed. Cloudy was sitting on the bed, sorting through a pile of clothes. He wore rumpled, baggy white pants and a loose white jacket. He must do some work here, at least part-time, Ned realized. It felt very strange to be there and to see Cloudy there, in an environment so completely different from the one in which they knew each other. The baithouse was shabby and poor, but it was also enchanting and magical. This place was simply drab. There was an air of unrelieved melancholy about it. Cloudy doesn't belong here, Ned found himself thinking. The old man was recovering from the shock of this unexpected visitor.

"Why, Mister—why Ned—well, I—"

"Hi, Cloudy."

"What're you doin' here? Not that I ain't glad to see you."

"I saw you on the street, so … I just wanted to say hi and see how you are."

"Well, come in, come in. Sit down here. That's mighty nice of you to come see me like this."

He patted Ned on the back and settled the boy in the armchair. But Cloudy seemed a little uneasy, as if he had been caught off guard at the wrong moment.

"I was sick," Ned said.

"You was? I'm sorry to here that, but you're all better now, ain't you? You look okay, still skinny but okay."

"I'm all over it now, but I was *really* sick, Cloudy. I heard my mom tell my dad she thought I was going to die. And there's a whole day I don't remember any of at all. The doctor came to see me a couple of times."

"My goodness, I guess you was sick at that."

"I had to say in bed for five days."

"Well, I'm glad you're better now. Ain't right, a fine young fellow like you gettin' sick at all, and bein' stuck in bed all the time, is it?"

"No, it's boring."

"'Course it is." Cloudy folded a shirt, set it aside and looked up stiffly. "You been around to the baithouse since you got over bein' sick?"

"No, I'm going out there this afternoon," Ned replied. "Today is my first day out of the house. I had to go to the post office this morning—that's why I'm in town."

"Oh, I see." Cloudy nodded, but his features seemed to be wrestling with themselves. The old man was trembling. "Oh, Ned, Ned … I have to tell you … Peeler died…."

Ned's mouth opened. Cloudy reached over, lifted the boy out of the chair and hugged him.

"In his sleep a few nights ago.... We was drinkin' and talkin' and singin' ... havin' a high old time, till we both just fell asleep ... in the baithouse.... Peeler, he never woke up. He's left this world, Ned. I'm sorry...."

He held Ned for a long time. The boy clung to his chest and cried until he was exhausted and there were no more tears, just deep, shuddering gasps. Cloudy rocked Ned gently in his arms. He wanted to say something more, to find words that would ease the child's pain, but there were no such words.

"The phantom took him," Ned spoke finally.

"No, no, no," Cloudy whispered. "He just died. It's death, that's all."

"That's what the phantom is."

"A man's time comes," Cloudy went on. "Nothin' you can do. It ain't easy, but that's the way it is. Peeler, he had a good life accordin' to his own way. It was his life, nobody else's, and if a man can say that, he's doin' pretty good. You understand what I'm sayin'?"

"The phantom came for me, and took Peeler instead."

"Ned, Ned, you ain't listenin' to me. Come on," Cloudy pleaded. "Peeler wouldn't want you to hear it any way but right. His time was up, and that's all it is. You understand?"

Ned was unsure, but he nodded anyhow. "Cloudy, where is he? I mean ... where does a person go when they die?"

"A better place."

"Really?"

"Has to be," Cloudy said impatiently. He knew he had to say or do something to keep the boy from becoming morbid about the subject. "The thing is, we can't sit around feelin' sorry for old Peeler," he said. "You think he'd like it if we did? The hell he would. And we can't sit around feelin' sorry for ourselves, neither. That's plain selfish. Even though it hurts, we got to remember to feel glad. Glad we knew Peeler, glad he was a friend of ours. You see? Glad he's in our hearts for the rest of our lives. We're damn lucky for that, and don't forget it."

"I won't."

"All right." Cloudy exhaled heavily. "Now I got to tell you somethin' else you won't like."

Ned gave a start, but the old man's arms held him close.

"What is it?"

"I'm movin' on from here."

"What? No! Cloudy, no!"

Ned struggled to sit up and look at Cloudy. Tears filled the boy's eyes again.

"I got to, Ned. I can't stay here no more. Winter gets in my bones, worse every year. And I'm tired of this place, I can't stay here. I got to go."

Ned's body shook as he cried within. He was sorry now that he had gotten better, sorry he had stepped outside to find his world changing so drastically and cruelly. It was several minutes before he could speak again.

"Where?"

"Florida. I got relations down there. It'll be better for me, it truly will. Otherwise, I wouldn't go."

"But you and Peeler were my only two friends," Ned said miserably. "And now you'll both be gone."

"You'll be okay, Ned. You know your way. You don't need us for that. If you did before, you don't now."

"But I do."

"Besides," Cloudy hastened to continue. "Even if they're miles and miles apart, friends are still with each other if they're real friends. You'll find that out, Ned, I promise you. Are you goin' to forget Peeler?"

"No."

"'Course you won't, and that means he'll be with you all the time, no matter where you are or what you're doin'. Same goes for you and me."

"I know that, but—"

"Ned, hey, Ned.... " Cloudy felt dull and inadequate. The boy was in a state and he had to bring him out of it. Even if that meant appearing to be brusque. There was another way. The boy had to accept what was. "Now listen. I got to go over to the baithouse and get a couple of things I left there. You want to walk with me?"

Ned was still taking in the second item of bad news and he couldn't think for a moment.

"How about it?" Cloudy asked.

"If I go there, I'll cry again. I can't help it."

"That's okay, Ned. I know how you feel. You want to cry one more time, you do it. But I'd like you to come with me this last time. Will you?"

"All right."

Cloudy changed out of his work whites and into his old suit. They didn't say much more until they were away from the center of town and on the road to the baithouse.

"Ain't you got school startin' pretty soon?"

"Monday."

"Sounds like you ain't lookin' forward to it."

"I'm not."

"I didn't care for it much neither, leastways not till I was out a few years. Then I wisht I was back in."

"Cloudy, when are you leaving?"

"Oh, a few days, I guess."

"By the weekend?"

"By then, I guess, yeah."

"Before you leave, will you go fishing with me again? For largemouth bass. Peeler said September is a good month to fish for them."

"I could do that, sure. But I ain't never caught no largemouth bass before, so don't expect me to know much about how to do it."

"Me either, but I'd like to try."

"Why not?"

Ned stopped when the baithouse came into sight.

"Are you okay?" Cloudy asked, touching the boy's shoulder.

"No."

Then Ned started to walk forward again. Cloudy felt good to see the boy struggling to be brave and strong in the face of grief.

"Cloudy."

"Hmmmn?"

"Did you ever make a scarecrow?"

"I can't recall."

"I'm going to make one. In the field out in back of our house."

"How come?"
"I don't know. I just want to."

ABOUT THE AUTHOR

Thomas Tessier was born in Connecticut and educated there and at University College, Dublin. He lived in Dublin and London for thirteen years, during which time three books of his poems were published and three of his plays were professionally staged. For several years he wrote a monthly column on music for *Vogue* magazine (UK).

His short stories have appeared in numerous magazines and anthologies, including *Borderlands, Cemetery Dance, Prime Evil, Dark Terrors, The Year's Best Fantasy and Horror* and *Best New Horror*. His first collection of short fiction, *Ghost Music and Other Tales*, received an International Horror Guild Award. In 2013, his second collection, *Remorseless: Tales of Cruelty*, was published by Sinister Grin Press.

He is the author of several novels of terror and suspense, including *The Nightwalker, Phantom, Finishing Touches* and *Rapture*, which was made into a movie starring Karen Allen and Michael Ontkean. His novel *Fog Heart* received the International Horror Guild Award for Best Novel and was cited by *Publishers Weekly* as one of the best books of the year. His latest novel, *Wicked Things*, was published in paperback by Leisure Books and in hardcover by Cemetery Dance Publications.

Thomas Tessier lives in Connecticut. He is currently working on a new novel, as well as more short fiction.

BIBLIOGRAPHY

<u>Novels</u>
Father Panic's Opera Macabre
Finishing Touches
Fog Heart
Phantom
Rapture

Secret Strangers
Shockwaves
The Fates
The Nightwalker
Wicked Things

Short story collections
Ghost Music and Other Tales
Remorseless: Tales of Cruelty
World of Hurt: Selected Stories

Poetry collections
Abandoned Homes
How We Died
In Sight of Chaos

Curious about other Crossroad Press books? Stop by our website:
http://crossroadpress.com
We offer quality writing
in digital, audio, and print formats.

Subscribe to our newsletter on the website homepage and receive a
free eBook.

www.ingramcontent.com/pod-product-compliance
Lightning Source LLC
Chambersburg PA
CBHW030252200626
46816CB00002BA/612